Bing

Bing

*From Farmer's Son to
Magistrate in Han China*

Michael Loewe

Hackett Publishing Company, Inc.
Indianapolis/Cambridge

14 13 12 11   1 2 3 4 5 6 7

For further information, please address
   Hackett Publishing Company, Inc.
   P.O. Box 44937
   Indianapolis, Indiana 46244-0937

www.hackettpublishing.com

Cover design by Abigail Coyle
Interior design and composition by Elizabeth L. Wilson
Printed at Edwards Brothers, Inc.

Library of Congress Cataloging-in-Publication Data
Loewe, Michael.
    Bing : from farmer's son to magistrate in Han China / Michael Loewe.
        p. cm.
    Includes bibliographical references.
    ISBN 978-1-60384-622-6 (pbk.) — ISBN 978-1-60384-623-3 (cloth)
    1. China—History—Han dynasty, 202 B.C.-220 A.D—Fiction. I. Title.
    PR6112.O28B56 2011
    823'.92—dc22   2011019150

For all those friends and colleagues, pupils and teachers,
who have helped the author to take a glance at the history
of Han China over the last fifty years, and for those who are
going to take a deeper look in the next fifty years.

Contents

A selection of images and illustrations follow Chapter Eight.

Prefatory Note

I owe a debt that I can never repay to friends and teachers who over the last years have lent me their unstinted encouragement, supplemented my shortcomings patiently, and corrected my errors in a forceful but kind manner. Impossible as it is to name them all, I select a few, now no longer with us, for special mention. Arthur Cooper was the first to engage me in a study of China; Walter Simon introduced me to the niceties of classical scholarship and bibliography, D. C. Lau to the treasures to be found in the writings of China's traditional scholars. A. F. P. Hulsewé was for a long time the only specialist in Han studies whom I could meet and consult, and he gave unstintingly of his time; Piet van der Loon, who suffered no fools gladly, yet allowed me the benefit of his guidance and deep scholarship, together with his friendship. Fujieda Akira and Ōba Osamu stood at my side with help at seminars held in Kyoto, and cooperated in work that we undertook in Europe. To my sorrow, Carmen Blacker was not there to call for a more lively narrative in this book or to poke fun at its characters.

For the present volume I can only express my deepest thanks to Deborah Wilkes for encouragement at an early stage, her editorial skill, and perseverance in bringing the book to fruition.

The Han Empire, 108 BCE. Identifications are restricted to provincial units (in capital letters) and cities whose names appear in the text; for further details, see Michael Loewe, *The Government of the Qin and Han Empires, 221 BCE–220 CE* (Indianapolis: Hackett Publishing Company, Inc., 2006), pp. 197–201.

Introduction

Writing two thousand years ago, China's historians and men of letters have bequeathed to us a wealth of information on the rise, decline, and fall of their empires. Archaeologists, working over the last century, have revealed untold riches, which serve to confirm or correct our literary sources and to supplement them over matters that do not feature in literature. But in none of this do we find a direct account of how individual men or women passed through the stages of life from childhood to old age, with their moments of triumph and disaster, their successful ventures or their abject failures, their moments of happiness and of grief. There is much that has not been recorded in situations that we can only imagine to have taken place; for example, as far as I know, there is no record of an official who was torn between his obligation to implement the laws and his revulsion at their severities; mention of such a difficulty in Chapter Fifteen stems from my belief that at least some of the imperial officials were also human beings.

The tale that follows draws both on the original writings and the material finds, and on the results of scholarly research of recent times. As always in a fictional account, it is not possible to find statements that immediately validate all the actions and events that colored a hero's life; but those related here are of a type that one may expect to see in the families of most cultures that have arisen in China or in the offices of the authorities that governed mankind therein. There can be no precise record of what our hero and his wife were thinking or feeling; their reactions and emotions are of the sort that can hardly be ignored in any account of human lives.

There is little to be seen in our surviving official records that tells of the emotions that bound together man and wife or relates their reactions to moments of joy or sorrow. Such a deficiency is partly repaired in China's early poetry and art, which reveal that the men and women of those days were by no means devoid of the loves and hates, the ideals and the ambitions that would seem to be inalienable parts of human nature. However, I should record that references which appear below to such emotions may derive from a writer's imagination rather than from hard evidence.

The life of Bing, for such is the name of our hero, is centered around 70 BCE when the Han empire had been founded for over a century. Both the sources of information that have been received for two thousand years and the wealth of manuscripts that have been unearthed more recently tell us consistently of most of the situations and experiences that are described, such as a soldier's service on the defense lines, the duties of a clerk or an official in government service, or the ways in which individuals sought to solve their personal perplexities. For some events, such as the conduct of the imperial cult of worship, the manner in which a magistrate would take up his duties, or the governor of a commandery would receive him on appointment, I have drawn on imagination with reasonable confidence that this has not strayed beyond control. There is no written evidence for some everyday events of a minor nature, such as the fall of a pot in a market stall (see Chapter One); there is evidence for activities that may on occasion surprise and require confirmation, such as an explosion that wrecked an iron foundry (Chapter Four).

The great majority of the sixty million men and women of the Han empire lived and died like Bing's parents and brothers, toiling alone on their farms and satisfying the tax collectors; and they may well have been ignorant of any other way of life, except that seen on a rare visit to a town. In imagining the figure of Bing, I have painted a picture of a somewhat exceptional person who, thanks to his native wit and persistence, was able to break free of that well-set pattern and to pass his life in a whole variety of situations, bettering himself along the way. To some readers it may seem too fanciful to suppose that it would be possible for an illiterate farmer's boy to rise to a reasonably high position in the civil service. That such exceptional cases were not entirely absent is seen in the records of a number of officials, most notably that of Gongsun Hong, who worked as a keeper of pigs but eventually took the post of chancellor, highest of all offices in the empire, from 124 to 121 BCE. The tale told of Bing is in no way to be taken as an example of what happened frequently.

Regrettably our sources provide little information about the daily lives, the joys, and sufferings of the women of these early days. We know of a few cases where one contributed to the growth of China's culture at this time, such as the poetess and writer Ban Zhao (died ca. 120 CE) who completed the main historical record of the Western Han Dynasty that her father had been unable to finish. I have allowed my fancies to run somewhat freely in the belief that before then a father might find it both delightful and possible to train a daughter in reading and writing and to inspire her with a love of literature.

I have unashamedly taken some liberties with the timing of certain events that are mentioned in the tale, in the belief that in so doing I am not treating some historical developments to undue violence. Scholars will note my assumption that laws known to be formulated in 186 BCE were also operative a century later; and they will be aware that references to a flood, and the coincidence of an earthquake and an eclipse are to events of 30 and 29 BCE; and that the account of a soteriological movement is dated in our records at 3 BCE (Chapter Sixteen). However, neither Bing nor his more intelligent wife are said here to have been drinking tea which, as far as we know, was not being enjoyed widely in Western Han.

This book is in no way intended to be, nor should it be seen as, an exhaustive historical account of Han times; for example attention is paid to the iron mines but the salt mines are not mentioned. Of necessity I can fasten only on activities and events for which reasonable evidence is available with the result that the account of Bing's life can only be selective. To ease the reader, proper names have been limited to a minimum. A short list of books that lend substance to these pages follows at their close. The endnotes that follow each chapter are in no way intended to give references to all events or activities that are mentioned, but instead to provide clarification or dispel difficulties, or to give warning where definite sources are not found to support a statement or an allusion; or they may point out where the timing of an event does not match with a life that was lived ca. 70 BCE. As the book is intended primarily for readers who are not familiar with Chinese written language, the notes do not usually include references to the original sources but lead directly to modern secondary writings that include the results of recent research.

The following brief sketch may be of help to readers who are approaching China's history for the first time and need some explanation of how the empire was being administered.[1]

---

1. For a fuller account, see Michael Loewe, *The Government of the Qin and Han Empires, 221 BCE–220 CE* (Indianapolis: Hackett Publishing Company, 2006).

The Western Han, sometimes called Former Han (202 BCE–9 CE), and the short-lived Xin empire of Wang Mang (9–23 CE) were ruled by the emperor and central government from the capital city of Chang'an (forerunner of present-day Xi'an); the capital city of the Eastern (or Later) Han (25–220 CE) was at Luoyang. At the head of the central government stood the Chancellor and the Imperial Counselor. The provinces were divided into a few kingdoms and more generally into commanderies, which might be as large as England or France, or as small as Luxembourg or Yorkshire. Each commandery, administered by a governor, consisted of between six and thirty-eight counties of which there were over fifteen hundred in the empire. Each county, controlled by its magistrate and including one principal and several other towns, comprised a number of districts; villages with their headmen, farmers, and their immediate kinsfolk peopled the countryside of the districts. The registered population of the empire was of the order of sixty million individuals, most of whom lived in households of four or five members (man, wife, son, daughter, and one grandparent); that of the kingdoms and commanderies varied from a hundred thousand to two million individuals; to such figures there should be added those of vagrants, criminals, and slaves.

Able-bodied men were obliged to serve for short periods as conscript laborers and for longer periods as conscript servicemen in the armed forces. Rich noblemen of high rank lived in comfort and luxury attended by servants and perhaps slaves in small numbers. Roving merchants of some wealth and substance moved around the empire; less-rich traders made a living in the markets of the towns. For some periods of time, the central government operated the iron and salt mines as an imperial monopoly. The emperor stood at the top of the social scale, followed by his immediate family and then the nobles; a distinction in social status permeated the rest of the population in some nineteen degrees. Officials were appointed by the central government and received a salary; and they could rise to positions of great authority and power. They enjoyed a high measure of prestige, enforcing obedience to the laws and sentencing criminals to punishment.

Bing

F OR THE FIRST TEN YEARS OF HIS LIFE BING HAD NO IDEA THAT THERE could be any other way of living than his own. Brought up on the farm, he saw his father and mother devote all their time to work, mainly in the fields. Bing usually joined them, along with his older brother and his younger sister. Occasionally the kind old woman who lived with them—his father called her "Mother"—would go out with them. Not that she was a great deal of help at much hard work for long; she was painfully thin and terribly frail, hobbling along with a pronounced limp. She could hardly carry anything heavier than a basket. In fact she spent most of her time at home, tending the fires and preparing a meal for the family to eat together once the day's work was done. It was always the same dreary food, but at least it filled you up, though it did leave you rather thirsty at times. Sometimes if you were lucky you would get a bite of a turnip or a taste of ginger or garlic, but these were very special occasions.

As Bing grew older, he began to wonder about the world beyond the farm, and how the family had come to settle where they were. One afternoon, when he and his father had lagged behind the others on the long walk home from their most distant field, Bing decided that it was a good moment for a question.

"Has our family always lived here?" he asked.

"Yes. My own father and his father worked these same fields. My granddad's father, I was told, was the oldest of several brothers and had been lucky enough to be chosen for a grant of land on which to settle and make a living. By way of exchange for that grant, he had to part with some of the crop every year. I've no idea what happened to his other brothers. When he died, the land and the farm passed to my father, your grandfather, and in due course it came to me." His expression became serious. "When my time comes, your older brother

1

will have the right to take it over. You may well have to fend for yourself."

Bing could only accept that this was the way it would be and that nothing would change it. Young as he was, he determined that he was going to make a better way of life than the one he saw around him. Of course he had no idea how things would work out, but he was sure that hard work, determination, and a little luck would help him find his way.

Bing had realized that the woman whom his father called "Mother" was his own grandmother, but he could not make out why it was sometimes difficult to understand what she was saying. Finally he learned that her family had come from a different and distant part of the land, way up in the north. His father told him what he knew of the story.

One day, many years ago when his grandfather was still young, something had happened to make that day unlike any other day of his life. He was working in the hot sun at the edge of his fields, when he heard a strange sound, not like any animal that he knew. He looked up from the ground he was working, shading his eyes against the glare of the yellow sun, but he saw nothing. It was not until his eyes adjusted to the brightness that he saw a young girl, leaning against the trunk of a tree, sobbing. She was too weak to walk without help, so he lifted her in his arms and carried her back to the farmhouse. It was many days before she began to come round. Gradually he got some strength into her, and she told him her sad story.

Her father had been convicted of a serious crime and sentenced to five years of hard labor. She, along with her mother and her brothers, were taken into custody and made to work as ordered. At least they had a means of keeping body and soul together. But they were treated more cruelly each day and, terrified that something worse might occur, she managed to run away. It never crossed her mind that while the others were still there, whatever else happened, they would be given food and shelter, and that once she had left them she would have none. Well, she soon realized her mistake, but she simply had to move on, scrounging for food as best she could and sleeping outside, wherever she could find some shelter against the bitter winds and snow. At times she had to escape from the leering threats of young ruffians, and on more than one occasion had just managed to avoid anything worse. Finding Bing's grandfather and the Wu's family farm had saved her.

Bing's grandfather told her to stay where she was and join in the work of the farm. Before long she was carrying his child and then became his wife. So, when years later her husband died, Bing's father had taken special care to look after her, and to treat her in the way he had been taught a son should treat his mother. It was only with some difficulty that Bing could understand all this and much of the story had to wait until later. But he did learn that the young girl in the story was the old woman his father called "Mother," and that her own family had come from a very long way away, where it was much colder. They spoke in a peculiar way there, and their ways of managing a farm out there in those days were quite different from what Bing was used to.

However it was not long before he was able to understand most of what his grandmother was saying. She didn't talk about the way she had lived as a child or of her family, but she spoke with fear in her eyes about some very cruel people whom you had to obey, or else they would take you away, never to be seen again. Sometimes she talked about the fighting that went on; men wearing strange clothes who would gallop in on horseback and take what they could. Anyone who tried to stop them would be killed. It was she who told him why he was called Bing.

"You had another brother, two years older than you, but he was a weak child and died soon after birth. Still, that made three children altogether, and the name 'Bing' means the third."

Their farm lay north of the great river that people called "Yellow" because of the yellow silt it carried. Every so often it would burst its banks and the floods would ruin all the countryside, but thank goodness Bing's family farm was too far away to suffer. There were several family farms within a short distance of one another and together they formed a small community or village. On the whole they all worked on their own but there were some things that had to be decided in common so that everyone would be satisfied. "Would all the farms benefit, or would some of them suffer damage if part of the river was drained?" was the sort of question that arose. Or "how quickly could they get a bridge that had fallen down repaired?" The villagers would meet together to talk it all out. Once they agreed what had to be done the headman of the village would take charge, seeing that the work was shared out equally. If necessary he would order somebody like Bing to leave his own farm for a few days to go and work along with his neighbors from the other farms.

Life was hard. Apart from the main cereal diet there was very little else except for the occasional bit of a pig or a chicken they had raised, or perhaps a fish from the pond. They had to be very careful with the salt, as it was so expensive. Most of the fields were sown with millet, along with some hemp from which the crude cloth for their clothing was eventually spun. There were just a few fruit trees, some stouter ones for timber, and a plot where vegetables and herbs were tended. Fresh water came from the well that they were lucky enough to have on their land, but there again you had to be careful, as it needed maintenance to prevent it from running dry.

As the farm lay some distance away from the others, they did not have much contact with neighbors. Only rarely did a stranger pass by. Once or twice a year the officials came to count how many people were living on the farm and to assess how much land they were working, or to collect the tax, or to take some of the youngsters away for the service they had to perform for the empire. Perhaps once in the spring or autumn a merchant might bring something on his wagon that he would try to sell them. Nobody else would likely be welcome, as they could be carrying a sword and would be out to steal, or they might be people who were running away from officials, and sorry as you might feel for them it was very dangerous to give them shelter. Bing's grandfather might well have been in for trouble if anyone in authority had set out to find the girl he had taken in.

The family—Bing was told that for generations they had been called Wu—were fortunate in the type of land that they worked, as it provided a good return if they tended it carefully, seeing that the seeds were properly planted and, above all, that they got enough water as they grew. There were times when it could be bitterly cold, when their rough clothing could not possibly keep out the wind, and the old lady would shiver in her thin wraps and keep asking Bing's father for furs. Other times it was scorching hot, and you would try to get some relief by wearing a wide straw hat, but they weren't much good, and come the midday sun it was all too easy to feel miserable.

Most often it was the supply of water that caused them the greatest worry. If, as sometimes happened, it looked as if the rain would never stop, try as you might you could not store rainwater for the time when, sure enough, the land would be parched. The ponds would dry up in the heat and water would evaporate in the large rough earthenware pots where it was kept. Then there was real trouble of two sorts, which might come from the nearby stream and dikes. As the winter was ending, these would fill up and overflow into the fields; in the late summer they might be so shallow that there was not enough water to keep the crops healthy. From early on in his life Bing was put to work at the pumps. You sat with your feet firmly placed, pushing pedals that lowered a chain of buckets into the river below, and raised them, full and heavy, to the level of the fields. The work was never ending, with never a moment's let up; and if you did happen to slack off, the fellow sitting next to you—probably sent there by the headman of the village—would soon give you a punch on the shoulder, or a hefty blow on the backside to get you to pull your weight.

In addition, each of the seasons had its own regular tasks that no farmer could avoid or put off. Winter after winter the fields had to be plowed before the seed could be sown; spring after spring you sowed the seed and then the weeds had to be pulled so that the earth would give its goodness to the growing crop; summer after summer weeding went on and then the millet had to be harvested; autumn after autumn the millet had to be stored so that it would not rot in the changing temperature. Of course, the rats had to be kept at bay. Finally, all the waste products of the fields had to be collected and burned.

At plowing time, both of the oxen that Bing's family owned, or perhaps just one, were harnessed to a wooden frame, which drew behind it the iron plowshare that they had bought from the local officials. Bing's father or his elder brother stood behind the animals, with ropes to control them and prods to keep them moving. Bing, less experienced, helped in whatever way he could, doing his best to keep them going straight. Up and down the field they trudged, leaving neat straight furrows behind them. During all this work they had to be particularly careful to choose where they directed the plow. Last year's furrows had been filled up and must not be disturbed; the new furrows must be dug just where the ridges of last year's fields had risen, so that year in year out some parts of the field would be left to rest while others would receive the seed. This was the modern way of raising a crop, Bing had been told. It had been tried out on some of the farms that the government worked and was now to be used everywhere. In the old way that his grandfather and father had long been accustomed to, you just cleared a patch, dug to a fairly shallow depth and scattered the seed in as widely as you could. But nowadays this was considered far too haphazard, and the farmers had to follow the strict instructions that they received about the amount of seed that they should use for their carefully measured plots. The new way of doing it could be tricky, but Bing always enjoyed looking at the straight furrows that they and the oxen left behind them.

While Bing's grandmother had nothing but scorn for these newfangled ideas, his father had to admit that he got a better harvest than he had with the old ways. But then they were lucky on this farm; not everyone could afford to keep an ox or two, and they made working the land much faster and easier, particularly now that a new longer furrow had been introduced, which was especially useful to those who plowed with oxen. Some farmers could not afford an iron plowshare and had to make do with one made of wood, unless they could manage to persuade the local officials to lend them a better one. Some households were very unlucky; they would scrape together enough money to buy an iron plowshare only to find that after a year or so it had become blunt and useless. Even though they had bought a plowshare of inferior quality, they had no recourse with the official who had sold it to them.

Farmers would fertilize their furrows with whatever they could find, be it the night soil from their stinking pits, or whatever droppings they could get from the oxen. Once the grain started to sprout there was the backbreaking work of pulling out the weeds, very often without the help of a hoe. Eventually the time would come to gather the crop and stack it, and once again they had to follow government regulations, which were intended to prevent waste. This meant that farmers had to measure everything, down to the fraction of the last bushel of the crop, and they had to fit straw matting in at the base, which was supposed to deter the rats.

"Why do we have to be so careful?" Bing once asked. "Why should anyone else worry about the way we get the job done?" Once more he learned that, never mind what it cost them in extra work, they simply had to obey the rules. At any time throughout the year they were likely to receive a visit from people who came from what were called the "district" or their superiors of the "county," and one of them would make a point of inspecting the stacks. What was worse, they had the power to punish any farmer if all was not being done according to regulations. Sometimes, if everything was not quite right, you could keep those busybodies quiet with a basket of fruit, or a nice fat fish.

Most of the buildings of the farm were little more than wooden sheds, some very thin and rickety. Bing would sometimes find himself holding up the branch of a tree or steadying a tool so that one of the others could cut a new piece of timber to size and shape for replacing a part that had rotted. There was one particular building that had been built much more sturdily, with walls that had been made with layer after layer of earth or clay. Occasionally there was a need to build another wall of this type and this meant hard work that was no less demanding than that of keeping the water pumps going. You worked with a high upright wooden frame just a foot or so wide, and you shoveled the clay or mud into the space between the sides of the frame. Then you hammered it down until it was as hard and tight as it could be. This went on for layer after layer. The higher the structure rose the harder the work would be, as you had to raise the mud higher and higher and then work at it without a really solid platform to stand on. At least, when the wall was built you knew it would last longer than the flimsy wooden shutters of the other buildings.

Bing was ever reminded that he lived in a poor household where there was always a struggle to find the money to buy necessities, such as the cloth for clothes and sacks. But he had noticed, and could not understand why, there seemed to be money around when the time came for those solemn meetings when everybody in the village gathered together to show their respect for their dead parents. Apparently Bing's ancestors, long dead, had to be given presents to prevent them from causing trouble, and some of these gifts, such as the pigs that had to be sacrificed, or that spiced drink flavored with pepper, must have been quite expensive. Before these events began, everyone would be hard at work cleaning house and sprucing themselves up. Once the proceedings started you had to take your proper place so that you were treating all members of your own family and the neighbors in the way that they deserved—elders always took their place before the youngsters. The two most important meetings took place every year in the winter and on the new year's day, and it was mainly on these occasions that Bing had a chance to get to know the people from the other farms, but there were also other meetings of this sort as the months went by, and even though they were not so grand they must have cost a lot. Sometimes the ancestors had to be content with the things that the farm itself could provide, such as eggs, leeks, or fish. Afterward, they usually had a good time with a special dinner to enjoy.

Bing never got a word of sympathy when he complained how hard the work was, not even from his grandmother or his mother. Instead he had to put up with his elder brother's taunts.

"Well, you'll be free of all this when the old man dies and I take over," he would say to Bing. "Not that that will help you much. You'll be too old to stay on as an extra male in the household, and anyway it would be against the law. As it is there are six of us here, while most of our neighbors have households of four or five. Six is too many. I'll be all right, thank you, with a boy or two of my own, and we'll be making a living here; but Heaven knows where you'll be or whether you'll have anything to eat. You may well be longing to be back at the water pumps, with a good meal in store for you at the end of the day."

Bing never said anything in reply; his brother wasn't telling him anything he didn't already know. Besides, he felt a bit sorry for his brother, whose life would follow a model prescribed by his inheritance. For Bing, the future was uncertain, and that meant it had promise.

Late one afternoon, at the end of an especially good summer, Bing's father was faced with a rather pleasant problem. As he surveyed the ample stores of fruit and vegetables that had resulted from a bountiful harvest, he saw that there was far more there than the family could use. The best option was to sell what they could not use for extra money before it went bad. That meant a journey of several days away from the family.

He looked out across the nearest field, where Bing was still hard at work, gathering debris from the spent furrows for burning. Usually he would take his elder son along with him on these trips, but it occurred to him that he might take Bing instead. "It will do the boy good," he thought, "to see something of the world. After all, he is the one who will have to make a living for himself."

The night before their departure, Bing was too excited to sleep. Instead, he closed his eyes and tried to imagine all the wonders of the town that he was about to see for the first time. When his mother came to rouse him at dawn, he was already ready to leave.

"Bing, I hope your excitement won't get in the way of helping your father," she said.

Bing thought for a moment about the best answer before he decided on a truthful one. "I hope so too, Mother."

At first, they made a solitary sight: the man, the boy, the laden oxcart traveling slowly along the rough path in the light of the rising sun.

Bing took a deep breath of the cold morning air. "How long will it be before we get there?" he asked.

His father laughed. "We've only just started and it's a long journey. I expect we'll arrive in about three days' time. We'll stop for supper, if that's what's worrying you. But we must take care along the way. We'd be an easy prey for robbers, so we must avoid certain paths where we might be trapped."

It wasn't long before they had passed the last of the neighbor farms that Bing was familiar with. They were in a part of the land that was quite new to Bing, who was all eyes and ears. Soon, they were sharing the path with others.

"Look," said Bing. "That group of men over there; what a strange cart they have!"

"It's built specially to carry containers of grain. But you see how narrow it is? That makes it possible to make safe passage up and down the narrow mountain paths." The cart was marked with a badge, or something like a badge, in bright colors, but Bing had no chance of asking what it meant. The gang of workers surrounding the cart were being ordered around by an overseer who looked to be a most unpleasant character. He was dressed in special clothing and carried a whip, which he did not hesitate to use if he thought that a man was slacking off. Bing was rather frightened.

"You'll be working like that yourself one of these days," his father said, "just as we all did." He went on to explain that they were all young men doing their year's service for the county. As they continued on, he pointed out another group, somewhat like the first, except they had no cart. "Much the same thing," he told Bing, "but those men are doing their time as soldiers and are probably on the march to the north where they will have to keep guard on the defense lines."

"How do you know?" Bing asked.

"I did it myself, my boy, years ago, just as you'll have to quite soon."

Bing said nothing, as he took it all in. It had been one thing to know that all young men such as himself had to work in the county's labor gangs and in the army, but quite another to see it all in action.

The sun rose high in the sky. Soon, the jostling of the cart lulled Bing to sleep. It seemed that just moments had passed, when his father gave him a prod and said, "Bing, wake up. You'll want to see this."

Bing sat up, yawning, and followed his father's gaze down the road. Coming toward them was a spacious carriage with red wheels, pulled by a pair of fine horses. Bing had never seen such glossy, well-fed animals.

"They could only belong to two sorts of people," his father said. "Either a high-ranking official, who is usually accompanied by armed guards, or a merchant who is rich enough to buy what he wants."

"I don't see any armed guards," said Bing. "It must be a rich merchant. I think we should paint our cart wheels red."

"I'm afraid not," said his father. "It is only very highly honored people who are allowed to have the wheels of their carriages painted red. There are others, rich traders who do it, but they are only showing off, trying to convince people that they are more highly placed or richer than they really are. Red wheels on a farmer's cart would not fool anyone."

Later in the afternoon, when this party had long since passed on its way, a different sort of carriage approached, and indeed there were armed outriders on this one.

"Make way for His Excellency!"

Bing's father pulled the oxcart aside into the mud and slush. Without a word, he leapt from the cart and Bing followed. They stood obediently in mud to their ankles, until the carriage had passed by.

"Better not get on the wrong side of them," his father said. "He's sure to be an official of the government of high rank, the sort who has authority to make you do whatever he likes, or else you're in for trouble."

After a few days they reached the town with its walls and guard posts. Bing's father showed the guards the register of his household and they were allowed through the gates. For the first time in his life Bing found himself inside a city, and he looked around in amazement. There was a large open space, squared off, with an imposing building on the north side. Wide streets divided most of the city into wards, also square, and surrounded by their own walls and gates. His father told him that people lived inside those wards, and Bing wondered how on earth they spent their days or how they lived; there could hardly have been enough room to raise a crop. "And another thing," said his father. "If you live in one of those wards you are not allowed to leave it after night fall; there are servicemen to catch you and punish you if you try."

They spent the night in a rather rough place where all sorts of travelers were to be found, and Bing's father took great care to see that his own belongings were kept safe from thieves. Somebody who had been to the city before took Bing aside and told him where to go and what to see.

"There is a high-towered building which houses a bell that tolls the hours of the day and night. You must see that," the stranger said. "And there is a very dirty building colored black from which smoke belches forth. Oh, and you must go see the execution ground where the officials have criminals put to death when it isn't done in full public gaze in the marketplace. Yes, and whatever you do, you must go to the marketplace. There you'll find all sorts of things your father can buy for you. There'll be an official there in his box to see that nobody cheats you by using false weights and measures."

Bing was going to the market in any case, as that was where his father would sell the fruit and vegetables he had brought. They set out early the next morning. Once there, Bing could only stand and stare agape at what he saw. He passed along row after row of stalls, finding each row full of people selling the same sort of things, so that if you wanted to buy something you could keep a sharp eye open to find the best quality goods at the lowest possible price. The fruit and vegetable stalls didn't interest Bing very much as there was little there that he did not know about.

"May I walk around a bit?" he asked.

"You may," said his father, "but don't be long, and don't stray too far."

He walked slowly by the stalls. The first were selling cooked meats and pickles, all carefully sealed in jars. Even so, a fine aroma was seeping out. Next along you could buy things to wear, such as sheepskins or pelts that would keep away the cold. Then there were the shops which sold the pottery jars that you needed in the kitchen, and beyond them there were a very few stalls that stocked iron-made goods, not only the vessels and pans used for cooking; there were plenty of things that Bing would have loved to have, either for his work in the fields or for cutting wood to the size and shape that was needed. He was allowed to handle some of these iron implements, finding some of them very heavy and others so sharp that he nearly dropped them. Bing found something forbidding about these particular stalls; they weren't reaching out to get your business as the others were, and this was because officials rather than ordinary tradesmen ran them. It was the government, not the private owners and merchants, that worked the mines and sold metal products.

The day went on, with Bing's father bargaining with customers for his wares. During the afternoon tempers flared in one of the pottery shops across the way and Bing nearly got involved. Suddenly, a large well-painted bottle fell, crashing to the ground, smashing into tiny pieces. The shopkeeper was sure that one of the customers had knocked it off the shelf.

"Your fault," he shouted at the crowd, "one of you must pay for the damage." The crowd stirred. "Nothing to do with us," someone called back. "We never touched the damn thing." Soon a full-scale quarrel had broken out with everyone shouting and threatening one another. The shopkeeper had picked on an old, grey-bearded man who he was certain had caused the damage. Some of the customers tried to protect him, while others spurred on the shopkeeper to fight for his rights.

"Wait!" shouted a voice from the crowd. "That young man saw everything."

Bing was aghast. The man was pointing at him. He was being pushed forward when he felt his father's hand on his shoulder, and he stepped back without saying a word, just as the market's warden turned up with a couple of men. The warden took one look at the shelf where the bottle had been and turned to the shopkeeper. "What do you expect? The rest are certain to come down if you don't fasten that shelf better," he said, and he threatened to take away the shopkeeper's license if there was any more trouble. Nobody wanted that and the crowd dispersed.

Bing noticed one row of stalls that was rather different from the others. Most of the people crowding in and jostling one another were women. They were examining all sorts of herbs that were on display and said to be very helpful in easing bodily pains and childbirth. You had to know which ones to choose and how to boil up their roots or leaves to make the right liquid. Bing recognized some of the roots, as they grew them at home, but there were others that were fetching an astonishingly high price and must have come from far away. He wondered whether they could possibly be worth such a cost.

It was new and puzzling to Bing to see so many people in the market and on the streets and finding out that none of them worked the land as he and his father did. Some of the men who were buying choice things to eat and drink turned out to work in a pottery or iron foundry. Bing met one of them, who had struck up a conversation with Bing's father at the stall.

"The foundry? Oh, horrible conditions. Hot and dirty. But you get good money." He pulled out a leather thong that was strung with coins. "It's the only way to keep them," the man said. "String them up, a hundred at a time."

"Does each string really have a hundred?" Bing asked, but only a burst of laughter answered his question. It was some time before he found out why.

Back home at the farm after all this excitement Bing had a lot to think about and a lot to tell his brother and sister, who got rather tired of his boasting. "He'll soon be off on his service," they thought, "and that'll teach him not to brag." But for the time being it did no such thing. Bing was longing to get away from the unending drudgery of the farm. Well, he would have to go off sooner or later; and he decided that once his year's service was over, he would seek a fortune in one of the towns. From what he had seen he thought he would be able to get by, but he would have to rely on his wits.

Notes for Chapter One
While the problem of raising water certainly existed, there is no certainty that chain pumps worked by foot were already in use in Han times, or that a team of pumpers would be made up by members of different households. See Joseph Needham, et al., *Science and Civilisation in China,* vol. 4, pt. II (Cambridge: Cambridge University Press, 1971), pp. 339–47, figs. 578, 579. Alternation in the use of land was in practice by ca. 100 BCE. The increase in the length of the furrow from 100 to 240 paces, as would be more productive for plows drawn by oxen, was introduced during the reign of Wudi (141–87 BCE). There is a hint that the usual load of grain that a wagon carried was 500 liters. The government's monopolies of salt and iron were introduced ca. 117 BCE. There is no certainty that herbs were on sale in the market stalls.

Chapter Two   *Conscript laborer and soldier*

BING HAD NOT BEEN BACK ON THE FARM FOR LONG WHEN, SURE enough, an official from county headquarters came round, with a long list of everyone who was living on the farms.

"Yes," he said to Bing, "you've just turned twenty-three; you can either come with me now for your service or wait another year. Once you've finished your year serving in the county, we'll have you back again for your two years as a soldier."

Longing for a change as he was, Bing was only too ready to get away, and he soon found himself in the company of some of the other young men he knew from the village. In addition to the locals, there were some unfamiliar recruits who came from farther away, and Bing could not understand a word that they uttered.

Some of the men who gave them their orders seemed pleasant enough. Bing felt that they were people of his own sort, and he could almost see them as elder brothers who showed the new workers how to do their jobs more efficiently. But as the months wore on and they were moved around from place to place Bing and his fellow workers sometimes had to put up with severe or even cruel treatment, as there seemed to be no limit to what some of those low-ranking officials could order them to do. Much of Bing's work was the same as what he had been used to on the farm, except that it took place in unfamiliar surroundings. The way the land ran, flat or hilly, and the feel of the earth, like clay or like sand, might be strange and make the work lighter or heavier. He might find himself in a part of the country where the soil was different and it was not so easy to get a plow moving.

For many days there he was again, stretched out at the water pumps, leading the plow, or carrying a load of wood on his back, just the same as it had been except that there was no family living on the farm where he had been sent to work. From what he could see, the place had been left to go to rack and ruin for some months, or even years, with weeds growing everywhere, trees torn apart by their fallen branches and the wellhead all broken down. He found out that the man who had held the land was now a convict. He had been caught thieving and sentenced to a long term of hard labor. "A lot worse off than you are," his informant had told him, "and I don't suppose that we shall see him or his family again. You boys here are to get the place in order for the next person the magistrate decides to entrust it to."

Sometimes when he was not engaged in this dull work Bing joined a team of workers who were taking loads of grain where it belonged. This meant carrying heavy loads on your shoulders as you stepped along the rough track across the fields, and you had to make sure that you didn't slip off of the narrow, muddy lane into the patch where a new crop was growing. One unfortunate man slipped and hurt himself, only to be flogged for being clumsy. But there were excitements. One day Bing was assigned to a team charged with taking a load to one of the county's larger granaries. Bing could hardly believe his eyes when he saw the size of the place. What enormous stocks it must hold! When the guards were not looking, he approached and looked inside, but he was immediately repulsed by the sickly stench of rotting grain. How to stop it, he wondered, when there is so much in store; and how good are they at driving the rats away? He had seen much smaller granaries that rested on stilts to keep the grain off ground level and free of all but the cleverest of rats, but no stilts would be able to support the load that was inside this store, which had been built in quite a different way. Just then one of the wardens came by with two fierce looking dogs on a leash. Perhaps they earned their living as rat catchers? Bing was longing to take charge of the dogs and took a hesitant step closer.

"Get back!" the guard ordered, "or they will eat you for their supper."

Some days Bing was sent to help the builders where a house was being put up or a tomb was being prepared. He knew well enough what some of the work meant, that endless pounding of the soil to get it to hold fast if it was to be any use as an upright wall. But there was also other work to which he was not accustomed. On one occasion, they were getting a tomb ready for somebody of a high rank. The man who had died was not a native of the commandery where he had lived, and he was to be taken to his birthplace for burial. A gang of conscript workmen, including Bing, was sent to a place called a "kingdom"—so Bing was told—but he had no idea what that meant. He did notice that the man in charge of the gang had to show a heap of documents to the guards as they passed from their previous workplace to the new one.

A deep pit had already been dug at the site where the tomb was to be. There were large amounts of good-quality timber stacked up, and it was on this that they had to work, cutting planks to cover the floor, and dozens and dozens of stout logs, long enough to measure halfway up your body or more. These logs had to be measured to the exact size that was needed and planed to be evenly smooth. Bing had no idea how they were going to be used. He had noticed that one of the overseers who regularly came around always carried with him a short bronze rod. Bing had tried to get a look at it but with no luck, and then one day the overseer left the rod behind. Bing saw that it was marked with ten divisions, each as wide as a thumb. When he next saw the overseer using it, he realized that the rod was a device for measuring the planks that had been cut to ensure that they were thick enough, and that the long, heavy pieces had been squared off correctly.

The tomb was to be built with several compartments that were separated from each other, and some of the doors that led from one compartment to another had been painted black and red. All those hundreds of long timbers that were so heavy were being laid one on top of the other to form a square of four solid sides around the interior of the tomb. These would provide a defensive wall, Bing was told, strong enough to prevent robbers from breaking in.

"Who would want to steal anything from a tomb?" Bing asked, and he learned that before the tomb was sealed all sorts of treasures would be put inside.

"No, I've no idea why," one of them said. "It's just asking for trouble, and anyway, what a waste of valuable stuff."

The tomb would be covered on top and sealed with a layer of white paint or another pungent liquid that they had in store, and this would keep the damp out. Finally, once the man had been buried and the tomb sealed, they would raise quite a little hillock on top.

During his year's service Bing was also put to work at keeping the roads in good condition so that officials could move around as their duties demanded without hindrance. Conscript workers had to make sure that the bridges over the waterways were safe and again Bing found himself working with wood, just as he had at the tomb. But unlike the carefully planned way in which the various parts of the tomb were measured, repair of roads and bridges required you to size up on the spot where a strut had to be replaced, or where the structure needed an extra support so as to hold it together. Bing became skilled at this sort of work and he liked to think of ways to prevent accidents from occurring. Soon he was seen to be so good at his job that the supervisors would ask his advice about what step to take next.

The worst of all things that happened to Bing while he was a conscript laborer was a stint at an iron foundry. A fierce explosion had all but destroyed the place while the men had been at work and a number of them had been killed or injured, and the government agency was short of labor. What really troubled the director of the foundry, a hardhearted man without much sympathy for anyone who had been hurt in the explosion, was the fear that he would not be able to deliver the required quota of finished goods; if he couldn't, he would be heavily fined. In one way he was lucky. In emergencies such as this he was entitled to ask the county for help, and as it happened the magistrate was able to oblige him by sending a party of workers, though nothing like as many as he had asked for.

Bing had never seen such a grim place. He could hardly breathe once he got inside close to the furnace. He had to keep shoveling logs into the fire nonstop. Not to mention the burning hot embers under the stove that he had to rake over to ensure that no precious scrap of metal had fallen through and was thus wasted. On several occasions his feet were badly scorched, but that didn't stop the foreman from insisting that he carry on with the work. They weren't turning out anything exciting, only loads of the arrowheads that the army needed by the thousands. It was all hard and thankless work, but Bing had to admit that he'd learned a few things.

Sooner than he had expected, the time came for his service to end and he was free to make his way back home. He'd had a difficult time working at the pace that was required but he had seen a lot and learned a lot about the world around him. Back on the farm, nothing had changed. It was almost as if he had never left. He was happy to see his family, but there were no excitements, just the same old dreary tasks, day in day out, and he soon found himself as sick of the routine as he had been a year before. Nobody who came their way interested him, except for one traveling merchant called Shang who managed to sell the household a few bits and pieces. Shang had actually spoken to Bing once when he had seen him complete a tricky piece of carpentry with only poor tools to help him. It was thanks to his work at that tomb that Bing had acquired a good skill at woodwork and Shang complimented him on what he had just done.

Bing was not sorry when the time came for his tour as a conscript soldier. He expected it to be hard going, for all of two years, but he was sure that he would get a chance to learn some new ways of making do on his own by the time his service was over. No, whatever happened, he was not going back to the farm where his brother had been getting more and more masterful and demanding.

Bing was over twenty-five when he was summoned to a nearby town by the county officials. Once there, his excitement was quelled when he understood that he was not as free as he had been when he had visited a town with his father. Discipline was strict and he was housed in bare barracks. Cold and hungry as he was, he told himself that he could take anything for two years, and he had heard that the food would be quite sufficient. He would be here for twelve months, they'd said. He would be taught how to use the army's weapons to best advantage, how to move around and act in formation with his fellow soldiers, and how to face an enemy in battle. There were other things he had to learn, what orders were being conveyed by the different beats on the drum, and how to distinguish at a distance his fellow troops from the enemy's. He was told that some of their own officers and commanders were martinets for discipline and immediate obedience, but although that could be harsh they probably kept you out of danger during a fight. Apparently, one of the generals was more easygoing with his men. In return the men would stick by him whatever was going on and would take all sorts of risks as long as the general was at their side.

One bright morning, Bing was astonished when the sergeant put a crossbow in his hands. He had never handled one before, and he noted its expertly fitted layers of choice woods that gave it both strength and flexibility. The sergeant showed him how to set the bronze trigger so that the arrow that he loaded would travel to the right distance. Bing soon got the hang of how to fix the mechanism at the right place on the scale, depending on whether the practice target was close at hand or almost out of sight, and he proved to be one of the most accurate marksmen of the recruits who were being drilled in how to use a bow. He was able to hold the weapon tight so that it was steady, and he always gauged the distance from the target accurately. His arrows nearly always struck home, and he was given good marks on his service record.

Soon the time came for Bing to move on to active service. He had heard tell of conscripts such as himself who were posted as guardsmen to protect one of the palaces in the great city of Chang'an. Others, who were kept in one of the commanderies, might be more likely to have to fight, if one of the kings took his own forces into the field against the Emperor and had to be suppressed. This did not happen often, and both of these assignments were likely to be rather dull, so Bing was excited when he learned that he was being drafted to serve in the defense lines of the north.

"You'll hate it at first," one of the sergeants told him. "Nothing but all that sand to look at and freezing cold nights." A soldier who had just come back from the north told him of the journey he would be taking and something of what he would be expected to do once he got there. "You'll be all right," he said, "but don't expect any comforts."

Bing was lucky that most of the other recruits in his detachment were from his own part of the world so they were able to understand each other. Later he found himself in the company of men from down south and what they said was incomprehensible. To his surprise they were accompanied by a few women and children and part of their job would be to protect them on the march.

"That means no fooling around by any of you," they were told. "Any squeak of a complaint from one of the women and you'll find how sharp this axe is; not that the culprit will have long to feel it."

Apparently these were family members of conscripts who were already up in the north and had been given a chance to settle down there, working as farmers. It can't be all that bad, thought Bing, if some of them are choosing to stay there.

The journey seemed endless, as they passed through countryside unlike any they had seen before. Hills rose suddenly from the plain. Fords took you across wide sluggish rivers of muddy water. Eventually they were trudging over sandy expanses on which no tree or bush could spring to life. There was little help for your sore feet when you camped down for the night and precious little water to drink, either on the march or later at the campsite. At last they were told that soon they would reach their new post.

There was still a long way to go, but finally in the distance Bing saw the faint outline of some buildings. As he and his companions got near, he could distinguish that these formed a line of small square forts joined together by an armed causeway. Merchants used to travel along that road with their caravans and the new recruits would have the job of ensuring that they could do so safely. He was told that some of the caravans would be really large, with hundreds of men and camels carrying all sorts of wares. Fierce men on horseback were continually waging attacks with the intention of stealing everything. Bing and his fellow soldiers would be responsible for defending those lines and keeping the buildings in a good condition, and they would always have to be on the alert in case of attack.

While he was taking all this in, a thought struck Bing. It would be impossible to raise a crop from the sandy wasteland around them, and he wondered where on earth they were getting food. They had been given a good meal on arrival. Where had it come from? Very soon the newly arrived men were each issued a set of working clothes—trousers, socks, and sandals—nothing special, just plain and rather rough.

"These will suit you fine," said the man who handed Bing his bundle of clothing. "Good and warm in the cold weather."

Bing unwrapped his bundle and examined the sandals he had been given. They were badly worn. He thought of mentioning this; perhaps a mistake had been made. But a glance around told him that his fellow soldiers had received sandals of a similar quality, and some of them decidedly worse.

He forgot about the sandals when a roll made up of foot long pieces of narrow wood was pushed in front of him. He was handed a brush and told to sign his name, if he could, or at least make a mark that would show he had received everything.

"It's all written down here, what we've given you," said the man who had handed him the brush. "Yes, you'll get a better pair of sandals if those wear out, but you'll have to bring those ones back and exchange them. Now, just make your mark here. Good. All right, next in line, your turn. Don't keep me waiting; hurry up." Bing wished that he had been able to read the thing on which he had put his mark. Once again, he examined the sandals. They were worse than he thought. It would not be long before they'd fall apart, and Bing expected that, when they did, he'd have an awful time trying to get another pair.

Next, the men were told how they were going to live. They would get a basic ration of millet and salt, sometimes more, sometimes less, depending on the work that they were doing. Already some of them were muttering to one another, wondering what sort of stuff would be palmed off on them. They knew very well what happened to millet if it was kept too long or left exposed to a hot sun; and they feared the worst if the garrison depended on what the merchants had to sell. To their great surprise they found that the rations were in fact in good condition, not too stale and fairly free of maggots.

"How do they get all this?" Bing asked aloud when he thought nobody was listening.

"You'll soon see," one of the sergeants replied. "It's all grown down there by the lake."

Some of the men did see this for themselves quite soon, as they were immediately posted to work on the farms that the service supervised, down along the banks of the lakes and the watercourses which joined them together. The farms were located on a line named Juyan that ran from south to north, jutting out from the main road and a defensive line that stretched out from west to east, and the farmers were growing grain for distribution to the units posted there. Where Bing was, on the line that ran out to the north, it was much easier to get fresh supplies than at the isolated posts farther west. The men who were posted to work at the farms found themselves working in much the same way as they had at home, except that the weather was different as was the timing of the age-old tasks of plowing, sowing, and harvesting. In many ways it was much easier to keep the crops well supplied with water. It was to these farms that the women and children who had made their way out with Bing's group went to join their menfolk.

Even before they had reached Juyan some of the conscripts had been detached to reinforce some of the units on the main defense line. Bing's first assignment was that of a runner who took official dispatches from one command post to another. Sometimes, after reaching the next post, you were turned back, and sometimes you were sent on for several more stages. No special training was required for this; all you had to do was to deliver the package where it belonged. There were labels attached to the postbag and others to the documents inside it; sometimes they were filled in with extra writing when the bag was handed over. Once again Bing wished that he was able to read what was being written down. After a while, he realized that the extra notes were made to record the times when he had set out and when he had reached the destination. He had been warned that a record would be kept of the time that he took and that he could face punishment if he was later than what the schedule expected. So the sergeant asked him when he had set out and then wrote something on the labels, and Bing guessed what was being put down. He learned that there were ways of ensuring that you would not be accused of being dilatory. This could be useful if you had taken a bit of time off, perhaps to chat with the messenger who was traveling in the opposite direction, and one of them showed him how to make sure that there would be no hint of any delay written down for an inspector to see. Had he already found out how time was counted and divided, and how anyone was able to measure it, he could have done so much more effectively and he might have made life much easier both for himself and his friends.

Duty as messenger became routine once you knew the way. As Bing discovered, the postal service that the army ran was not much different from one of the ways in which the government's mail was carried from the capital city of Chang'an to the commanderies and then the counties in the provinces. Ordinary mail went by foot, according to the schedule, stage by stage. Urgent dispatches went by riders on horseback. Neither Bing nor any of the other messengers had any idea of the contents of the wooden scrolls that they were carrying; they were not supposed to look at them, and in any case they could not read. However, one day a friend who was taking mail in the opposite direction stopped to share a snack, and he noticed that Bing's bag had come unfastened and that one of the rolls had fallen open.

"Let me see that," he said, and he took the roll in his hands. He was able to read, or so he said, and he told Bing that the roll was listing the criminal charges that an officer had to face. When he took out another roll, Bing tried to stop him, as he had been ordered not to open any of the documents that he carried. "No matter," his friend said, "nobody will know. Look here; this one reports the promotion or demotion of staff. Let's have a look at another one. Here we have a report of what a patrol saw of some marauders." The longest of the lot, so Bing was told, was a monthly return of the grain that had been collected and then issued, down to the smallest details.

"Put them all back," said Bing, "and do it neatly, before we get ourselves into trouble!"

One time he was delayed setting out because two officers, unknown to him, insisted on going through all the mail to look at its contents. They were talking quietly, in the hope that nobody would hear, but Bing could make out much of what they were saying. Months later, when tongues began wagging, he guessed that he had been carrying some fairly explosive material; a complaint that a conscript soldier had been making for repayment of some money that an officer had long owed him. There was also another document that might have stirred up quite a lot of trouble if its contents had become generally known; it reported the complaints that some of the men had been making because they hadn't received their full allowances of salt. Bing made a careful mental note to watch what he was being given.

Bing had been amazed when he first saw the command posts with all their equipment, everything stowed away so neatly, and no obvious flaws in the walls or towers. As it happened the commanding officer had just given orders that a number of extra rooms were to be built on to the guardhouse. A large number of bricks were needed for the job and Bing was sent to make them. Before the sun was up he had to shovel up mud from close to the river, check that it was free of rotting wood and take it back inside the courtyard of the post. Once there he had to fit the mud into wooden frames, all of equal size and shape, while it was soft enough to handle but not too full of water. When the sun broke through it soon started the work of drying out the mud and hardening it into bricks that would be ready to use. Eighty bricks a day he had to prepare and the officer would come around to count how many were ready. Not for the first time Bing wondered at all this insistence on counting everything and writing down a record of what the inspectors had seen. Little did he know that the time would come when he himself would have to be just as diligent in keeping records of this sort of activity, if he was to avoid a reprimand. But he was not yet through, as he had to get the newly baked, hard bricks out of their frames and stacked neatly for the builders.

There were other materials that the builders needed, such as bundles of reeds, which they laid out to form alternate courses between those of brick, as this was the best way of building up a high watchtower. At times Bing was sent to cut the reeds from the lakeside, strip off the twigs and leaves and tie them into bundles of the right size. Sometimes when he delivered them, the men who were building the walls asked him to take a turn at their work, plastering over any crevices with horse dung, or whitewashing them with coat after coat of paint.

There were other forms of work, such as cropping fodder for the horses and stacking it, and just as Bing hated some of the jobs he had to do, he loved it when he was sent to the stables to rub down the horses or feed them. He took care that nobody was looking when he gave them the freshest hay he could find instead of the stale, dried-out stocks that had been moldering for so long. Then there were fish to catch from the lake, mainly for the officers' meals but occasionally the men got a mouthful. In winter some of the catch was set aside for packing in ice and delivery elsewhere. He heard of one occasion when there had been real trouble over this, as the carter had been accused of selling off the black ox that drew his cart while it was still on the register of the county. He'd been very sly and pocketed the money, but he was soon found out.

Bing also had to take his turn at forestry and lumber work, or tending the vegetable plots, and even once as a cook. What he really liked and was good at was carpentry; not just the rough-and-ready hewing of timber for burning but the more choice and skillful assignment of making furniture for the officers, or hanging their quarters with doors that had to be measured accurately if they were to fit properly.

Eventually Bing's turn came for what would surely be an interesting assignment. He was drafted to keep watch on the walls of the command post. This was a small compound, built foursquare, with a somewhat higher part built as a platform. You had to be careful when making your way in, as all around there were hundreds of spikes buried in the sand, and hardly visible. These had been made of wood with sharp tips so that they would severely injure any man or beast that accidentally trod on them. Beyond that dangerous network the sand was always raked smooth, so as to form a wide even spread; any intruder would leave a telltale footprint or hoofprint, and the command post kept a lookout to see if anyone had penetrated there in the night. Come morning, the men had to sweep it all smooth again.

Inside the compound there were the buildings or huts in which the officers lived or spent weary hours keeping their records, and buildings where supplies and weapons were stored. The outside walls of this fortress rose above everything and when you climbed to the top you found yourself on a broad pathway that ran all the way round. It was here that Bing was posted. At his side stood the heavy crossbow that he had now been trained to use, far more powerful than any he had seen before. A series of special devices, made of wood, had been cut into the walls at regular intervals, each with an opening where the bow could be lodged. Bing found that you could then swivel the bow from left to right or right to left, so as to face any direction; at the same time, the wall itself gave you some protection against anyone who was trying to shoot at you from outside.

The bow that was now in his charge was fitted with the same sort of bronze trigger that he had already used when fitted to a lighter weapon. The trigger had a scale which enabled the marksman to adjust the weapon so that the arrows would reach the target. Powerful as this bow was, it took an enormous amount of strength and concentrated effort to load, as you had to stretch it out to the limit, pressing as hard as you could with your feet. It was a beautiful weapon, far better than those inferior ones on which he had been trained before getting to

Juyan, and Bing had been given some oil and grease to keep it in good trim and working to full capacity.

"That's nothing," said one officer, when Bing mentioned the range of his new weapon. "At least, nothing compared with one I've seen. That was a wooden framework on wheels, to which at least two bows were installed; and somehow it was possible to get them all shooting at the same target simultaneously."

Bing was fascinated. "Did you see it here?"

"Good Heavens, no," said the officer. "I haven't heard of anything like that at this god forsaken post."

Stretched out along both the west-to-east main line and the south-to-north line of Juyan, the command posts had orders to keep in regular touch with their neighbors so that everyone would quickly know of any danger or of any signs of intrusion. For this purpose every command post was equipped with a high pole up which signals could be hoisted, by flags during daytime or fire baskets at night, and sometimes a signal was sent by smoke. In addition the command posts always kept a pile of dry brushwood and light timber, which could be set ablaze in no time if there was a real emergency.

The officers regulated all this with the help of a written set of rules that they had to follow. In normal times a flag would be raised at the prescribed time, and the next command post up or down the line would acknowledge it by hoisting just the same signal. In all cases, the officers duly made an entry in their reports to record what had been done, noting the exact time when the signals were exchanged. Bing took a hand at this work on which the inspectors kept a sharp watch. Their first concern was with the wood that might be needed in emergency, to see that it was dry and well stacked so that it could be brought into use as quickly as possible.

It was cold for Bing up there on watch, looking not only for signals but also for any hint that marauders were at hand. Strict silence was ordered among those on watch duty so that they might keep their ears open for the slightest odd sound; in any case, if they did start telling smutty stories to one another, they would lose the concentration that was needed. Every so often an officer would come around—never at regular intervals—to see that they were awake and to let them know when one of their own patrols was expected back.

Bing had looked forward to duties of this sort, expecting to be involved in exciting activities, but the long nights seemed never to end, nothing ever happened and it was all tedious. So he was glad when his turn on watch was over and even more pleased when his squad was given special rations and arms for going out on patrol. Sometimes these patrols were quite short, six days, but they could last as long as thirty. On this particular occasion they were told to make their way to a hill, which they could see clearly from the top of the command post. But it was a starless night with no moonlight when they set out, and even with a guide it was difficult to know for certain that they were heading in the right direction. If there were any bandits about, they would probably be able to spot Bing and his squad from a distance.

The squad moved in twos and threes in silence, listening for telltale sounds that might disclose where an enemy lurked, under cover of a sandbank or down in a hollow. But the whipping winds made hearing difficult. As they were approaching a copse of tamarisk trees, a figure struck out at a sprint. Two men darted after him, and it took them some time to catch up. Sure enough he was armed, with a sharp dagger and a sword, and in the fight that broke out both he and some of Bing's squad were injured. Eventually they got the man down on the ground and bound, and they brought him back to the command post to explain himself. Who was he? Where did he come from? How many others were there, and where did they operate? Who was their leader? If they meant no harm, why was he armed?

"Would any one of you go out there by night unarmed?" he asked the interrogating officer, who had no answer. He was taken away, and Bing never knew what became of him.

It was while he was posted to duties of this sort that Bing became friendly with one of the officers. It was from him that he found out how an accurate count could be made of the hours as they passed. Altogether the day and night are divided into twelve hours, he was told, but that much he had already gathered.

"In addition," the officer told him, "some of the hours are divided into seven, and some into eight, short periods." Then the officer showed him two jars, an upper one connected to a lower one by an upright tube. "Water in the top jar drips down through the tube to the lower jar," said the officer, "where, if you look, you can see a number of straight lines marked on the side."

"Yes," said Bing. "I see them."

"As the water fills up the lower jar, you can see the level it has reached and count off how many hours or parts of an hour have passed."

Bing leaned close to the lower jar and stared.

"I have heard of a different way of telling the time of day," said the officer. "You do it with the help of a large, round, flat disk, into which an upright post is slotted. Around the rim of the disk, there is room for 100 divisions to be marked, but only 69 are shown. I'm not quite sure how it works or what it shows, but I am told that if you set the disk in the right position you can see how the shadow of the post moves around from one of the divisions to the others, and you can measure the passage of time in that way—but only in the daytime, of course, and only when the sun is bright enough for the post to cast a shadow."

Interested as he was in the ways of measuring the passage of time, Bing was even more excited about learning how to read and write, and he was terribly grateful to that same officer for giving him his first lessons. He showed Bing some of the simplest records that they had to keep, lists of the men and their units.

"Look at this," the officer said. "Here are the names of a new group of conscripts who got here ten days ago—that lot from down south who talk in such an odd way. You'll find the names of their squads first, then the place where they come from, and then their names, like this." And he showed Bing how all that had been put down, always in that order. "You can take this away with you if you like, but make sure that I get it back in one piece."

Bing was just longing for a bit of leisure while it was light so that he could take a long look at what he'd been given. When Bing did take it back, the officer was astounded to see how much he had mastered so quickly. Bing could easily recognize which signs were for numbers and which for names of the men and their units.

"I'll tell you how to understand the rest," the officer promised, and Bing was soon learning how to copy out what he saw. They had found him some worn-out materials with which he could practice, an old brush with half of its hairs worn out, and some slats of wood that were too short for proper use. Soon Bing was writing down the names of the units and command posts on the wooden slats from memory and doing quick sums, such as working out the total amount of rations needed to feed the troops who, a document said, would be joining them soon. Once it was known how useful Bing could be, he was ordered to help some of the officers in work which they themselves hated, calculating how much money they had to account for, or making good clean copies of a document.

"Who are those families down on the farms?" Bing once asked one of the sergeants.

"Some of them started as conscripts just like you, men who were sent here for a year's service. Well, we need to keep those farms running smoothly and I don't have to tell you what happens once they are left untended. The only way to keep the farms going is to get families settled there who will make their living and grow crops for all of us. It's no use having people there just for a year at a time, longing to get back home. Now what happens when one of the men gets a girl from close by into trouble and wants to marry her? They let him do so and settle the happy pair on one of the farms. Or else, you may get someone such as yourself who is sent here and fancies settling down, if only his wife and children could join him. You probably saw something of this on your way up here?" Bing did indeed remember the women and children who had made their way with him. "How about it?" one of the officers chimed in. "Can't you picture a life on one of these lush farms with all that lovely water close at hand?" No, thank you, thought Bing; he wanted a better life than that.

Notes for Chapter Two
An incomplete copy of the laws that were in operation in 186 BCE shows that gangs of conscripts who were moved from place to place required passports. A complete dossier that has been found records the legal case of a carter who had sold a black ox, illegally, in 28 CE. Numerous examples of foot rules and other objects show that the Han foot measured 23 centimeters. An example of a tomb of the pattern described, with a barricade of timber logs, may be seen at Dabaotai, Beijing. Multiple bows were listed in the inventory of an armory for 13 BCE. We know nothing of the quarters where troops posted to the garrisons slept, or of the conditions in which those detailed for farming work lived with their families.

Chapter Three *At the pass*

ALL DAY AND ALL NIGHT THE COMMAND POSTS ALONG THE LINES were responsible for keeping a check on travelers, military and civilian alike, whether they wanted to pass out from the Han commanderies into the outer world or to be admitted in. The commanding officer had made a point of telling Bing and his fellow troops about these duties as they would be performing them sooner or later.

"You must first establish why people want to go out and decide if there is any reason to detain them. Ask them their names and where they come from, and why they want to go out. You'll have to remember their ages, count how many family members are with them, and note their sex. Oh, and of course you must see what they are taking out with them, horses, mules, or carts, especially valuables. Much the same for anyone wanting to come in; find out where they want to go and why. Don't forget to include the time when they reach the lines. You'll be asked for all this information in the office up there. They will ask these people the same questions to see if they get the same answers. They will make out a written report."

With even the little knowledge Bing had of writing, he was luckier than the others who had none. It usually fell to him to go and tell the office what was going on and once up there, when they saw that he could just about read, they would ask him to help with the book work that had to be done. He still had no idea why it was necessary; why couldn't people come and go as they liked? All the officers said the same thing. It was all due to the Emperor's laws.

Then there was a rather special incident, from which he learned a lot.

A strange-looking man and his family came from inside the commandery with a coffin lying on a very simple cart that they were trundling along. It was his dead father inside the coffin, the man said, and he was taking him for burial to one of the settlements where his family had come from years and years ago, because his father had wanted to be with his ancestors.

"Very good," said the officer in charge, "but just let me have a look inside that coffin."

Well, there was nothing there except for the body in its shroud. Bing observed this and he could not understand why the poor man had had to open up the coffin. "It's a miserable thing to have to ask someone to do," he said.

"Maybe it is," said the officer, "but it's the law. We've got to see that they are not hiding anything that is not allowed. That includes anything precious: valuable dishes and pots of bronze or perhaps even of gold and silver, the sorts of things used in sacrifices. Also iron tools or sharp weapons of the sort that would fetch a high price. That's absolutely forbidden." Even members of the Han forces, who wanted to take a journey outward, were checked.

Bing learned that rules applied to certain types of animals as well. He was once ordered to examine some of the horses that a traveler wanted to take out and report what marks had been branded on them. In the process he narrowly missed a kick from one of the stallions who were not allowed out. This was because all sorts of regulations required that all valuable animals taken out must be brought back at set times, and they had to be identified by their color and measurements of height and girth, and by the brand mark which told where they had come from.

Indeed, there had been something suspicious with the man and the coffin. The officer had not been satisfied and the animals were all detained.

One of the officers usually took part in judging whether a man or woman who wanted to leave the Han lines should be allowed to do so. Anyone who had been condemned to hard labor as a convict for some crime or other was easily recognizable; no hair, as it had all been shorn off; tattoo marks on the face, or signs where some horrible cuts had been inflicted. But it was not so certain that, as they would claim, they had completed their sentences. Had one of them been able to make a getaway? Had a young man, of Bing's age, done his time as a conscript laborer and soldier, or was he just trying to escape from those duties? Should he be held on suspicion of being a deserter?

The first thing that the officer would ask for would be the man or woman's card of identity. This was a small slat of wood, some six inches long, on which all the necessary personal information had been written, such as name, place of domicile, age, coloring, height, social status of the man and his family members, together with the date when it was issued. If anyone who wanted admission to the empire did not have such a card, he would have to explain himself. If he did so satisfactorily, he could get a document of some sort, but it might take a few days for the officials to make up their minds, after some rigorous questioning.

It was from one of these incoming travelers that Bing heard of the long routes that stretched out over the sands, of the intense cold at night out there, with little shelter from fierce animals. Usually people traveled together in small groups, so that when they settled down for the night they could take turns keeping watch, and before they made ready for sleep they would have a round of singing and music to keep their spirits up.

If you went far enough, Bing learned, you would come to a grassy settlement where there was plenty of water, at least enough for the people who lived there but they did not welcome strangers who came to share it with them, and they had some very odd customs.

"Who on earth would want to go to such places over all those routes that stretch forever over the sands?" Bing asked. His friend told him of vast caravans led by rich merchants, their camels loaded with bales of silk, pots and pans for cooking, and valuable goods of bronze. "These bands are made up of several hundred men," said the traveler. "It takes them months to make the round trip, sometimes on the most dangerous mountain passes that you can imagine. Of course, the camels get on all right, so do the yaks."

Bing looked puzzled. "Yaks?"

"What? Never seen a yak? Very sturdy, they are, and they walk ever so slowly. They love to be right at the edge of the path, staring down the precipice; quite scary."

In exchange for the goods they sold, the merchants might pick up some furs to sell back home, or some felts made from the wool of the mountain sheep and goats. Or they would be paid with peculiar coins, very different from the simple bronze disks with a hole in the middle that Bing was used to.

"Yes, I have got some," said the traveler. "Look at these."

They were much larger than the coins Bing knew and much heavier, with no square hole in the middle, and instead of the dull-colored bronze, these were gold or silver and shone brilliantly, especially when the sun caught them. Bing turned them over in his hand. Each side was decorated, one face with the figure of a man, the other with a mounted horseman, and there were marks that looked like writing of some sort. The stranger could not read any of it except the figures which told the value of the coin, but he did know that, curiously enough, the writing went in horizontal lines rather than in columns and it was read from left to right. He had no idea where they came from, he'd been given them at one of the markets down the line where he had been selling some skins, and he knew that he could get a good price for the coins, simply for their value in silver.

Bing got to know a lot about the way this part of the service worked and he learned even more when one of the officers asked him if he could write. He was confident enough—and he hoped not foolhardy—to say that he could.

"We need a copy of this document," he was told, and he was given the materials with which to make one. Luckily these included a knife, as Bing made a number of mistakes on the wooden strips and was able to peel them off and start again.

It was a long list and turned out to be a record of officers who had been let inside the lines for legitimate purposes. Some had been summoned, so that they would proceed to take up another and more highly ranking post. Some were making their way in voluntarily; they had realized that they had committed some offense or even a crime, such as a small dereliction of duty, and they knew that if they delivered themselves up with a confession they would be treated far more leniently than if they were charged and punished. This could happen easily if somebody wanted to do them harm and denounced them to the authorities. One officer came in after buying medicine for his men, probably at the great trading center of Dunhuang in the west, and Bing wondered if it was from there that those strange coins had come. Others were officers who came in to draw the rations of grain or salt to which their men were entitled, or to draw their own pay.

The register told of one man who wanted to come in to lodge a claim for money that was owed to some of those under his charge. And there was the case of one person who was not a soldier. As far as Bing could make out, he wanted to buy a coffin that he could take to bury a kinsman outside the lines. He explained that there were no solid trees out there to use for that purpose. What surprised Bing was the number of civilians who came from all parts of the empire, from the capital city or even the commanderies in the south, to ask to be let out of the lines.

One fairly senior officer had been inspecting the defense lines and was on his way back to headquarters to report. Another was personally bringing reports on his subordinates' records of service. This was a highly confidential document for delivery to the governor of the commandery and he had not wanted to entrust it to anyone else, for reasons that Bing could well understand. While working in the office, Bing had accidentally seen a report of just that type, showing how long the officers had served, down to the number of days, and the degree of merit they had attained. The clerks in the office had no business leaving it lying around for anyone to see and by mistake this one had actually been put with the list that Bing was copying. They made him swear that he would never talk about it or even say that he had seen it. In return he could sometimes extract a favor from the officer who had been responsible, and who knew that Bing could denounce him if he felt like it.

There was one incident that Bing would never forget. A party of five arrived from down south, asking to be let through. The man and wife, each forty to fifty years old, were accompanied by an old woman whose head was bound up by several layers of clothing. There was a seven-year-old boy and his younger sister with them, and they all looked worn out by the hardships of travel. They had their goods stacked on a well-used cart of a type that Bing had not seen before and which looked as if it had seen better days before it had fallen to their lot to pull it. Rather ill at ease, they presented their card of identity.

"Why do you want to leave with all this family?" the officer asked. "Isn't it good enough for you down in Henan—oh no, I see it's

Donghai you come from. I'd always heard that it was easy going and a fine life down there by the sea."

"We've got relatives out beyond there," the man said. "We want to see my grandfather before it's too late; he must be very frail by now."

There was something about the wife's behavior that the officer could not quite place, and he knew very well that out there in the beyond, however much a son wanted to show respects for an elderly relative, the family would not relish having to house and feed five mouths beyond their own.

"How long are you going to be there?" was the next question.

Before he could be stopped, the young boy piped up, "Forever!"

Now the officer was on the alert. "Any of you ever been charged for a crime and sentenced to punishment?"

"Oh, no," the man mumbled. The wife nodded while the old woman kept silent.

The officer's gaze rested on the old woman. "Let's get a look at your head."

She had no choice but to unwrap everything. "I do feel the cold at my age, Sir, and the wind is very bitter. May I keep this last one on?"

"I'm afraid not. Well now, how come your cheeks are scarred like that when you said you'd never been punished for a crime?"

Out came their story, which went back to the old woman's father. An impressionable youngster, he had joined a group of rebels who were scheming to remove the Emperor. Heaven knows what they were planning to do after that, none of them even bothered to ask. Probably their leaders, no less than seven kings of the empire and relatives of the Emperor himself, had their ideas, but no word came down to the rough-and-ready gangs who were fighting for them. Of course, they had all been soundly defeated in the end and just wanted to limp back home. It was only thanks to a wonderful act of grace by the Emperor himself that her father had been allowed to return to his homeland in Donghai.

"And then?" Bing stood by with his ears wide open to hear it all.

The old woman shivered as she spoke. "Despite the pardon, even down there, and for so many years afterward, it was not easy for a family known to have taken part in that incident. What's more, the officials kept a sharp eye on all of us, especially on my son here. As a youngster he was careless and was reported one night for stealthy behavior. No, he hadn't committed any crime, he was out with a girl, but, suspicious activities had to be reported, and he was brought before the magistrate for questioning. Luckily, he was released with nothing more than a warning."

The official sighed. "Your story is very long and it seems to be going nowhere. It has nothing to do with those tattoo marks on your cheeks, does it?"

"Sorry," said the woman, "but I've left that out. You see, they questioned me as well, several times, and at one point, so they said, I contradicted myself. That was their reason for branding me in this horrible way. All this was years ago but you know what it's like in a village. There's always somebody who enjoys picking on the misfortune of others. Years of taunting became unbearable. That's why I finally persuaded my boy here that we must take to the road to make a fresh start."

The officer on duty had heard this sort of thing before and found himself torn. His plain duty was to consult all those rolls of the empire's Statutes and Ordinances to see what he ought to do but that would take him all day, and in any case he had a human heart. Fortunately, only Bing, his personal assistant, had been near enough to hear any of this. Dare he let the five of them go out, where they would never be pursued? Must he report the whole thing and send them to the magistrate to decide? He was quite at a loss.

He turned to the younger woman. "What is the name of your husband's relative you are going to see?"

Caught up by a fit of coughing she could not reply.

"Well," he said, "let's see what you've got in that cart," and Bing was ordered to have a look. Most of the things were household goods and equipment, such as pots and pans and earthenware jars, and there were some provisions sealed in some of the jars. Once a stack of clothing had been removed, there was a pungent smell seeping from the jars.

Bing was about to report that there was nothing there of any value, when his eye caught a glint from something between the rough folds of fabric. He drew up a string of coins. But it was not that string of dull bronze disks that had been shining. Concealed even deeper there was one of several beautiful vessels of lacquered wood, or perhaps bronze, inlaid with gold and silver. There was a bronze mirror decorated with all sorts of figures and something in writing, and several other items. At the time Bing had no idea what all these things were used for, but he was told later that they were the sorts of items buried at funerals.

"I thought so," said the officer, perhaps proudly, perhaps grimly. "You've no right to be taking all these valuable pieces outside the boundary and you'll be charged with a criminal offense, just as the statutes here say. You'll have to explain it all. No, this is all beyond me; it's got to go higher up. We'll keep you here under guard while I write up a report and send it on, and the commandant will send his orders. Take them away."

Bing wondered how on earth they had come to possess such valuables that Incense burner, shaped like a mountain, and that lamp stand, why you could set a dozen candles on it to burn all at once. He never learned what happened to that family. Probably the man had been sentenced to a few years of hard labor. He'd be lucky if one of his feet had not been cut off. His wife and children would probably have been taken to work in government service, just as some of Bing's earlier relatives had been. He hated to think what might have happened to the man's mother and felt very sad about the whole episode. He knew that all orders and laws had to be obeyed, however harsh they might be, and he knew that they were supposed to be there to make life safer for everybody. At least that was what the officers had told him, though they seemed to say such things in a stilted way that suggested a speech, something they'd had to learn by heart. But what did it all mean? Here was a family that had stored up their treasures and wanted to start a new life away from any trouble or bad treatment. Old and young, they were human beings and he could not see what harm they were doing, especially the children.

"Don't be a simpleton," one of his friends said. "Can't you see that they must have stolen all those valuables? They may even have dug them out of a tomb, for all that you or I know, and been planning to sell them at one of the markets down the line where they are not so strict as they are here and no questions are asked."

Bing didn't know what to think, but there would come times in his future when he would relive this incident, and the lessons he had learned from it.

Notes for Chapter Three
For the revolt of the seven kings in 154, see Denis Twitchett and Michael Loewe, eds., *The Cambridge History of China,* vol. I, *The Ch'in and Han Empires, 221 B.C.–A.D. 220* (Cambridge: Cambridge University Press, 1986), pp. 141–44. Legal records of 217 and 186 BCE refer to the control exercised over movements of horses. For trading contacts between Han China and communities in Central Asia, and Han knowledge of Greek coins, see A. F. P. Hulsewé, *China in Central Asia: The Early Stage, 125 B.C.–A.D. 23* (Leiden: E. J. Brill, 1979). For the activities of the troops on garrison duty in the northwest, including controls exercised at the passes in and out of Han territory, see Michael Loewe, *Records of Han Administration* (Cambridge: Cambridge University Press, 1967).

Chapter Four

In a nobleman's mansion

ALL THE MEN WERE LONGING FOR HOME AND EVENTUALLY THEIR stint in the service was over, and they were to return to the place where they had come from. Until they reached the county offices there, they were still under official orders and they would be free to go only when they had been dismissed. On the return trip, they were all in good spirits. The hard work that had been their lot for so long had come to an end, that wretched place to which they had been assigned was behind them, and gradually the fields and trees of their own home lands were coming into view.

The officer responsible for managing the return trip was in a good mood, too, cracking jokes and looking forward to the pleasures of life in a town once more. He had in fact made a pact with his men; he would give them as easy a time as he could, so long as not one of them attempted a getaway. Anyone who did would be hunted down and, if found, subject to arrest on a charge of desertion. What's more, his friends would be charged for abetting him. It went without saying that the officer himself would be in severe trouble if he could not account for each soldier on his list. Bing thought that it was a fair deal. Several times, when the snow was falling, or they had stopped to rest in the thick of a forest, he saw how easily he might slip away, but he stood firm by his promise. Besides, the temptation was not so great. He had no idea where they were and could not possibly have found his way home without guidance.

The journey was uneventful and at last he arrived at his native village. He was officially dismissed, and made his way to the family farm. He was of two minds about returning home, for he knew that life on the farm would not have changed in his absence, and he was eager to make a new life for himself somewhere else.

Bing had not counted on a warm reception, nor did he get one. Nobody seemed the slightest bit interested in hearing about what he had seen and learned in his time away. The morning after his arrival, his father had him right back to the same old boring work. He had no one to talk to. His brother was always reminding him that he could not stay there forever, and it was not long before he planned to get away from it all. He was in a far better shape now to find his own way. He was able to read up to a point and he had become a skilled carpenter. Most important of all, he knew much more about ways of the world beyond the dreary farm.

Before he set out, he attended one of those village meetings, where everyone gets together to pay their respects to their ancestors. He stopped to speak with some of the friends he knew from the village, all the while keeping an eye out for a particular young girl. Although she was from one of the neighboring households, she was nowhere to be seen.

"Oh, she's married and gone away," he was told, and he felt more than a slight pang of regret. An inquiry about some of the old ones brought the news that they had died in the last winter, which had been severe.

Early the next morning, Bing set out for the town where his father had once taken him. The sights along the way were not new to him now, and he passed the time thinking through his plans. He intended to go straight to the market, and finally arrived there to find that, sure enough, everything seemed to be much the same as it had been before. He got there just in time to lend a hand to a team who were packing up their stall for the night, and he earned enough to cover the cost of a modest supper. The next day he was back at the market and found a small job, helping to repair a vegetable stall. As he worked, he felt that he was being watched, and looked across the way to see Shang, the merchant who had once complimented him on his work back at the farm. Bing saw him again the next day. This time, Shang was making a purchase at a fruit stall, and Bing observed the proprietor cheating him with a flawed set of weights.

"Excuse me," said Bing, "but that scale is reading too high, about half as much again as the fruit actually weighs."

The proprietor bristled. Shang nodded to Bing and paid the proprietor a just price.

"You're a sharp young man," said Shang, as they walked away. "And talented as well. How would you like a small job? I have a broken axle on one of my wagons that needs fixing."

Bing took on all sorts of work, mostly small jobs that required a few hours of his time, and he would get a meal or a few coins for his trouble. Sleeping out in the rough was pretty wretched and it could be dangerous. There were plenty of thieves around and the magistrate's patrolmen were always on the watch for people like Bing, whom they called "vagrants" and treated as criminals. Short of money, he was nearly always hungry. At times, he wondered if leaving the farm had been the right decision. He'd always assumed that there was a better way of life than the backbreaking work in the fields, which anyone could do. Repairing carriages, working on houses, running a shop.

A chat that he had one day in the market gave him something to think about. There were no odd jobs to be had that day, and there had been none the day before. Bing could feel his belly tightening with hunger, as he sat beside another young man, likewise hungry and looking for work.

"We could always get jobs in the ironworks," said the young man. "I hear they never have enough people to get the work done."

Bing hated the idea. After his experiences as a conscript, he knew what the ironworks would be like. But this was no time to be fussy, he thought. There was no other way out, and he had to get something to eat.

As Bing expected, the ironworks was a grim place, but sure enough they agreed to take him on. What's more, whatever the job he was assigned, they would pay him with coins. Bing was soon using his strength to full capacity at a job for which no training was needed, except when he was cutting down trees and splitting branches or trunks into logs to fit the furnace. In addition to wood, there was a supply of a sort of fuel he had never seen before—heavy, dark black lumps that gave off a peculiar dirty smell and burned to a terrific heat. But the really heavy loads that he had to carry or, if he was lucky, take by cart, were rocks, which were taken inside and heated until they were so hot that the precious liquids inside them would start to ooze and then to flow out to become iron or copper. Inside the building there were some highly skilled men at work. It was so hot that they hardly wore any clothes. Their job was to pour the liquid into molds while it was still hot. When the liquid cooled and hardened, there were the finished products such as plowshares or arrowheads. Then there were the smiths hammering away at the hot metal to beat it into the right shape. So long as he had to work outdoors Bing did not worry, but long spells inside were killing, as the place was always filled with smoke and steam and you couldn't get free of the dreadful fumes.

Sometimes Bing found it difficult and very painful to breathe and he would come out gasping and choking, only to have the foreman threaten to cut his pay because he wasn't working full time. It became clear to Bing that he would have to give up this work and find another way to stay alive, and he made that decision none too soon. The day after he quit his job, there was a devastating accident at the ironworks, and many of the men lost their lives.

Exactly the same thing had happened when he was working in a foundry as a conscript. Work had been proceeding as usual, when the whole place started echoing with a series of unearthly noises, like a deep guttural roll of drums followed by claps of thunder. Most of the men dropped their tools and ran for their lives, just before a terrific explosion tore the place apart. Bing for one had managed to get out, but some of his fellow workers had not and were killed. All that was left of the foundry was a deep blackened pit in the ground.

Bing decided that he had to find work in the town, and he now knew far more than he had about various ways of getting himself taken on. Before long he was lucky enough to become attached to one of the largest and richest houses there. It had been built by someone who had had real power and must have been very rich. At one time, this man had been a senior official of the central government, away in Chang'an city, but he had had enough of life there and wanted to spend his last days in comfort, away from the capital where all his former rivals, and some enemies, still lived. He had deliberately chosen a site for the house that he would build in one of the smaller towns, knowing that his rank would guarantee that he would be treated with respect. Rather than live in the middle of the town with all its noise, and the ban on going out after the curfew, he chose somewhere on the west side, where there was a good view and shelter from the worst winds. He was very careful to choose a site with a natural way for good fortune to come in and where evil influences would be kept at bay.

Bing had to show his identity card before they would take him on. There were quite a number of slaves, all clothed in red, employed in the house to do the menial and unskilled tasks. Bing knew nothing of slaves and had to be told what being a slave meant.

"You can buy and sell them," one of his fellow workers explained, "and once you have them, you can make them do any sort of work at all and punish them if they don't do it properly. Why, I heard about a slave master who put a slave to death, probably because he had an eye for one of the ladies of the household. But we don't expect any trouble from this bunch here. They've been here a long time and know that no harm will come to them if they behave themselves."

Nonetheless, Bing was glad not to be a slave. He was a servant of the house and found that he got on well enough with the other servants, who were in a class above the slaves, and he worked well with the overseer who gave him his orders.

This great house had been built of wood, with walls and partitions inside that separated one sort of activity from another. When the master and his wife were dining, perhaps with some guests, the room would not be filled with the steam and smells that came from the kitchen. Some of the inner rooms had tables or other pieces of furniture of far better quality than anything Bing had ever seen. He just marveled at the choice woods from which they were made rather than the rough timber that everyone else used. The walls were covered in finely embroidered curtains, and there were plenty of cushions for comfort. Up toward the roof, the house had not been built with plain planks of timber straight from the forest; the beams and struts had been expertly planed and oiled before being painted or carved. Bing could only admire the skill that had gone into producing all this.

The tableware with which dinner was served was particularly fine. Some of the vessels were inlaid with silver. Some had gold worked into the handles. There were specially shaped cups, again with some gold, that came from a place in the west called Shu. Bing had even seen

decanters made of jade. He wondered what his family would make of
all this, especially if they saw the sorts of things that the kitchen staff
produced for dinner. There were vast quantities of roasted meat and
fish, with sweet or sour relishes and seasoned with the finest of herbs;
and there were some very expensive delicacies, such as rare fruits, that
Bing had seen for sale in the market.

Bing noticed similar differences when he thought of the rough
clothes of hemp that they had to make do with back on the farm, or
the very ones that he himself was wearing. Ladies in this great house
wore silk weaves of all sorts of colors and patterns, even embroidered
silks. He was told that the best of all was the very rare "ice white"
brand. This was fine enough in the summer; for cold winters there
were the delicate woolens that merchants brought in from the north,
and furs and fur hats to wear. Sleek, well-fed horses drew these people
around in luxurious carriages built with awnings to shelter them from
sun or rain and fitted with ornamental fastenings and handles. There
was no shortage of entertainment in the house. Lest anyone feel bored,
there was often some sort of a show that the home orchestra would put
on, with bells, drums, and flutes. Sometimes for entertainment there
would be a clever troupe of dancers, acrobats, or wrestlers.

The head of the house was a nobleman, a member of almost
the highest-ranking order in the land. When the time came for the
nobleman's mother to die, Bing saw for himself how people of high
rank buried their dead, never mind how much hard work was spent
preparing the tomb, or the value of what would be put inside. Some
years earlier, a deep pit had been dug out in the fields. The sides were
stepped with ledges so that you could move by easy steps from a higher
to a lower level. Down at the bottom, a structure was built of very
fine timber, the sort that would last forever, with its columns carefully
joined together. This whole frame, which was large enough to contain
a house, would be the resting place for a series of coffins, nestling one
inside the other and finally housing the old lady. In this way she would
be protected by stout walls, which would withstand all changes of
cold and heat, damp or drought, and be safe from any harm that men
could do.

Bing watched as those four coffins were being finished. Artists
and their helpers were at work painting the sides and lids with a

magnificent pattern of designs, mainly in black, red, and gold. They let their imaginations run wild. Sometimes they kept to formal patterns; sometimes their brushes left delicate lines of lacquer that wove around in curls; sometimes they painted creatures that were half human and half animal, leaping from one side to another.

There would be plenty of room to spare down in the pit and Bing assumed that it would be a long and arduous task to fill it up. But he soon found out that the empty spaces would not be filled entirely with earth. The nobleman's chief aide took Bing into a large room in the house, where a whole array of objects, both rare treasures and ordinary items, had been placed on tables.

"Here's the written list of what should be here," the aide said. "I know you can read, so it will be your job to check the items against the list. You must let me know if there is anything missing. And before you begin, let me warn you; in the old days anyone who saw all this before a funeral would be put to death and buried in the same tomb with the corpse, so that he couldn't tell anyone what treasures had been buried. We don't do that sort of thing nowadays, but remember that these pieces are all marked, and if any of them turn up in the market for sale, you'll be the one to be charged and punished."

Bing thought of that family of five he'd seen at the pass—the old lady with her head wrapped in layers of cloth, and the valuable items that they had tried to take out. Of course, they must have been goods stolen from a tomb of this sort. He set to work with the inventory and soon found himself in great difficulty. He could easily match up many of the things on the list with what he saw on the tables and mark those items off on the list, but he couldn't make head or tail of some of the writing. What's more, he had never set eyes on anything like some of the potteries or bronze wares on the tables. Sometimes he found that there were differences between the quantities entered on the list and the numbers he found on the tables. The list showed five square containers for grain but there were only two to be found. He made sure to make a note of this to pass on to the aide.

There they were, cups and platters in lacquer, storage pots of bronze, painted food containers. There were also the supplies needed for the banquet when these would be in use, grains and liquor, stored fowl and fish. Then there were the rolls of silk, some in just the same pattern as the clothes he had seen the ladies wearing. There were hampers made of straw with all sorts of clothes and sandals inside, and sets of small boxes, black and scarlet, all fitting neatly into a large round container. There were combs with them and he thought that these must be the sorts of things the ladies used when dressing themselves up.

Bing was puzzled when he came upon strings of coins; some of them were real enough, but some were made of pottery and would be of no use in the markets that he knew. Then there were the fairly small figurines, sets of men and women made of wood and gaily painted, each one of them carrying the musical instrument which he or she had played. Tucked away on an upper shelf lay rolls of narrow strips, bundles and bundles of them, that obviously carried written texts. The rolls had been tied together tightly to ensure that none of the strips would drop out, but that had not prevented some of them from being broken and falling to the floor. Finally, Bing found a box in which squares of silk, painted with pictures and columns of writing, had been stored.

As he did his best to check the list against the items, Bing could only marvel at the wealth of what he saw. Why on earth, he wondered, were all these lovely things going to be buried, never to be seen again; and what was the point of all those rolls of writing? He would have liked to unroll them and try to decipher what had been written down. What a dreadful waste it all seemed.

There was a delay before the funeral took place, as there were some wise men who had to choose a day when it would be lucky to hold the funeral. When the day came, Bing was told to go with the procession so that he could attend to any breakage or mishap that might occur, perhaps to one of the carriages. Many relatives of the dead woman had come to pay their respects and before they set out to the tomb they had to take their correct place in the family line; the older ones, who were much more closely related than the younger ones, went first. Ahead of the carriage that carried the coffin, there was a smaller one in which a high pole had been mounted, and a long richly colored banner was hung from the top of the pole. Bing was not close enough to see the banner clearly but he could make out a picture of the sun and the moon at the top.

The procession moved slowly, pausing every so often when somebody called out something in a loud voice. Once they reached the gravesite, every move that was made had to fit a set of rules; every stage was marked by the reciting of verses or prayers and some sustained wailing. Slowly the coffin was removed from the carriage, no easy job when you thought of the weight of its four pieces. On and on went the wailing as the coffin was lowered into its final home in the structure at the bottom of the pit.

It was at this point that a series of other carriages made their way to the front. Bing watched as all those things he had checked so diligently were unpacked and taken right down. Some of them, still in their straw cases, were placed around the coffins; some of them were set out in formal fashion as if in preparation for just the sort of banquet that they held in the great house itself. Bing simply could not see the point of it all. Then he heard someone saying how splendidly the master was looking after the soul of his mother and caring for her after death in just the way that he had while she was alive, and Bing began to understand what some people thought happened to you when you died. Well, maybe so, he thought. His duty was to stay right to the end of the ceremony to watch while the tomb was being sealed, in preparation for the high mound that would be raised above it. He had to make certain that none of the workmen left a sign or a secret means by which a robber could make his way in and steal all those wonderful treasures.

There was usually something of interest going on in the nobleman's house, what with guests arriving and needing attention, and Bing thought how much better life was there than it could ever be in the town, where there were always people to see that you were not breaking any rules. Of course, the style of living was infinitely better than anything they could dream about back on the farm. But as time wore on he became restive. He had seen a lot on that journey north as a conscript serviceman, but there was much that they had passed by without stopping to look. He wondered whether he would ever have a chance to go back and see what life there was really like. By luck his chance came quite quickly.

Notes for Chapter Four

We have no certainty that choice of the site for a house depended on considerations of *feng shui* at this time. Accounts of the extravagant style of life practiced by the opulent, as seen in two written works of respectively ca. 48 BCE and 150 CE (*Yantie lun* and *Qianfu lun*), are partly supported by archaeological evidence; a less restricted use of "ice-white silks" is castigated as a sign of decadence. It cannot be known how far coal was in general use, but it was probably not widespread. Nor do we know to what extent hired labor was used in the iron foundries or how far they were staffed by conscripts. For accounts of explosions in iron foundries in 91 and 27 BCE, see *Han shu* 27A, p. 1334; Donald B. Wagner, *The State and the Iron Industry in Han China* (Copenhagen: Nordic Institute of Chinese Studies, 2001), pp. 46–47; and Anthony J. Barbieri-Low, *Artisans in Early Imperial China* (Seattle: University of Washington Press, 2007), p. 99. The funeral and burial arrangements as described are based on an example in the south, at tomb no. 1 Mawangdui (168 BCE), and may not necessarily have been practiced in the north.

Chapter Five

On the road

Some of the rich merchants, who dealt in luxury goods, made a point of calling at the nobleman's house when they had anything special to sell. Bing was always interested to see them arrive and set out their wares. One day when a party like this turned up, Bing recognized the leader. It was Shang, the man whom he had met back on the farm and for whom he had done a small job in the market. Managing to get close to Shang, he made sure that he would be recognized. Shang spent some time with the nobleman's steward, who saw that he got a good meal before he made his way farther afield.

"I've seen that fellow over there once or twice before and rather like the look of him," Shang told the steward. "As it happens I need a spare hand at the moment and have a good mind to take him with me—that is so long as you have no objection."

The steward knew when he was on to a good thing. Of course he could not sell Bing as if he were one of his master's slaves, but he knew enough about some of Shang's dealings to see that he would not part with Bing for nothing, and Shang knew how to make it worth the steward's while to do so. The two men soon came to an agreement and settled it over a pot of home-brewed beer that the steward had in store.

Shang asked to see Bing and told him what to expect if he joined him.

"Life on the road is fairly hard," he said. "But our travel ends before winter, and we settle down comfortably at my home for a few months. Yes, you will have good solid food the whole time and I will pay you in cash as a hireling."

It didn't take Bing long to make up his mind. He reckoned that, if he kept his eyes and ears open, he would learn how to run a business.

He'd already had a good look at Shang's carriages and thought how well furnished and comfortable they seemed to be; and the horses looked as if they were being well cared for. Yes, what a fool he would be to refuse this golden opportunity.

So off they set, Bing in high spirits with hopes for a prosperous future. At the first town that they reached Shang took Bing to the local officials to make sure that the card on which his personal details were written was in order and would not cause any difficulty as they traveled. He had been badly delayed once before when he met just that sort of trouble and had even had to part with money to get himself out of it.

Shang's carts were laden with some of the goods that Bing had seen on sale in the market, such as pottery wares for the kitchen. He had quite a stock of silk, still in rolls, and some furs and woolens from the north, which would fetch a high price in places where it was not possible to herd sheep. One wagon was given over to luxury foods such as dried meats, fish, and fruit; and there were jars of pickles and sauces, and a few of those very rare spices that gave a fine flavor to meat that was beginning to go off. Shang said that he had sold most of his stock of these jars at the nobleman's house and that he needed to pick up some more from farther west. One wagon was full of something that Bing had hardly ever seen before, jars that contained raw lacquer, drained straight from the trees. In fact there had been two or three of these jars in the room where the artists had painted the old lady's coffins, and he was amazed to find out how expensive they were.

There were some things in which Shang never dealt. Some of his colleagues had been paid large sums by officials to deliver cargoes of grain to distant places, even as far as Dunhuang where food could be in short supply. But Shang had not been tempted; grain was bulky and soon started to rot. Some types of timber could fetch a high price, particularly those heavy trees that came from the west. The wood was long lasting, and people liked to use it for coffins; but here again there were problems in transporting and handling such bulky wares. Animal skins were another commodity that Shang avoided; whether of horses, cattle, or sheep, they all needed special treating or else they would smell and breed flies. Nor had Shang any wish to deal with live animals that needed regular feeding and tending, and which could not be moved far away from the place where they were used to living. He had known some people who traded in horses or cattle, or even slaves, but they had rarely found it worth their while.

Before long they reached one of the points where their documents were checked and their goods examined. Neither Shang nor Bing was surprised at what went on as Shang knew all about it as a traveler, Bing as an assistant to the officials who carried out the inspection. Here he was, on the other side now, and he could give Shang some suggestions such as how the inspectors liked to be addressed and treated—a small present by way of greeting could work wonders and save a good deal of time. Shang was only too grateful for Bing's friendly guidance, especially when it came to having something to read or write. They passed the checkpoint easily. Shang was relieved. Bing didn't say so, but he thought the officials had been rather slack.

As the days went by along the rough roads, sheltering from rain, and later in the year from the sweltering heat, Bing did various jobs, checking all the wagons, greasing their wheels, and seeing that the goods which they carried had not suffered from pilfering. When they settled down for the night Shang asked him to take charge and see that everyone was looked after properly, including the pregnant wife of one of the drovers. In the towns Bing saw how skilled and experienced Shang was at driving a bargain; how unlike Shang's approach was from the simple way in which his father had brought his spare vegetables to market. Bing was surprised at the way prices varied from place to place and from season to season. He'd never thought of such large sums of money passing from hand to hand, and as Shang had asked him to keep a written account of all that came in and went out, he soon became an expert at sizing up whether it would be worth Shang's while to step in quickly with an offer to buy a stock of something or to hold off until the sale price had dropped.

Long, long hours they spent on the road and there was much that drew Bing's interest as they passed through a landscape that was always changing, past farms and houses of all sorts, and granaries built in a variety of strange shapes. Everything was new and different, or so it seemed, until one day Bing looked around and sensed something familiar. He began to recognize where they were, not far from his home village and the family farm. Part of him longed to stop and see the old folk. Were his parents still alive? Part of him feared that they might see him as a stranger and resent the easy way of life that he was now living. With a shudder he thought of the endless time he had spent stamping earth to build walls, and the plain, sometimes meager suppers that ended the day. Shang settled the question. "We've simply got to get on," he said. "There is no time to linger."

Occasionally, they gave shelter to a wretched beggar when they caught up with one on the road, but not as often as Bing would have liked. Late one afternoon, as they were preparing to stop for the night, Bing thought he recognized one of them, trudging along with hardly a stitch of clothing on his back.

"Can't we feed that poor devil?" he asked.

"Certainly not," Shang answered, "they're all vagrants, too frightened to go into the towns without a card where they would be picked up as deserters and punished. They have nothing to do but turn to crime, working in a gang under some ruffian's orders. You see, it's part of a scheme. One of them is let loose to beg a meal from the likes of us. Come nightfall the whole band of them has surrounded you. They are well armed, and they steal anything they can get their hands on, taking whatever they like and killing or wounding anyone in their way."

As Bing got to know Shang better he knew that it would be best to refrain from pressing such matters; nor did he openly express his sympathy with the groups of convicts they met, traveling under guard.

One afternoon, they passed some vagrant travelers and, as usual, refused to offer them food or shelter. It's likely to be just as dangerous to ignore these people as it is to help them, Bing thought, but it would be no good telling that to Shang.

The rest of the day passed uneventfully. They stopped to make camp. Darkness fell and all was quiet. Bing was going over their plans for the following day, when a shrill cry broke the silence. Shouts and screams followed, and suddenly the camp was in an uproar. Bing rushed to the wagons. There were some members of his own party, bleeding, lying motionless on the ground. Most of the robbers had made off by the time he got to the last of the wagons. Its coverings were ripped off, half its cargo—sweet fruit and spices—was strewn on the roadside, and the other half was missing. Bing was about to rush back to aid the wounded, when a rustle in the underbrush caught his attention. He picked up a hefty stick and began to beat the thicket, until somebody was forced out.

Heavens above, thought Bing; it was the same man who had been tramping the road a few days earlier and this time Bing had no doubt who he was; it was his old friend from the village. He hadn't been injured, and he attempted to run, but after a chase Bing was able to grab hold of him and drag him back to camp. Ye gods, thought Bing, here is a man of my own age who came from the farm next to my family home, and he had been a good friend.

Bing thought quickly. He signaled to the man to keep silent and took him behind the last wagon where they could talk without being overheard. The man blurted out his story. He hadn't had anything like Bing's good fortune. Like other second or third sons he knew that he would have to leave home, and while fulfilling his year as a conscript laborer he had decided to take a chance on making a getaway. Since then, he had lived in the shadows, unknown and unseen, dodging government officials. Eventually, he had joined a gang of criminals.

"What the hell do we do?" Bing asked. "If the master hears about this he'll hand you over to the authorities, and he'd probably send me packing. He's keen to keep on the right side of the law. Luckily, it seems quiet now, and I don't think anyone saw you. If it helps, I'll get you back to the woods. We'll be on our way at daybreak. Now, whatever you do, steer clear of the gang who sent you here."

The two men talked for a few moments about how the years had passed. Bing learned that both of his parents had died during the last winter. He managed to get some food for his friend and to settle him down in the woods, away from the roadside. Poor devil, he thought; it might just as easily have been me.

Up and down the land Shang took his team, buying goods when they were plentiful and cheap and selling them for a good price where they were hard to come by. Rather to Bing's surprise, Shang had bought a cartload of apples up in the north, all green, stored in sacks. "They're too sour to sell," Bing remarked after tasting one, "and stored in sacks like that, they'll all go bad before long."

"Just you wait and see," Shang answered. "They'll last long enough for us to get them down south where apples don't grow, and the people there pay anything for luscious fruit like that. Try one yourself in seven days' time, when they've turned red, and you'll be surprised."

Then Shang explained to Bing what he had in mind. They were going to move around in the north for a while, picking up good stuff to sell down south where they would shortly be moving. "It's a different way of life down there," he said, "and you'll see all sorts of wonders."

So down they made their way to warmer and warmer places. They had to choose their way carefully, after making inquiries, as they had already seen for themselves large stretches of land that were under water, with no chance of saving any crop that had been sown there.

"If it's always like this," Bing asked, "how on earth do the people here keep body and soul together?" Shang shook his head in silence. It was only when he got talking to some of the locals one night that Bing found out more.

"No," said an old man with a thin white beard, "not always. In some years, like this one, all the rain and snow from those far hills pours into the river; whatever you do here you can't stop that fast stream from bursting its banks and everything is flooded. Eventually the water level drops, and you never know which way the river will choose to settle, this side of the hills or the other. There are some places, I believe, where they are able to build high dikes which rise over the water, however much there is, but even there they can't save much.

"It's all the fault of the God of the River, the river whom some call 'Yellow,' and I'll tell you what used to happen. The old men of the villages were held in such respect that anyone would do whatever they ordered him to do. Well, year after year, at midsummer, if I've got it right, they would force everyone to go to the river's bank, men, women, and children. They would have quite a little ceremony going on; you know those old women of the village who utter strange sounds and think they can tell you what the gods want? Well, they would all take their turn, and there were some of the men chanting prayers as well. There would be a raft waiting there, beautifully decorated in colored silks, with all sorts of cushions and shading against the sun. They called out for all the young girls from the village to come forward to the front, and they led, or probably dragged, one of them to take her place on the raft, tying her on very tightly. Then they set the raft loose to float downstream. The poor girl didn't have a chance; she couldn't get free however hard she tried, and even if she had, she couldn't swim. Off she went. 'A bride for the God of the River!' they called out as she floated by. Maybe she was, but not for long, as the raft would break up and she would drown. Why did they do this, you ask? They thought that the God of the River would accept her as the village's sacrifice and see that no harm came from the river that year. Thank goodness the practice has all but disappeared."

There were other years, Bing learned, when there wasn't a drop of water to be had, however much they prayed for rain. The farmers saw their year's work ruined, and the next winter there was nothing for them to eat. Bing was horrified to hear that that was why there were so few girls around.

Soon Shang had Bing on the move again and there were other things to think about. As a conscript laborer he had spent plenty of time getting the produce of the fields carted to where it had to go, and he had seen some large granaries where it was kept. But these were nothing like the size of one they passed called Ao. Bing could not fathom why it had to be so big and how it could ever be filled.

"Oh," someone said, "that was built years and years ago as a place to keep any amount of food in reserve for the soldiers when a war broke out. But the trouble was that it was such a rich and plentiful site that the kings fought each other as hard as they could to take it, and by all accounts there was a terrific amount of blood spilled, just where we are standing. They are taking good care now to see that such a thing doesn't happen again; look at all those troops on guard."

Down south they visited a place that used to be named Chu, spreading on either side of a great river of which Bing had heard tell and which some called the Yangzi. Bing did not recognize the crop that was ripening in the fields, and it was at his first meal in those parts that he tasted it—rice. Quite different from the millet they grew on the old family farm, and Bing learned that the best way to grow this crop was to plant the seedlings in a field that had been flooded. The rice farmers needed an endless amount of water. There were places where the farmers had been very clever and got water to run from one level to another, up and down the terraces that they had built on the hillsides. This grain was nice to eat, but tended to be sticky on the tongue and made you thirsty.

They were not very far from the river itself and Bing could hardly believe his eyes when he saw its breadth and imagined how long it would take to get across. Everywhere there were people cutting the reeds or fishing and they all looked well fed and healthy enough. One elderly man, who didn't look too happy, gave Bing a word of warning.

"There's a god who lives in that river," he said "and at times he can get really angry. If he doesn't get enough meat and drink from us to keep him satisfied, he'll see to it that the river destroys your hearth and home. We go out of our way to try and keep him amused and to show him how much we are afraid of his strength. Come back here at the right time of year and you'll see the youngsters on their boats, playing out a fight, all in good fun. That seems to keep the river god happy for most of the time, and everyone enjoys the day. At least the youngsters do; it's too much for me, at my age."

As they moved west along the great river, it passed through a whole series of rocks and cliff sides. The narrower it got, the faster the current ran and there were some stretches where it was almost impossible to get a boat upstream; you needed quite a large number of people to team together on the bank and pull on the ropes. They were bound for a place called Shu, Shang said.

"Very rich; it's an isolated stretch of lush country and you'll see bamboo bushes that are far stouter than anywhere else. All sorts of people live there, as the area is abundant with homegrown supplies of food and timber. If you've never seen a salt mine, you'll see one here. They have several. And, yes, I expect we'll do a good business."

By now Shang knew that there were some parts of the business that he could leave Bing to manage on his own, while he himself wandered off to be entertained in some of the houses of the rich. Sure enough Bing picked up some of those silver coins that he had once handled, as they were again changing hands, this time from one of the more select stalls to another. Bing noticed some strange, dark-skinned people in the market. They came from a place called Shendu, or Indy as some called it, or so they told him. Apparently it was also from

Shendu that some beautiful pieces of wood and horn, now on sale, came from. They commanded a very high price and Shang had asked Bing to make a point of seeing just how much those rarities would fetch. He himself was far too well known to get an honest answer that he could trust, but Bing was unknown here, and he looked innocent enough.

There were ivories, tortoise shell, and pearls. Bing did not think much of the pearls, until somebody told him how they were ground down and taken as a medicine, which did all sorts of things for a growing man. Perhaps the most precious things on sale, and there were not many of them, were some drinking cups made out of the dark brown horn of an animal that was rarely seen. It just had the one horn and it could be very fierce. "Really fine to look at," the shopman said, "and, what's more, if you take a drink from one of those you can't possibly be poisoned; it's all some form of magic."

"Too expensive for me," said Bing.

Shu was a large enough place. Range after range of hills closed it off from the rest of the world. There were plenty of rivers, but Bing heard no mention of floods.

"They've been very clever here," Shang said. "I'll take you to a place I know and show you."

This was at the Min River where some years earlier a highly energetic and ingenious governor had worked out how to prevent the floods that used to rise from time to time. At the same time, he had worked out how all that rush of water need not run to waste but could be used to water the farmers' crops. Broad as the river was, he managed to divide it into several channels by laying canister after canister full of stone that would dam the excessive inflow and divert it where it could best be used. He had calculated what was needed so cleverly and exactly that the whole scheme worked perfectly so long as it was cleaned and repaired when need be. Bing could well imagine the hefty work that had been involved and thought that the governor must have put the labor gangs on to the task.

It was elsewhere in Shu that Bing saw some enormous waterwheels that rose high into the sky, and raised the water from one level to another as they turned. As they traveled around the countryside, he saw even more places where the farmers had built their terraces and planted their crops on the hillsides.

No wonder Shu was such a rich place. Shang sold quite a number of choice pieces of jewelry, of jade or bronze, to some of the great houses there. Bing asked if they were going farther to the west or perhaps to the south. He had heard that down there most of the population led very crude lives; some of them, women as well as men, went around without any clothing and thought nothing of it. They had no formal weddings after which a couple would set up living together. He'd also heard that the farmers made more by raising animals, mainly cattle, than sowing crops.

"Don't they also have a festival once a year when they worship their gods and pray for good fortune, but instead of sacrificing animals they put a man to death instead?" This was another occasion when Shang turned silent.

"No trade worthwhile down there," he answered finally and rather brusquely. "No, we're going back north to my home in Luoyang for the winter; but we'll have a quick stop at Chang'an first." But on their way there, something else of interest happened.

Notes for Chapter Five

It is not certain how far, or in which areas, wet rice farming in terraces was being adopted in Han times. A writer of 220 CE remarked on the primitive state of civilization in the deep south, to the point that in some areas men and women were running around naked. An anecdote records the circumstances in which the sacrifice of a girl to the Count of the River was suppressed; see Michael Loewe, "He Bo Count of the River, Feng Yi and Li Bing," in Rachel May and John Minford, eds., *A Birthday Book for Brother Stone* (Hong Kong: Chinese University Press, 2003), pp. 197–206. For the highly skilled work designed to control the Min River, in present-day Sichuan (the Dujiangyan), see Joseph Needham, et al., *Science and Civilisation in China*, vol. 4, pt. III (Cambridge: Cambridge University Press, 1971), pp. 288–96; for waterwheels, ibid., vol. 4, pt. II, pp. 356–62, figs. 593–95.

Chapter Six   *A state occasion*

O N THEIR WAY NORTH, SHANG MADE A POINT OF VISITING YONG where he hoped to sell a large consignment of warm clothing. To their surprise they found that the town was in a festive mood. Every third year, the Emperor made a solemn journey to Yong with all his attendants to pay his respects to the Five Deities who protected the different parts of his realm. The Emperor would take his proper part in the occasion, offering worship to unseen gods and prayers for the welfare of his people and his land. He was expected any day now.

Shang and his party learned all this once they were inside the town, and what a business it had been to get there! The guards at the gates were taking no chances and it took hours before they could get the team and their wagons passed as fit to enter. One young man in Shang's team had lost his pass and that had cost Shang a fee, and a long bout of questioning, before he could get it replaced. Shang took it all calmly, even the need to pay a substantial sum for bringing his merchandise inside the town's gates, but once he realized that he had very little chance of making much of a profit, his anger was roused. Someone had been there before him and captured the market so that hardly anybody wanted to buy. It was small consolation that customers compared his goods with those they had already bought, and felt pretty angry that the goods they had purchased were inferior to Shang's.

As usual, Shang intended to call on the magistrate and make sure that he would remember him with favor. But because of all the work that the magistrate had to do to prepare for the His Majesty's visit he had no time to spend with Shang. Instead, he had to attend on his superior the governor who had come there for the occasion and await his orders. What added to Shang's discontent was that there was hardly any chance of getting a decent room in the town. The magistrate's men had commandeered all the most comfortable places and put them at the disposal of the Emperor's staff. They wanted to ensure that their guests were comfortable and content, and they were powerful enough to dictate their terms to the innkeepers. The innkeepers had to be content with whatever they could get out of the deal. Bing saw how his master had been obliged to part with far larger sums than he had anticipated to get his goods accommodated safely, and secure a place where they could all spend the night, not to mention proper care for the horses.

Bing soon discovered the best place to go for a good view of the next day's events. Everyone knew where the shrine was and how difficult it was to get into it unless you were a member of the Emperor's own party or a high-ranking official. First, there were the soldiers on guard who wouldn't hesitate to send you away with a shove or a kick, or a blow from their truncheons, if they felt like it. Even if you could somehow get around them with a carefully placed handful of cash, you would have to get past their officers, who demanded to see your special pass.

Crestfallen men hobbled back from where the guards were posted. Bing walked as inconspicuously as he could around the whole site looking for a way of entry. This meant quite a long journey, as the site was ringed by hills, some of which were studded with trees and bushes. Eventually he found what he was looking for, a slight break in the fence at the top of one of the hills, hardly visible unless you were looking for it. And just beyond it the undergrowth provided some cover. Once inside, Bing made his way silently and with the utmost caution, and eventually found that he could look down on the center of the site, with an unobstructed view of the proceedings.

A square wall ran round outside the enclosed site, capped with grey and brown tiles. Inside the square a circular mound rose up, built in several stages, with stone walkways and steps, and low screens that separated a lower from a higher layer. At the top of the mound a flat surface of evenly polished stone formed a square platform. Everything was in excellent condition, with nothing in need of repair. Right in the center there was a special stone, circular in shape and engraved with markings that Bing could not make out. At one side there were frames set out on which a number of musical instruments were hanging, sets of bronze bells in a whole series of sizes, jade stones oddly shaped, and an array of drums. A few men dressed in yellow robes were busy laying out pieces of furniture and equipment. There were large vessels of bronze and earthenware, larger than any that Bing had seen, both round and square. Some of the flasks were brightly colored, some may even have been inlaid with silver or gold. Four sets of these were laid out, one on each side of the square and there was another one on a table placed on the south side outside the platform. With each of these five sets there was a pole from which a brightly covered device was hanging in the wind—a green dragon on the east side, a scarlet bird on the south, a white tiger on the west, and a black tortoise and serpent on the north. On the set that was outside, to the south, there waved a flag with a brown circle on a yellow background.

Bing presumed that the largest of these vessels were there to contain water, as he had been told that all these rituals included turns at washing. Then as he watched, one of the serving men who had bent down rose up rather clumsily. He could not catch himself in time, and he knocked one of the vessels over. Liquid poured out. Poor devil. They soon dragged him away and Bing hated to think what punishment would ensue. And, what on earth was the liquid? If it was plain water, why were they scurrying about, trying to get rid of all signs of the upset? Water would dry off quickly enough, and it would not harm the stonework in any way. Why were some of them crouching down and, as it seemed, trying to smell what was left? As he peered more closely Bing saw that the liquid was red. Could it be blood? There was only one other liquid that was red, as far as he knew, though he had never seen it. It was said to be made from grapes, which smelled strongly and which, when drunk, cheered you up wonderfully but left you nearly unconscious.

By now the sun had risen to its full height. The entrance to the circular site at the south was marked by two tall pillars, of polished stone and through these there advanced an imposing figure, moving in a measured tread, and preceded by his attendants. Then there were those who carried baskets of grain, vegetables, and herbs or fruit. A special group of men and women, all wearing robes of the same colors and pattern followed, some of them carrying pipes that showed they were musicians. Behind them came another band, which turned out to be made up of singers. They all seemed to know where to go and

what to do. They took their places. And then came a solitary figure—
ye gods, it could only be the Emperor himself! Bing had never dreamt
that he would see him!

Decked in fine multicolored robes, mainly yellow, he slowly made
his way to the south side of the central, square platform, and then
to take up his position on its east side. Once he was there the music
began, shrill notes from the pipes and some of the strings, a lower
pitch from others, steady beats from the drummers, while some of the
musicians struck the bells or struck the jade stones to resound. Very
slow and solemn it was, nothing like the jolly tunes that Bing had
heard in the towns, and after a while, it became tedious. At last the
choir, men and women, took the place of the orchestra, but try as he
could Bing could hardly hear what they were singing. Occasionally he
caught a word or two, something about the sun, moon, and stars, but
it was in a strange sort of language that was not easy to follow.

When this was all over, the moment came for the Emperor to
take a part. His servants handed him the fresh supplies that they had
brought; in turn, he offered these things to the gods by placing each
item in the particular vessel that awaited it. When these vessels had all
been filled, he took a lighted taper from his staff and set fire to the twigs
and faggots that lay underneath one of the large bronze vessels. That
will soon be far too hot to handle, Bing thought, and then he realized
what the purpose was of the two stout loops fitted on facing sides of
each of the pots. Obviously you could push a wooden pole between
the loops and lift the whole thing easily, without being burned.

To Bing's dismay, the musicians struck up again, but soon the
music halted, to his relief. Three men, one old, one middle-aged, and
one young, strode forth in their specially shaped robes and headgear.
They intoned something in unison, but again Bing could not hear
what it was that they called out. "Harmony," he thought he heard
repeated. Years later, he learned that they were mouthing a series of
prayers offered to the gods in the hope that all manner of good things
would be forthcoming from the earth, that all the spirits of creation
would bestow their blessings upon the Emperor and his people and
avert all evil, and that the seasons of cold and heat, of darkness and
light, and the forces of decay and growth would all follow one another

in their due seasons, in perfect balance and without a contest with one another.

All this had taken a long time. As the ceremony proceeded the Emperor went around to the other sides, repeating all the steps that he had taken; to the south, then the center, then the west, and finally the north. It was all much the same except that the songs and the prayers varied each time. For the east side, they had been chosen to suit the season of spring; for the south, they told of summer; and from the set outside the platform, they suited the time when the sun was at its highest and hottest point; for the west side, the subject was autumn; and for the north, the winter.

Still the bells rang, the drums beat, and Bing's head began to ache with the continual boom, boom, boom. It was all the louder because Bing had been able to move closer to where everything was taking place. Not that he could make head or tale of some of it. The Emperor had at last been led to a seat. With him was a basket, which contained dozens and dozens of long straight branches of a plant, all very evenly matched. Sitting opposite the Emperor there was another man. Very old he was, with a couple of young lads at his side. He took the branches or rods in his hands, slowly counting off how many he had; usually these seemed to be about four or five, as far as Bing could see.

Every so often this man signaled to his attendant, who walked over to where a large dish full of sand lay flat on the ground. With the help of a shovel, he drew out a straight line in the sand, sometimes right through to its end, sometimes breaking off in the middle and leaving a gap between the two halves. Altogether this took place six times, forming a pattern of six lines, each one set higher than the last. Sometimes he drew out a second set of six lines. Once this was complete they pointed to another very old man and called for him to join them. Stooped and stumbling he made his way to where the dish was and sat down. For a long time he stared at the pattern, and Bing wondered whether he was capable of doing anything else, let alone speaking. Complete silence reigned; everyone, even the Emperor, waited for what he was going to do. What was he muttering? He could hardly be speaking like a normal person, but the attendants had cupped their hands to their ears so as to hear. At last he stood up, as straight as he could, to call out what he knew, and everyone shouted it out after him. "Encouragement and success. All is going to be well," he had uttered, and a great shout went up through the crowd to show that everyone had heard and understood his message.

Separated as he was from all this, Bing sensed a feeling of immense relief down below. The Emperor made his dignified way out, through those high pillars at the entrance. Somewhat mystified by it all but nonetheless overcome, Bing made his way back to where his master had settled him for the night, to take a meal that he had long needed. Dare he trust anybody if he revealed where he had been and what he had seen? He didn't have to decide, as there was an elderly man staying there who had seen how dazed Bing looked and evidently guessed. He'd done just the same when he was younger, he said. All he knew was that that old man who examined the lines was said to possess unusual gifts or powers beyond those of ordinary people. Somehow he was able to make direct contact with the gods or whosoever it was that decides what fortunes are destined to come to a man or woman. Quite inexplicable, but there it was. These gifted men were nearly always right.

Notes for Chapter Six
We have no direct account of how the imperial cults, either to the spirits addressed here or to others such as Heaven, were performed; the description given here draws on details found scattered in the primary sources (see, e.g., *Han shu* 25B, p. 1256).

Chapter Seven   *In Chang'an and Luoyang*

Here they were at the gates of Chang'an. Bing had heard much of the great capital city. "You won't believe how big it is," he'd been told, and as Bing had already seen some large bustling cities, such as Chengdu, he wondered what to expect.

The usual procedures were required before they could enter, and Bing could have told the guards what questions to ask. Their passes and identity cards were examined, and finally their goods were searched. The officials on duty were not the sort to miss anything. Shang's carts made it through all right, but he had some explaining to do about one of the horses, which the guards inspected closely. They seemed most concerned with the marks branded on one of the animal's flanks. Eventually they were satisfied, that this was not the horse they were looking for, and they were allowed to pass through the gateway. Its towers were massive, and Bing could not believe it possible to build anything to such a height.

"Do those walls go around the whole city?" he asked Shang.

"They do."

"At the same height and width? It all looks so solid."

"Oh yes," Shang replied. "You'll see for yourself. Way back, when our dynasty was founded and the city of Chang'an was chosen to be the capital, where the Emperor and his officials would live and work, it became clear that it must be protected against enemies that might appear, either from the north, or from the east. There were plenty of people there who would be only too ready to force their way in and seize power. Work began almost immediately, and vast numbers of conscript workmen were called up. If you'd been living in those days, you'd likely have been one of them, as nearly 150,000 were needed, women as well as men, with orders to complete the job as swiftly as possible. But work could not progress in all seasons, and it took about two years to finish it. No, the walls don't form an exact square; you'll see the odd way in which they run."

Bing well remembered the much smaller walls he'd worked on as a soldier and how difficult it had been to construct them. As they made their way to their lodging place, he marveled at the wide streets that ran straight from one side of the city to the other, east to west and north to south. As far as he could tell, these streets divided off the living quarters for the inhabitants into wards, each enclosed in its own wall.

"Here we are," said Shang. He had stopped before a modest inn. "I have much to do and some friends to visit. Feel free to stow your belongings and have a walk around the city. But be very, very careful. There are all sorts of people living inside these walls; many of them are out to rob anyone they can, and I suspect it's got a lot worse since I was last here."

"Why is that?" asked Bing.

"Some time ago, a very smart official did an excellent job suppressing all the thieves, and he did it by way of a trick. He got all of the ringleaders together and invited them and all their men to a great feast. Nearly every criminal in the city showed up. Of course, they had no idea who was providing such good food and drink, nor did they care. Well, it was so good that they all got drunk, and the officials took the opportunity to give each one of them an identifying mark: a smear of red on their clothing. The next day they were arrested by the hundred. But that was some time ago. I'll bet there are plenty of them at it again."

Bing took no chances and kept to the main avenues, but he nearly got himself into trouble by crossing one of them from one side to the other. He hadn't noticed an especially smooth lane running down the middle. Almost immediately two patrolling soldiers stopped him. "Don't you know that's forbidden?" they asked him.

Bing looked askance. He had no idea what they could mean.

"That path in the middle of the road is reserved for none other than the Emperor. May Heaven preserve him! How dare you walk there! It's strictly off limits for you and your lot."

Bing was abject in his apology. "I'm new to the city," he explained. "I only arrived this morning."

"Let's see your pass then. Where are you staying?" Thanks to Shang's precautions he was able to show them his card and give them the address of his lodging house.

"This looks all right," said the officer, "but don't let us catch you violating the rules again."

Large areas of the city were walled off with no admission for ordinary people, and Bing learned that those walls enclosed the palaces where the Emperor and his family members lived.

"All five of them?" he asked Shang later that night. "Why do they need so many palaces?"

Shang suppressed a smile. "It's not a subject I would bring up with just anyone," he said. "But between the two of us, I'll tell you that one of the palaces houses the Emperor's mother, and the others some of his consorts. They all have to be kept in separate places to prevent them from quarreling or sometimes even fighting with one another. As the palaces take up such a large part of the city, the rest of the population—cooks, gardeners, carpenters, carriers, and such—are badly cramped together, while most of high-ranking officials are able to live comfortably."

On one of his walks, Bing noticed an ironworks situated close to one of the palaces. It was far larger than any he had seen or worked in, and the fumes it produced were suffocating. He stood by watching as great plumes of smoke belched forth. There must be times, he thought, when anyone inside the palace or living nearby would suffer terribly. He was not inclined to watch for long, and he continued on his way to the market. He loved the markets. There were two, each one stocked with all sorts of goods—fresh food, pickled food, fine clothing, ironware. As much as there was on display, there was no sign of the wonderful fruits he and Shang had enjoyed down south in Chu.

There was yet another palace, Bing learned, outside the city to the west. It was slightly cooler there than in the city and the Emperor would go there sometimes in the summer to enjoy the beautiful gardens and ornamental lakes. Bing was eager to see it, because it was there that all the exotic animals that were sent as gifts to the Emperor were kept. One day he met up with a man who drove one of the carts that made deliveries to the palace, and Bing was invited to come along for the ride. The supplies in the cart were nothing grand, just the usual tubs of millet, and nobody would notice who was going along with them, and that was how Bing was able to get inside the precincts of the palace. As compared with the palaces in the city, it all seemed to be very relaxed. The watchman knew the carter well enough and asked no questions, when he handed him something in a quiet way. Once they were inside, he sent a young man to take Bing on a tour of the whole site, where he could admire the wonderful trees and flowers that were growing so brightly. The lakes with their ornaments and carefully directed spouts of water made you feel cool, a refreshing change from the city.

At the edge of the park Bing stopped and looked out over rows and rows of bushes of a sort that he had never seen. They went on and on, far into the distance.

"You should see them in autumn," the young man said. "They bear clusters and clusters of berries, some green, some dark blue, and all wonderfully sweet to eat. But not much of the fruit reaches the Emperor's banqueting hall in that state. The berries, or grapes as they are called, are nearly all taken away and crushed so that the juice runs out. This is kept and treated in a particular way until it ferments, and you get the most wonderful drink. It makes you forget all your worries and sends you to sleep. There's a name for the fruit, which I can never remember. No, I've no idea where the bushes came from, they've been here for twenty years or so."

All that land made over to grapes, Bing thought, luxury stuff for the palace and its fat servants, when often there was not enough food in the city—plain nourishing food that they needed there, and which could easily be grown instead of grapes. Still, the grape bushes were planted on the Emperor's lands and nobody else had a right to plant anything there. But people would get very angry if they saw so much land put down to a crop that wouldn't feed anyone at a time when the millet harvest had failed.

Bing watched the walls of Chang'an disappear from view, as they headed to Luoyang. It took about ten days to get to the city. It was well known in Chinese history as a seat of kings and a center where writers, scholars, poets, and musicians had lived. It was well known now as a place where important roads came together and where busy traders were forever coming and going.

On the way, Shang and Bing passed along the foot of a steep mountain, which was called Huashan. Bushes and trees led up to the top.

"It's very odd people who pass their lives up there," Shang told him. "They spend their time trying to find out why life is worthwhile, whether we are any different from the animals, and what's the best way of living. They're some really peculiar people too; they don't mind the cold in the slightest—probably take a shower under that waterfall when there's snow lying on the ground—and all they have to eat are pine kernels. They keep their hair very long and do their best to be friendly with the birds and animals, as if they shared the mountain with them. Not," Shang added, "the sort of life for you and me."

There were long stretches on the road when Shang and Bing would talk and talk about all sorts of things. They got to know each other and, despite the twenty-five years between them, they became friends. Shang had come to rely on Bing for a lot of routine work, keeping the wagons in good repair, adding up sums of money, or helping him with something that he had to read. Shang knew pretty well which were the best roads to take and which were the towns that they had better avoid. But he was not as young as he used to be and, when it came to scouting ahead to make sure that the road was clear of trouble, he was glad to leave such energetic and potentially dangerous work to Bing. Likewise, the rest of the team were content to trust Bing on such matters and obey his orders. Bing realized that he had much to thank Shang for; he had taught him how to make a good living, what tricks to look out for, and how to make the best of the seasons.

Luoyang wasn't nearly as large as Chang'an, and it seemed to have been built in a much more regular shape, with nothing to interrupt the straight walls on its four sides. There were no large sections of the city set away from the public, attended by guards, or walls enclosing a palace with its multitude of attendants and servants. As he had expected, Bing found Shang's house spacious and comfortable. It was situated in an open part of the city where the streets were lined with sophora or ginko trees. Life there was pleasant and easy, with plenty to eat and drink, including a fine beer made from grain, and occasionally some of that grape juice, which he'd heard about in Chang'an. Supposedly these were among the luxuries that merchants were not allowed to enjoy, along with silk clothing, but the rules didn't seem to bother Shang, or his wife who dressed in lively colored finery.

"She couldn't do that in Chang'an," Shang said. "They would be sure to clamp down there; but life is much easier here."

Bing thought that the house was large enough for all of them, but nothing would stop Shang from his plans to extend it with a new room or two. However, there were two things that worried him, and Bing could help with both of them. First, Shang had to know what day would be the best to start building so as to make certain that the construction would be done properly and would not suffer any ill fortune. He showed Bing a bundle of wooden strips covered with small writing which, he had been told, stated clearly which days of the year would be lucky ones for beginning a new project, such as constructing a house, starting a new job—perhaps as an official—setting out on a journey, or celebrating a wedding. Shang admitted that he could not read the strips, the writing was too cramped for him to make out, he said, and he asked Bing if he would try. Luckily enough, Bing could cope with this sort of rough writing; it was very much like what he'd seen when he was up north.

The signs for the days themselves were clear enough, but the small columns underneath were defeating him, and these were the ones that mattered. After looking at it for a long time, Bing made some headway and Shang was very pleased when Bing told him the days when it would be fortunate to start building.

The other problem was the cost of construction. Shang pulled another roll of wooden strips down from his shelf. This set was supposed to show you how to calculate this sort of thing. The roll was written in a far clearer hand than the other one and there were quite a number of diagrams that went with the written text. Bing took this set away and spent a long time studying its columns. He could read the figures easily enough, and there were plenty of them, but just what they meant and why six was followed by five and then by thirty, or what a run of twelve, two, and ten meant he did not know.

One evening, they had a visit from an elderly friend of Shang's, Mr. Li, who was leaning on his stick and anxious to see Shang. Before long they summoned Bing to join them and to bring that roll of strips with him. The strips were spread out before Mr. Li, who looked them over carefully for some time. Finally, he looked up at Shang and Bing with a smile. "I'll show this young man how to read this," he said, and it was some time before he'd finished and stood up to take his leave.

"I'll come back in two days' time," he said, "just to see how you are getting along."

Bing had liked Mr. Li. Eager to make a good impression, he worked hard on the set of strips, and by the time Mr. Li returned, he was ready to explain what he'd learned. "Well," said Mr. Li, "Bing has got it all worked out. The amount of wood planking required is correct, as is the quantity of plaster you'll need to keep the walls sealed up and dry. If the builder says you need more and wants to charge you extra, don't you believe him."

Sometimes Shang would talk about his earlier days on the road. So as to make a good profit, he had always made sure that he knew if anything special would be going on in the cities. Those sorts of occasions drew large crowds from some distance, people who had left their comforts back home and would be ready to pay good money to make their lives easier. So when Shang learned that a high-powered leader from the north was coming to pay his respects to the Emperor in Chang'an, he made it his business to be present. In fact, this was the first time that an Emperor had deigned to receive such a visitor in person. Even more astonishing, the Emperor would ride out of the city to meet him and conduct him into the palace.

Shang made his plans carefully; there would be many visitors to the city who would be spending the night outdoors, so he laid in a stock of warm clothes, woolens, furs, and pelts, which he was sure he could sell. Sure enough, vast crowds gathered to watch the events. Shang had never seen such an array of Han soldiers, all lined up in their ranks by the roadside, some riding as escorts before and after the Emperor's carriage. The great visitor himself was attended by his own party and horsemen and followed by a number of wagons, which, Shang was sure, carried gifts that he would present to his host. It was a wonderful sight, and Shang did a good day's business.

Such things did not always go so well, and Shang had once missed out on a golden opportunity. It was in a year some time back when one of the emperors had died, quite suddenly. He was a fairly young man, and there were some people who suspected foul play but had been silenced. The unexpected death caused great difficulty. Usually there would have been plenty of time to prepare for such an event, so that the tomb would be ready and all the treasures, furnishings, and equipment needed for the final ceremony would be waiting in storage for the time when they were needed. But this Emperor was young, and his death had happened too quickly. Even though there was always a delay, sometimes of up to seventy days, between an Emperor's death and his burial, the officials had made no advance preparations. They now had to get a lot of building done with the utmost speed, but they could not lay their hands on enough of the sand or timber they needed, let alone the very hard woods required to build the coffins. Even the materials needed to build a tumulus once the funeral was over could not be procured. It would have been the ideal moment for Shang to turn up with a load of such supplies, but unfortunately he arrived too late on the scene to make much of a profit. The heavy trunks of catalpa trees could only be found far to the south, and he hadn't been able to get hold of any.

"You would have done well at that time," he said to Bing. "They were short of craftsmen particularly of skilled carpenters; they would have paid you thousands."

Shang's talk of future plans had always been full of optimism and excitement about their prospects, but lately his talk had taken a melancholy turn. One evening over dinner, he said to Bing, "We need to have a serious talk," and Bing thought that he was off again on some new idea he'd thought of.

"The good old days are over," said Shang. "Things simply aren't what they were. We used to have a fine free market in iron goods, yes and salt; just the things that everybody has to have to keep alive. If you kept a good lookout, you could make a fortune, especially if you knew a rich person who had an iron or salt mine on his land. You could deal in grain far more easily then than you can now. As it happens, I hardly ever did, because you had to decide on the right moment and to choose the right place, buying when and where it was plentiful and cheap and selling it in areas where they'd had a poor harvest and would pay a good price. Well, that's all going now, with these plans to set up granaries in the counties or districts which buy it at a high price but sell it cheap, so as to help the poor. All very well, but it means that freelance merchants will be squeezed out. All that will be in the hands of the officials, and those officials never did like us merchants. I hate to think what they'll come up with next."

"So, what are you saying," asked Bing, who was beginning to feel worried.

"I tell you, I'm getting on in years now and I've got enough saved to last out my lifetime. I don't need to travel, and I've had enough of that sort of life. It's all right for youngsters like you. Now, you've been a good friend to me and helped me a lot. I'm arranging for a man in town to take over all my stock, and he'll be starting off on the road come spring. Would you like to go on with him? I could easily get him to take you on if you like, he'll need the help, but as I've just been saying, I don't think that there's much of a future left in this business. Think it over, will you?"

Bing was now very worried. It never occurred to him that Shang might give up his business so soon, and he did not like the idea of starting over again with someone who might turn out to be far less of a friend than Shang had been. He decided to discuss his qualms with Shang.

"Well," Shang said, "I've got another idea. You remember old Mr. Li? In his day, he was a junior official over in Chang'an. After that time you worked through those sums for the building, he told me that he was impressed with you and that he had a high regard for your talents. He said you were good enough and smart enough to go into government service yourself, if the idea should ever appeal to you. He even offered to give you some training in tasks of the sort you'd have to handle in a government office, work on written texts and doing really difficult sums. You'd have a head start over the others when the time came to take the tests. What do you think of that?"

Bing didn't have to ponder the question for long. He had enjoyed his travels, and he had made the best of his time with Shang, knowing how lucky he was to be working with such a master. But he also thought how differently his life might turn out if he accepted this challenge, and how such an opportunity might never come his way again. He had never had any contact with those high-ranking officials who drove around in their plush carriages, but he had had some experience with some junior officials when he was a conscript soldier in the north. He had even taken part in some of their work.

"Would that really be possible?" he asked Shang. "Does he really mean it? How on earth would I be able to thank Mr. Li? I would never have dreamed such a thing was possible."

Shang happily agreed that it was a very good opportunity for Bing, but he kept some quiet thoughts to himself. He knew very well that Mr. Li had two daughters, and he'd taught one of them to read and write. She had turned out to be quite an accomplished scholar. He was sure that Mr. Li would involve her in drilling Bing, and who knew what might follow from that?

Notes for Chapter Seven

For Zhang Chang's exploit in suppressing crime in Chang'an, ca. 61 BCE, see *Han shu* 76, p. 3221. For the introduction of the grape to China ca. 10 BCE and the widespread planting of vineyards at the emperor's country estate west of Chang'an, see A. F. P. Hulsewé, *China in Central Asia: The Early Stage, 125 B.C.–A.D. 23* (Leiden: E. J. Brill, 1979), pp. 135–36. There is no direct evidence of a popular protest against using land for this luxury. State monopolies over salt and iron were introduced in ca. 117 BCE; at the same time, measures were taken to prevent undue profiteering by merchants at times of acute shortages of staple goods; see Nancy Lee Swann, *Food and Money in Ancient China* (Princeton: Princeton University Press, 1950), pp. 62–65. A text named the *Jiu zhang suan shu* was a set of mathematical examples and problems of a highly practical nature that would be of invaluable help to officials; the date of compilation is not known for certain. A number of copies of almanacs, showing which activities would be suitable for particular days of the year, have been found in tombs, written often in very small writing. Zhaodi acceded as emperor at the age of seven in 87 BCE; he died in 74 BCE. For merchants' profiteering at the time of his death, see *Han shu* 90, p. 3665.

Chapter Eight *Pupil and junior clerk*

THROUGHOUT THE LAST YEARS, WHENEVER HE COULD BING HAD seized every opportunity to learn more about reading and writing, but he had never found anyone who could and would give him professional teaching.

In Luoyang, time lay heavily on the hands of Mr. Li, who relished the chance of having a pupil whom he would instruct and who in his turn would treat him with the deference due to a teacher. First of all, he must make sure that Bing knew how to handle the wooden boards or narrow strips on which he would write. Thinking back to what he had seen used when he was up on the guard posts, Bing had brought a stout knife with him when he went to see Mr. Li. Mr. Li was anything but impressed.

"You don't suppose you can use that thing, do you?"

Bing stammered that he had indeed used it when he was working with the junior officers in the army. The knife came in handy when they needed to remove something that had already been written.

"Yes," said Mr. Li, "that's what a knife is for, but you need a far better one than that blunt object. Here you are, take this; you're going to need it a lot. You're going to write, write, write so that you'll end up with a good clean hand instead of that scrawl of yours. Yes, I know very well that your writing has been useful enough, so it would be for the army, but it is not nearly good enough for the sort of work you'll be doing in one of the offices at the capital, or when they send you out to one of the provinces. You'll find it much easier to strip away something you've written by mistake, now that you have a decent knife to work with. It won't tear the wood to pieces, and it will leave you a smooth surface—that is, if you learn to use it properly."

As a carpenter Bing had learned to work with a steady hand and this helped him as he held his brush poised above the wood to copy out what he had been given. Some of it was written in very different forms from what he was used to seeing, rather like some of the books that Shang had shown him, and there was much that he simply didn't understand.

"Get on with it," Mr. Li would say. "Learn, learn, learn; repeat, repeat, repeat; no, don't ask what it means, you'll find out. Now, I think you'd better peel off all that you've done and start again. I can see at least five errors. No, no, no; find them for yourself."

Bing couldn't find a single one, and it was actually Mr. Li's daughter, called Yu, who pointed them all out to him. It was she who had shown him how to tie a number of two-foot-long wooden strips together so that he could write out a long passage from one column to another, and it was Yu who taught him how to roll it all up when he had finished so as to make it into a scroll. As the days passed, Bing began showing Yu what he had written before handing it to Mr. Li. For his part, Mr. Li was more and more pleased with the rate at which his pupil was advancing. Not that he'd say so, of course, but there were certainly far fewer peelings of wood on the floor than there used to be.

One day, Mr. Li told Bing to take out the very book that they had consulted to estimate Shang's building costs.

"The time will come when you'll be responsible for measuring or calculating all sorts of things, the tax that a farmer has to pay, the time needed to deliver a cargo of grain from one place to another, or how to settle the price of a sheep. Maybe you're used to some of it but it can get very tricky. You'll find the answers to all sorts of problems here and the book will tell you how to work them out for yourself.

At last the time came when Mr. Li thought that Bing had learned enough to go to the capital city, where he would be tested by officials to see if he was fit to be one of their underlings.

"Anything wrong?" Shang asked him one morning. Bing seemed listless and sad, just staring into space. "Aren't you looking forward to the next stage in your life? We're giving you a wonderful chance that doesn't come everybody's way."

Bing felt ashamed and was at a loss to know what to say, as he tried to stammer out his thanks. "Of course, of course. You have treated me with such kindness; and I owe so much to Mr. Li! But . . . if only Yu could come with me."

Shang could hardly suppress a smile, but he did his best to put on a serious face. "Well, it is certainly high time that you took a wife, but I have no idea what plans Mr. Li has for Yu. He'll want to know all about your family background. Anyone called Li in your family? You don't know? That's a pity. Well, not much we can do about it. I'm not going to talk about it now."

Of course Bing went to see Mr. Li before he set off and thanked him whole-heartedly for what he had done for him. And Mr. Li was able to cheer him up.

"You've been to Chang'an, haven't you? Did you see those fine carriages with outriders taking a man through the streets; did you notice the special hats that they were wearing? And their formal clothing? Well, watch out for all that now. Those men were some of the thirty thousand officials who live and work in the city; one of these days you'll be riding around like that yourself."

Bing started out from Luoyang by himself to make his way to Chang'an, trying as best as he could not to think about Yu, but he never failed to wake up with her on his mind. Though he was used to travel, the journey was long and lonely with no companion to talk with. After some time, he found himself close to the mountain called Huashan that he had passed with Shang when they were going the opposite way. Bing now knew how to write the mountain's name.

It was a beautiful spot but it seemed likely to be lonely as well, and it suited Bing's mood. As he drew closer, he caught up with a stranger on the path, and they began to walk together. Bing supposed it was one of those strange men Shang had told him about. He was about fifty years old, Bing thought. He wore his hair very long and had hardly a stitch of clothing on his back. His feet were bare and Bing could see that they had been bleeding. It must surely be painful, but the man made no complaint. Indeed, he had a bright and peaceful look on his face.

"I'm on my way up the mountain," he told Bing, "about which I've learned a lot. I've had enough of what goes on in the towns, where everyone seems to be looking for money and never thinking about anything else that lasts a bit longer. I've not met anyone for years who bothers to wonder why we've all been born, grow up, and die, just like that flock of birds over there. Let alone if there's anything that can give you a better life than money can, and I've had plenty of it in my time. Once I'm up that hill, I'll be free of all those petty worries that plague people down here. I'll be able to live the sort of life that nature has given to all creatures who breathe, great and small."

Bing was intrigued. "What about sustenance?" he asked. "And a warm place to sleep? Comforts?"

The man smiled. "Up there, they grow what they need and no more. They eat what they need and no more. They have all they need to keep alive, and no more, with plenty of time to think about the world and our place in it."

There was something about this that Bing found attractive. He had never thought of such a life, because he never knew that it existed. What would it be like to abandon all his plans and spend his life pondering these immense questions? Would it help him to forget about Yu? But could he really dismiss everything that he was used to and enjoyed? How could he contemplate those great questions when the wind froze him stiff, as it surely would? Then he thought of the way Mr. Li had told him, time and time again, of how fortunate men and women are as compared with the animals, as they can live together in a group harmoniously. And then Mr. Li and and Shang had done a great deal to make him fit for life as an official, and they had done so for a reason. They had faith in him. They wanted him to succeed. His success would also be theirs. This man who was set to go up the mountain had said nothing about such things. He seemed to think that one could drop out of one life and assume another, with no shame or hurt to anyone else. Bing knew how ashamed he would be if Mr. Li and Shang knew that he had even considered abandoning their plan. Much of what the man said had indeed enticed him, but he realized now that of all the things he had mentioned, he had never spoken of a man's duty to his family or his fellow creatures. Yes, he would go on to Chang'an.

Shortly after arriving in the city, Bing found himself inside a hall with many others, all waiting to be tested to see if they were fit for employment in the government service. Most of them appeared to be from the countryside, fresh faced and nearly all of them younger than Bing. They had been sent up from the provinces to see if they could make their fortunes and bring their home villages some credit. Bing struck up a conversation with a group of them and learned that they had all spent the last three years preparing for this, and he realized that it was not just anyone who could be admitted to take the tests. It would have been impossible for him if Mr. Li had not sent in a strong letter of recommendation.

Taken into an inner room, they continued to wait. Finally, three very senior officials arrived, each one wearing his robes and headdress, each one looking more severe than the other. Bing found out later that they were the heads of three important departments in the government: astronomy, divination, and prayer. Some of the young men were to face practical tests of their abilities in just these matters. Could they explain how the stars move and what a change in their movements would mean? Could they operate the square and round implements that they carried and tell you if it was an auspicious time to start out on a journey or get married? Had they been properly trained so that they could call out the prayers and supplications at a sacrifice to the gods and make them sound loud yet solemn? They had all been trained to take a job in the service and the three officials would decide if they were fit to be chosen.

The first thing Bing was instructed to do was to write out a long section of the laws and, thanks to Mr. Li's strict teaching and his own abilities, he did an excellent job of producing a formal document. Next he had to write out something on a stretch of silk, the first time that he had ever done so. Then he was asked to recite some texts by heart; fortunately they were texts that Mr. Li had taught him. Repeat, repeat, repeat, he remembered his teacher insisting, and now he knew why. It was Yu who had listened to him reciting these very texts, and she had helped him understand what they meant, and how to make his words sound important.

The most difficult part of the test came when Bing was shown pieces of writing in all sorts of different styles of script, not just the rough scrawls of the old command post which he could manage, and not those highly formal characters that Mr. Li had made him practice. Some of the writing that he was now asked to read was not done on wood; it had been fashioned on bronze vessels or painted on pots. These entirely defeated him. Then there was a large square piece of silk with two blocks of characters, one running one way and one the other, with twelve curious faces drawn round the edge. Bing couldn't make anything of that. He had better luck with some drawings of clouds shaped rather like animals to which short captions had been added. When asked, he correctly replied that these told you what your luck would be if you went to war.

The outcome would depend not only on the skills that Bing had demonstrated, but also on the abilities of all the others there, as the examiners had to decide which of them were most likely to make good officials.

Once the testing was finished, there was nothing to do but await the results. Bing noticed that some of the young men were behaving strangely, down on their knees, clasping little statues and mumbling under their breath. Others couldn't stop fidgeting. Some of them were pacing around and around.

It was not long before several clerks came in and called out a short list of names. "You all may leave," one of them said. "Your services will not be wanted." Bing watched as those whose names had been called left the room, their heads bowed in shame.

Now the clerks came around to each of the remaining applicants, asking where they had come from. The clerks would leave the room, then return to inform some of those waiting that they had been accepted and posted to jobs in the country, nowhere near their homes. This went on and on, until Bing was one of only a handful of applicants still awaiting word of their fate. At long last he was called and asked a number of questions about how he had spent his life. One of the three examiners was not too pleasant. He kept reminding his two colleagues that Bing had been moving around with questionable company in the towns and on the road. "Vagabonds," he said. "None of those merchants can be trusted."

Then the three of them went off for a private consultation for quite a long time, leaving Bing feeling utterly humiliated and dejected. Maybe he should have opted for a life on Huashan after all. Obviously, he had no chance of being taken on here.

Finally, two of those stern officials returned.

"You did very well with all the writing," they told him. "Where did you learn?"

"Mr. Li was my teacher," Bing replied. "I studied with him in Luoyang."

"Mr. Li?" one of them said. "Tell us more about him."

Bing told them what he knew, mentioning that Mr. Li had spent many years working in government service.

"Of course," said one of the examiners. "I remember your Mr. Li; he and I once worked in the same department. I should have recognized that fine hand of his in your own writing. Once you got a brush in your hand, it was clear that you are far and away above the others."

Bing could hardly control his emotions. "Thank you!" he said.

"Thank Mr. Li," replied the examiner. "Now, we will be sending you to a job in the Secretariat where so many important decisions are made. You'll have every opportunity there to learn how the empire is organized and governed. With luck you'll be in a fine position to start a long career in the service."

What an opportunity! He'd be living right here in Chang'an! Suddenly his life seemed perfect . . . except for one thing. His smile waned. Could it, would it be possible for Yu to join him? He could only hope. In the meantime, he must get on with his work.

The man in charge, his immediate superior, was of an unfriendly character, brusque and short-tempered when he gave Bing his orders.

"As you know there are twenty kingdoms and eighty-three commanderies under the skies, all enjoying His Imperial Majesty's kindness and protection."

Bing did not admit that he hadn't known this, and he realized that he must find out what the kingdoms and commanderies were called and where they all were.

"The kings and the governors of each one must have an accurate copy of the calendar for each year, otherwise they can't collect the taxes and call up people for work. And they need to receive it promptly before the year begins, as they have to make copies to send to each of the counties—fifteen hundred of them altogether. So there's no time to lose. I'm told that you're good at writing; well I hope that you're quick too. You'd better get cracking."

There were others there who were already hard at it, and it was not the first time that Bing worked as a copy clerk. Back in Juyan he had helped out by copying lists of men and their families and the rations that they had received. That task had taken a long time to do, as he was inexperienced and the list he had to work from was clumsily written. Now, the work was much easier. He had had some experience, and the calendar before him was clear enough. Mr. Li had taught him exactly how the calendar worked with its signs for each day. On closer inspection, the one he was to copy contained some extra characters, obviously put on the document after it had been finished, as they were in a different hand. He had no idea what they stood for and this worried him, until he discovered that none of his fellow workers understood the extra characters either, except for one elderly man who believed they had something to do with a way of counting the days and months that was different from the regular way they all knew.

"If you look carefully," he said, "you'll see that those extra characters were not written by the person who made out the rest of the document."

Bing didn't say that he'd noticed this, but he went on with his work just the same.

The work was not exciting, but Bing was determined to do the best he could, boring as some of it was. As time passed, he learned more and more about the tasks performed in the other offices and how the Emperor's government operated. Sometimes he was given an interesting job that required some thought. Once he was taken to a room where there were piles of rolled up documents, some of the wooden pieces broken off and lying on the floor.

"The last man left here in disgrace," he was told. "Got drunk and left this terrible jumble. Don't think he wasn't punished! Your job is to sort everything out and stack the rolls properly so we can see what's here."

Well, those rolls of documents were a mess! There were tax returns sent in from all those kingdoms and commanderies over the last few years. Some of the rolls had labels attached telling what they were, with their proper titles and dates; others had none. Bing began to work, trying to put the documents in order. Sometimes he found that the wrong label had been attached to a roll; for those with no label he had to make one himself. Clearly, the last man had been careless, but Bing had good reason to thank him for the mess he had left behind. After working through that vast pile of documents, he could name all the different parts of the empire, and he knew the names of most of the senior officials and where they were posted. Still, there was much more that he needed to know!

As it happened, he soon got another opportunity to increase his knowledge of the way the empire was run. A governor of one of the commanderies wrote to report that a fire had damaged his copy of the laws, destroying part of the document, and he urgently needed a replacement. The governor explained how this had happened and hoped that he would not be charged with careless treatment of government property. Here was another copying job for Bing, but this one really was attractive. Only one copy had to be made, and the document to be copied was full of interesting information. He had never seen so grand a document. It was written in the clearest of hands on long strips twice the length of the ones he usually handled. He would never have imagined that there were so many "ordinances" and "statutes," which he learned were the technical terms for these orders that the Emperor gave, or that they went into such detail. The document contained all of the rules and regulations of the land, including those that they'd had to follow back at the family farm about how to manage crops and store them. It laid down how travelers had to prove their identities and how their goods were to be inspected. Now he knew why they'd had to be so careful back on the farm; everything had to be done according to rules, which were all set down here in writing.

In addition to the rules, Bing also read about the punishments that followed if the rules were not obeyed, or if a man committed something called a "crime." There were many grades of crimes, and this made a difference in the punishment. If a person stole something on his own, that was one thing; if he stole something while working in a gang it was another, and the penalties were different if you got into a fight and injured an official or some ordinary person. Some of the documents specified how officials were to be graded, or the food to which they were entitled if they traveled on official business. All this interested Bing, as it provided a glimpse of what might lie in store for him in the future. He wondered what had become of his predecessor. Did the poor man get into trouble for losing documents in his charge? Mistakes could happen to anybody, but someone always had to pay the price, and the punishments were horrible—hard labor for years and, if you were unlucky, with a foot chopped off.

The rolls also contained a whole host of provisions that concerned the way in which ordinary people up and down the empire lived: how households in farming areas were established; how land that was covered in bush was to be reclaimed; schedules for sowing and raising crops; and a ban on felling trees at certain times of the year. In his time with Shang, Bing had often been offered coins whose edges had been clipped off, or some that were not of the usual shape or pattern. Now he learned of the penalties for damaging coins, or melting down the metal to use for other purposes.

While Bing was learning where his duties lay and gathering experience in official life, his friends in Luoyang had not been idle. Old Mr. Li hated the thought of parting with his daughter, Yu, who often read to him, now that his eyes were hurting. She had a talent for making the tales and poems sound so beautiful, especially when she sang. But Shang, at last, was able to persuade him that it was high time for Yu to have a home of her own and that Bing's humble origins should not stand in the way of letting him take her for a wife. The two old friends struck a bargain, though neither of them would have put it that way. Yu was to go to Chang'an, whether she wanted to or not, and Shang would transfer the management and stock of his business to Li's younger son. He had often accompanied Shang on the road and was keen to earn his fortune by running the business himself.

Bing could hardly believe it when he received a letter, carefully written on wood, telling him to expect Yu very soon. He had barely finished making preparations, when she arrived. This was the first time she had been there and she didn't like the way in which the soldiers or guardsmen were forever patrolling the streets, or how officials seemed to be riding around in their carriages everywhere, so that you had to make way. Life in sleepy old Luoyang had been so much more pleasant. However, there she was.

Every so often officials, even of Bing's low rank, were entitled to take a day off from their duties, and Bing's request to do so was granted. On that day, Bing and Yu went through the formalities, pledging themselves to each other. After the ceremony, there was quite a feast. Yu's younger brother, who had brought her to Chang'an, had also brought a stack of money with him.

The celebration did not last long and Bing was soon back in his office. Thanks to his record of service during the last year and the report that his superiors had sent in, Bing was promoted. He would have a new set of duties now, and he would be working with some of the most senior officials of all. These were the nine commissioners who were each responsible for one of the major tasks of government, such as collecting taxes, providing guards to keep crime down, or arranging the great ceremonial events that took place when a high-ranking foreign dignitary came to pay court to the Emperor. If any one of these offices or their smaller departments was short of staff—if someone died or went on leave to mourn the death of a parent—Bing would be sent to help out. In this way he learned how the whole structure of the Emperor's government worked.

One morning, he was sent to the office of the Commissioner of Trials, the office that received reports from up and down the land of any criminal case that local officials had not been able to settle. In some cases, they simply lacked enough authority, in other cases an appeal had been lodged against a judicial sentence, or perhaps the facts of a case were anything but straightforward, or it was unclear how the laws should be applied. Very often this meant drawing up long documents that set down all the evidence and recorded all the steps that had been taken, including the questions that had been put to a suspect and his or her answers.

One particular case had been going on for over a year before it reached the commissioner, and as it involved the integrity of some officials of fairly high rank, it was a serious matter. The incident in question had taken place down in the south, where some elements of the population were not of Han origin. They lived out in the backwoods and, unlike the settlers from the north, had no wish to lead the Han way of life. Apparently, some of them had become restive, attacking Han farms and fisheries and flouting Han authority. They had damaged some of the Han peoples' homes and wounded or killed some of them, before making off to their lairs. The Han officials had not been able to round up all the ringleaders, nor had they been able to recover the weapons that had been stolen from the government's store. The governor had instituted a thorough investigation as to what those officials had been trying to do and why they had failed. Some of them had been judged guilty of cowardice or refusal to fight, and that meant the death penalty.

Bing was assigned the immense task of writing all this up in a formal report. The form of the documents had to be strictly observed, as in the examples he was shown. Bulky as they were, these samples were a great help. They were written with scrupulous care, and Bing found them easy to read. Even so there were a number of unfamiliar technical terms, which someone explained to him. He never knew the outcome of this case. As soon as his work was done, he was called away to a job in another office.

There were other things on his mind. Yu had not been feeling well. Finally, amid her blushes she whispered what she knew would make him happy.

Well! This was news indeed! But would it be a boy, who would carry on his name? This was not a question Yu could answer. Was there any way of finding out? Bing posed the question to one of his friends in the office.

"If I were you," the friend advised, "I would go down to Diviners' Row. Find one of them there who works the 'Changes'; he'll charge you a lot but he's more likely to be reliable than the others."

Bing had heard tell of this alley. It had a poor reputation and was hidden away in an unsavory part of town. It consisted almost entirely of the stalls or booths of specialists of all sorts, who all swore that it was only they who could practice the methods required to predict the future and solve one's difficulties. Some of them turned over the strips in a roll such as the one that Shang had given Bing; others talked in a superior and refined way about the cycles of birth, death, and regrowth, or about the way in which all fortunes depend on the forces of yin and yang. One old man sat behind his table spinning a circular disk around in its square seating and would read off the answers to which one of its lines pointed.

The most superior of all these specialists, or so they claimed, were the ones whom Bing was looking for. As in the markets, these men were in fierce competition with one another and there was a considerable difference in the fees they charged, according to the methods that they used. The lowest were those who went straight to the books and read off an answer, telling the client whether the time was right or wrong for what he was proposing to do. Bing could read these books himself and had no wish to waste his money. He had no idea of the mysterious ways in which some of the others worked or produced their answers, but he took the advice he had received and went to one of the professionals who had bundles of stalks on his table. Very grand these people were, calling themselves "Masters," and the one he went to certainly took his time, performing an elaborate ritual of manipulating the stalks. Bing observed closely and noticed that they were the same motions that he had watched the Emperor make when he had performed his religious rites. Time and again the Master divided the bundles into smaller ones, taking a few off in his hand each time before he uttered a word.

"This is the wisdom of the secrets of the past of unending years," he finally called forth, and taking hold of a writing brush he drew a single horizontal line on the silk square in front of him. Once again he went through the whole procedure, this time drawing a line that was separated into two halves. By the end, he had written out a pattern of six lines, some complete, some divided, rising one on top of the other. Just the way that Bing had glimpsed the patterns being drawn in the sand at that ceremony at Yong.

"You may now ask your question," he told Bing in lofty tones.

Bing cleared his throat. "I wish to know whether the child in my wife's womb will be born male or female," he whispered.

"Take it in turns," the Master said. "First we will ask the age-old unquestionable source of truth whether it will be a girl."

Silence prevailed for quite a time, and Bing wondered whether he had spoken loudly enough for his question to be heard.

The answer came in six words that the Master uttered and which Bing could in no way understand. In very different tones the Master agreed to explain the message of the "Great truth that we have been fortunate enough to hear," and Bing waited.

"The message is that we must always be patient and await the outcome. Perhaps you have another question?"

Bing said nothing as he produced an additional sum of money.

"Very good," the Master said, as he took the second, larger fee.

Once again the interminable wait while the Master created six lines of a pattern completely different from the first.

"Let us ask if the child will be a boy," Bing said with a hint of pleading in his voice.

As interpreted by the Master the answer to this second question was, "On no account get into a fight."

Bing strode out in a fury, disgusted that these so-called professionals enjoyed such exalted reputations.

"All that money wasted on that charlatan!" he thought. "I'll make sure that nobody I know ever goes to Diviners' Row without fair warning. It's a good thing I didn't tell Yu where I was going."

One day Bing had to take some documents under safekeeping to what was called the "Lesser Treasury," a very large set of offices that were housed inside one of the palace's compounds. Bing showed his special pass and was allowed into a large room, where a number of officials were busily engaged with their clerks. Some of the clerks were working with sets of oddly shaped objects. As Bing drew nearer, he saw that they were piles of small fragments of bone on which some writing had been roughly scratched. Indeed, it was even worse than the writing on the strips that he had seen up at the command post. These bone fragments evidently served much the same purpose as the strips, as they were mainly filled with figures and dates on which payments had been made or goods transferred. Bing helped to sort these small pieces into different piles according to their subject.

The clerks were most grateful and they offered to show him around the whole set of offices.

"It's no bother at all," said one of the clerks. "And so long as nobody important is watching, we'll take you up to the roof and then you really will see something."

It was a lovely spring day with all the trees bursting into blossom. When they reached the roof, Bing could only gaze with amazement. It was a view that gave him a completely new idea of what Chang'an city was like. He could see how the hills were situated to protect the city from attack, and the passes where careful guard was always kept to prevent an enemy getting through. Almost due north he could make out three high towers side by side, the one in the middle higher than the other two.

"Those are the tombs of earlier Emperors," he was told. "The founding Emperor in the center, and his son and grandson on either side."

"They look enormous," said Bing, gasping with wonder.

"Yes, and they must have cost Heaven knows how much to build, never mind all the workmen required to build them. Each of those towers is built on top of the tomb itself and there is a large park set aside to enclose it all. There's another one out to the south, behind you; and if you go far enough to the west, you'd find several more, I'm told. You can't see them from here. Oh yes, the Empresses are buried there too, in their own tombs, not as large as those of their menfolk, and there are even some smaller tombs for the Emperors' less important women. They're all inside the parks, closely guarded, so that robbers can't get in."

As it happened, Bing did not have too long to wait before he saw one of these tombs for himself.

Notes for Chapter Eight

It was not permissible for two persons of the same surname to marry. Rules for the ways to test clerks are given in recently discovered texts of laws of 186 BCE. Instruments used for divining that depend on coincidences of the calendar and astronomical cycles have been found in a number of tombs. For a square silken document of the type described, see Tsuen-Hsuin Tsien, *Written on Bamboo and Silk,*

2nd ed. (Chicago and London: University of Chicago Press, 2004), p. 136. Some calendars carried a key character, such as *jian,* from time to time to indicate a day of special importance in a somewhat esoteric series of dates, auspicious or inauspicious. For the laws of 217 and 186 BCE, see A. F. P. Hulsewé, *Remnants of Ch'in Law* (Leiden: E. J. Brill, 1985); and Michael Loewe, "The Laws of 186 BCE," in Michael Nylan and Michael Loewe, eds., *China's Early Empire: A Reappraisal* (Cambridge: Cambridge University Press, 2010), chap. 9. The particular case that is discussed is the subject of a legal dossier of 220 BCE found at Zhangjiashan.

Image 1: Granary, mainly of wood, built ca. 100 BCE, 62 × 26 meters. Reconstruction based on remains found 150 kilometers east of present-day Xi'an. From *Xi Han jingshi cang* (Beijing: Wenwu chubanshe, 1990), p. 15, figure 13. See pp. 16, 57 above.

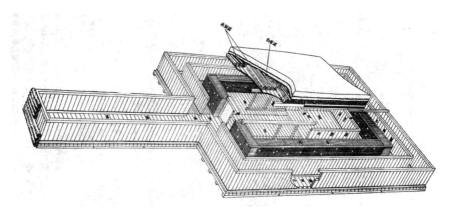

Image 2: Tomb no. 1 Dabaotai, ca. 10 kilometers southwest of Beijing, as reconstructed. Wooden structure with corridors and inner chambers surrounded by a wall of 15,000 superimposed timbers each 1 meter long. Built for a king of the Han empire who died in 44 BCE. Main structure is 25 × 20 meters. From *Beijing Dabaotai Han mu* (Beijing: Wenwu chubanshe, 1989), p. 10, figure 13. See p. 17 above.

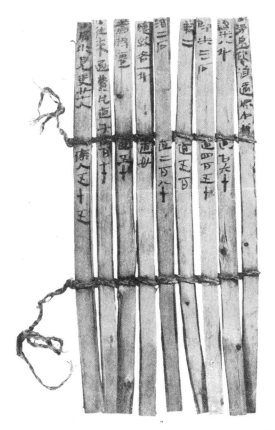

Image 3: Complete document on 9 wooden strips, 23 cm (1 Han foot) long, bound by cords; found at Juyan, Gansu province. Text gives accounts for the expenditure of official stores, dated 22 CE. From *Wenwu* 1978.1. Plate 8:2. See pp. 22, 23 above.

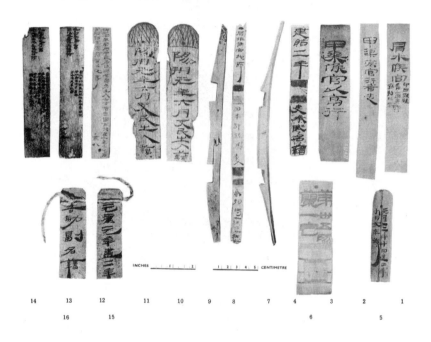

Image 4: Wooden labels attached to rolled wooden documents, with title (no. 4 dated 31 BCE; nos. 10, 11 dated 24 BCE; no. 16), time of delivery (no. 1), destination and means of dispatch (nos. 2, 3); from a command post at Juyan, Gansu province. From Michael Loewe, *Records of Han Administration, Volume I: Historical Assessment* (Cambridge: Cambridge University Press, 1967), Plate 4. See pp. 23, 84 above.

Image 5: Incense burner, bronze and inlaid gold, shaped like a mountain, with design of a hunting scene; height 26 cm. From the tomb of Liu Sheng, one of the kings of the Han empire who died in 112 BCE (tomb no. 1 Mancheng, Hebei province). From *Wenhua da geming qijian chutu wenwu* (Beijing: Wenwu chubanshe, 1972), p. 5. See p. 39 above.

Image 6: Kitchen scene. Engraved stone from a tomb in Zhucheng county (Shandong province), probably dated in Eastern Han; 1.52 × 0.76 meters. From *Wenwu* 1981.10, p. 19, figure 7. See p. 45 above and p. 136 below.

Image 7: Part of an embroidered silk roll, blue and red on yellow, with cloud scroll pattern; from the tomb of Lady Dai (tomb no. 1 Mawangdui, Changsha, Hunan province); dated not later than 168 BCE. From *Changsha Mawangdui yi hao Han mu* vol. 2 (Beijing: Wenwu chubanshe, 1973), p. 117, Plate 126. See p. 46 above.

Image 8: Entertainment with musicians, dancers, and acrobats; painted ceramic, 67 × 47.5 cm; second century BCE. From a tomb near Ji'nan (Shandong province). From *Wenhua da geming qijian chutu wenwu* (Beijing: Wenwu chubanshe, 1972), p. 125. See p. 46 above.

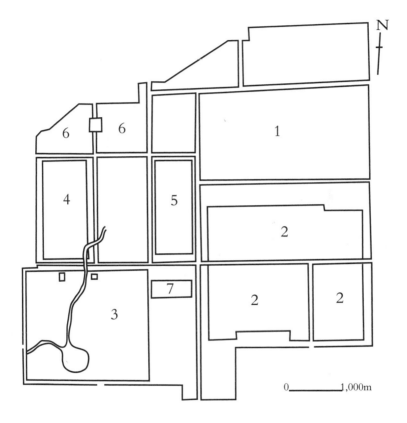

Image 9: Chang'an, Capital of the Western Han Dynasty
1. Mingguan Palace
2. Changle Palace
3. Weiyang Palace
4. Guigong Palace
5. Beigong Palace
6. Eastern and Western markets
7. Arsenal

Image 10: Officials, of low grade. From a wall painting (red, yellow, and blue) at tomb no. 1 Wangdu (Hebei province), late second century CE. From *Han Tang bihua* (Beijing: Waiwen chubanshe, 1974), Plate 13. See p. 83 above.

Image 11: Lamp, held and operated by a domestic servant; bronze, height 48 cm. From the tomb of Dou Wan, consort of Liu Sheng (tomb no. 2 Mancheng, Hebei province), who died after 112 BCE. For Liu Sheng, see image 5 above. From *Wenhua da geming qijian chutu wenwu* (Beijing: Wenwu chubanshe, 1972), p. 1. See p. 106 below.

Image 12: Official receiving his subordinates. Engraved stone 1.51 × 0.75 meters. From a tomb in Zhucheng county (Shandong province), probably dated in Eastern Han. From *Wenwu* 1981.10, p. 20, figure 8. See p. 126 below.

Image 13: Tripod of lacquered wood, with pattern in red on a black background; height 28 cm. From *Changsha Mawangdui yi hao Han mu* vol. 2 (Beijing: Wenwu chubanshe, 1973), p. 141, Plate 154. See p. 130 below.

Image 14: Queen Mother of the West, attended by armed guardian, three-legged crow, dancing toad, hare with herbs, nine-tailed fox, and suppliant for the gift of immortality; 46 × 41 cm. From a molded brick found in Sichuan province, dated in Eastern Han. From *Sichuan Han dai diaosu yishu* (Beijing: Zhongguo gudian yishu chubanshe, 1959), no. 61. For an explanation of the iconography, see Michael Loewe, *Ways to Paradise: The Chinese Quest for Immortality* (London: George Allen and Unwin, 1979), pp. 101–12. See p. 173 below.

Chapter Nine   *Assistant to the Imperial Counselor*

Promoted once again, Bing was now appointed assistant to the Imperial Counselor, whose rank and authority were higher than those of all officials except the Chancellor. When Mr. Li heard of this, he wrote to Bing to warn him of the dangers he would face. "You'll be blamed for all sorts of things that you can't possibly have anything to do with; it's a fine job, but watch out."

Bing already knew that he would be trusted with highly confidential matters that might seal the fate of any one of his colleagues, however highly placed he might be in the government, or whatever favors he might enjoy from one of the palaces. The Imperial Counselor was a half brother of one of the Emperor's consorts—not the Empress herself, but one of the minor ladies of the court—and there had been a lot of loose talk about how she was trying to take the place of the Empress, possibly with the help of her brother. Bing soon realized that he would be in grave danger if he misused or leaked any of the information that came his way and that there would be plenty of people who would do their best to pump him.

"Yes," the Imperial Counselor warned him, "there will be those who try to bribe you to reveal state secrets, especially when you're sent to evaluate how thoroughly and honestly an official has been carrying out his duties, or to inspect his accounts." Despite the heavy responsibility of his new job, and its dangers, Bing was proud to carry the new seal of office, to which he was entitled, and he took special pride in showing it to Yu.

Bing's first mission took him north of Chang'an city to the tombs of some of the earlier Emperors. A number of officials who had to meet the expenses of the palaces had been muttering about the high cost of keeping so many of these tombs in order and properly guarded, not to mention the offerings rendered to their shrines every day, every

month, and every season. Some of them argued openly that there
was no need to continue maintaining all the tombs. Bing was to see
whether the claims sent in for expenses were accurate; they varied so
much from tomb to tomb that it seemed unlikely that they could all be
correct.

These tombs were not far outside the city walls, and as he
approached them Bing took in the great height of the highest of their
towers. They were even more majestic close up than they had looked
from the rooftop inside the city, where he had first seen them. He
had been advised to make a detour to avoid one of the settlements
that lay close by. It was called Changling, the same name as that of
the first tomb he was to visit, that of the founding Emperor. All sorts
of people lived in Changling. Many years earlier, the government had
deliberately set the place up for occupation by moving a large number
of families there from the east. Some of them were related to a much
earlier branch of the local kings of the area; but they still resented
having to take orders from an emperor who was not one of their
own, never mind his officials, and there were signs that they might stir
up trouble. Bing agreed that there was no point in provoking them,
which might well happen if he drove conspicuously through their
village in his official carriage, and his driver was able to skirt the area
without much loss of time.

Walls built of stamped earth surrounded the large parks in which
the tombs of the early Han Emperors and each one of their Empresses
lay, the Empress on the east side. Within their own compounds, the
tombs rose from a base that might measure 150 meters wide to a flat
plateau of 50 meters at the summit. But these were by no means the
only buildings in the park. There were the shrines given over to the
reverent service of remembrance, displaying the wooden tablets that
bore the names of the deceased Emperors. There were two small
chambers named the Chamber of Rest and the Chamber of Ease, and
it was at all three of these that the offerings were regularly presented.
At the tomb of one of the emperors Bing noticed an area that had been
fenced off. He was told that it was a mass grave where the convicts
who had been engaged in building the tomb had been buried. Once
their work was done, they had been put to death to prevent them from

revealing to anyone how to force their way in and rob the tomb of its treasures.

Bing's first step was to make a thorough inspection of the whole site, as he needed first of all to find out whether it was being kept in good repair. On the whole it had been well maintained, though, as an expert carpenter, he could see where some of the wood had not been treated properly and needed replacing; he also noted gaps in the surrounding wall. Anyone could force those weak spots and enter the park. He duly paid his respects at the shrine devoted to the memory of Gaozu, the first Han Emperor, and tested the gateways to see that they could be locked securely. The tomb itself was well kept; there were no wild shrubs or trees sprouting at the top, and as far as he could see reasonable precautions had been taken to keep the rats away from lesser buildings such as the storehouses.

So far he had not observed anything serious to report, but he knew that the trickiest part of his work lay ahead, when he was to determine how honestly the staff were accounting for the goods they used in the offerings. To do this he had to witness examples of all types of ceremony, for the day, the month, and the season. Fortunately he had arrived during the last month of spring and by staying there for about twenty days he would be present when the summer season began. As the food and drink, the grain, and the animals were brought in for each of the services, every day at the Chamber of Rest, every month at the memorial shrine, and every season at the Chamber of Ease, Bing watched carefully to see that all the vessels were really full, making a note of how many had been placed on the altar. For several days he did little else, and the attendants took him to be no more than a silent observer whom they could disregard.

Then one day he was rewarded for his patience. One of the grain containers was accidentally dropped and its contents spilled over the floor. With a quick glance, Bing could see that it not been packed full, and other signs told him that a careful examination was in order. When all the staff had left, Bing stayed behind to take his time and inspect the contents of each vessel. Just as he suspected, much of what they held was old and stale, obviously being offered day after day. Some of the containers were only half full. Some were packed with weeds hacked from the fields by hoes, with only a thin layer of millet on top.

Bing calculated the discrepancy between the amount of supplies actually used and the amount that had been reported for each day. He went on to do the same for the monthly and seasonal offerings. When he worked out what the difference would be for a whole year, he was staggered at the extent to which the treasury in Chang'an was being cheated. He would now call at the storehouses where these supplies were kept and issued for use. Thanks to his rank, he could demand to see the duplicate copies of the returns that were sent in for payment for the last five years.

Bing drew up his report with some misgivings. He knew that it would inevitably give rise to further investigation and judicial proceedings, and eventually to the infliction of severe punishment on whoever was judged guilty of the misuse of government stores. Only time would show who was going to suffer. He hoped that it would not be the staff members who had looked after him in such a friendly way at Gaozu's tomb, as he was fairly certain that they were simply obeying the verbal orders they had received. The person who seemed most likely to be charged for these malpractices would be the official at the top who was in charge of the tomb site, but in Bing's view it was more likely to be his immediate assistant, who had managed to pull the wool over his superior's eyes. Bing had noticed what a mean sort of man he was. But it might be much more serious. If things went badly and somebody high up in Chang'an wanted to exploit the case for personal reasons, a charge might even be made against a really senior man, such as the Commissioner for Ceremonial, who bore overall responsibility for all the imperial tombs. Bing knew that some of that man's colleagues had a grudge against him and would not hesitate to seize an opportunity to bring him down. For his part, he had been instructed on no account to let anyone at the tombs know what his business was or what he had found out.

Bing had attended and enjoyed some of the musical performances that accompanied the presentation of the sacrifices at the shrines, and he had admired the skills of the troupes of dancers. He had also witnessed another ceremony, which drew a large number of sightseers from the city. It took place once a month when the robes and headdress of the last Emperor were conveyed by carriage from the Chamber of Rest to the shrine. The crowd stood solemnly as the carriage passed. Some people were in tears, as they explained to their children what they were looking at. "They're taking the dead Emperor from where he's sleeping to a place where he will receive visitors who want to express their loyalty and respect." Bing did not know what to make of it, and much later he described the scene to Yu.

"It's all playacting," she said, "but it is also very important, as it makes everyone believe that their Emperor is always there, looking after their needs and receiving their services."

The next task assigned to Bing was of a totally different nature. The Imperial Counselor was taking a very serious view of a fire which had broken out in the city's arsenal, destroying a great deal of equipment before it could be brought under control. He wondered whether it had been due to an accident, or careless warehousing, or whether it had been set on purpose, and he sent Bing to see what he could find out.

The arsenal was located almost in the center of Chang'an between two of the largest of the imperial palaces. It was under the charge of the Commissioner for the Capital, whose men patrolled the streets to keep order and arrest anyone who behaved in a suspicious manner.

There were more storehouses there than Bing had expected, all very large, and he insisted on being shown around all seven. Only one of these separate stores had been set on fire and from the others Bing could see how the different types of military weapons and other equipment were kept, some of them neatly arranged on wooden racks. In all there were over two hundred types of objects. Only a few of some items were kept in stock, but there were arrowheads by the thousands. He could hardly believe it when he was told that the last report listed a total of over twenty million items.

"How often do you oil the crossbows?" he asked the sergeant, who stood beside him, and he made a note of the answer. "And where do you keep the oil that you need for that?" The sergeant told him that most of it was away in an outbuilding and that inside the sheds they kept just enough for immediate use.

As he entered the next building, he stopped short and gazed at a row of trolleys on which several crossbows could be mounted and moved around so that they could all shoot at the same target. He'd been told about such things when he was a conscript soldier, but these were the first he'd ever seen.

"How many of these have you got?" he asked and was staggered to learn that there were no less than five hundred in stock. If only we'd had a couple of those up on the fort, he thought. Obviously, it was from here that the generals drew the shields, spears, and bows they needed when setting out on a campaign. But what a chance it would be for anyone who wanted to stage an armed fight with the Emperor. All he had to do would be to light a fire in one shed and pilfer what he wanted from the others. The Imperial Counselor was quite right to be concerned.

Fortunately, the shed that had been burned had not been gutted and some of the iron weapons lay in heaps where they had fallen from the racks. Bing ordered the official in charge to make out a list of everything that had been destroyed and an estimate of what would be needed to repair the damaged building. There had been no lightning on the night of the fire, he determined. The Imperial Counselor himself wanted to know what those present that night thought about the cause of the fire. Bing needed to find that out, and also how they had tried to douse it.

Not so easy. There was something decidedly odd about the way some of his questions were being answered, but Bing couldn't quite put his finger on what was wrong. One of the men kept on talking about the sheds that had not been damaged, repeating himself as if he had been given strict orders what to say. When Bing eventually saw the inventory of the items destroyed or damaged, he compared the figures with those he had been given verbally and they didn't quite tally. So, he really had two things to worry about: how the fire had been allowed to break out and why the figures were so different.

The only thing to do would be to have the director answer these questions, but Bing was far too junior to do that. In his report to the Imperial Counselor he made it quite plain what needed looking into, but the Imperial Counselor ordered him to think no more about it.

It was only years later that Bing found out what had really happened. One of the generals had come back from fighting in the north and faced serious charges of dereliction of duty. In the course of his trial, he confessed to all sorts of things that he should never have done, which included returning weapons to the arsenal that were damaged and making sure that it would not be reported. In fact, he had bribed the director of the arsenal to admit the goods without asking any questions.

All this had been some years earlier. But the director had been due to retire shortly after the time when that fire had broken out, and he had realized that he would be in great trouble if his successor was sharp enough to check everything personally. Destruction of the damaged equipment by fire would remove any evidence that the director had acted criminally. Interestingly, the fires had broken out exactly where they were needed. The general had been punished for his crimes; somehow the director had escaped scrutiny. But his family used to say that he never passed a night without shouting.

Time had passed since Bing's visit to Diviners' Row. Though he had given up on trying to learn whether he was going to be the father of a boy or a girl, the question was always in the back of his mind. One day, he returned home from his office to find Yu in great pain, and he knew that he would soon know the answer. Yu had been far too weak to go for help, but the disagreeable, roughly spoken woman who used to sweep the streets was there. Trust her to be anywhere there was any excitement, thought Bing, and don't expect to hear a word of comfort from her.

The light was dim and Yu lay in the cool shadows, but Bing could see beads of sweat on her brow, her face contorted in pain. A trickle of blood ran down her chin from her lower lip, which she had been biting.

"We all have to go through it, dearie," the dreadful old woman was saying, quite smugly and without a trace of sympathy. "Doesn't matter if you're a rich merchant's wife or a beggar or a one of them street girls who's got herself into trouble; it doesn't get any better."

Bing was frightened. Yu had not said a word. She seemed not to know he was there. The look in her eyes told him that she was frightened too.

They needed help, and Bing thought he knew where to find it, as he had a friend on the medical staff at one of the departments where he worked. This man would know where to find an experienced midwife. But Bing would have to leave right away.

As it was, the dreadful old woman was actually tucking blankets around Yu. At least she was doing no harm, so better than getting rid of her, he would leave her here with Yu, rather than leave his wife alone.

He knelt down and held Yu's chin in his hand. "I will be back with a midwife," he told her. "I will be back . . ." he said, but Yu seemed to have fainted.

"She's looking quite poorly," said the woman, shaking her head.

"Keep her warm," said Bing. "I will be back with help."

Bing's friend in fact knew just the right person. The woman he had in mind had actually attended to none other than one of the Emperor's consorts.

"Your wife is in safe hands," his friend told him, after they had delivered the midwife to Yu's side and were waiting outside.

"We must leave them now," he said. "Just for the time being. You come away with me, and they'll let us know when it's time for you to come back. Believe me, it's all for the best."

Hour after hour passed as Bing tried to contain his anguish. It was no good going to the office, he would not be able to concentrate. He spent the afternoon wandering the streets with his friend and, come nightfall, they moved to an inn, where they spent a sleepless night with a few drinks.

It was almost dawn when a messenger arrived with the news that it was time for Bing to return home. He approached his house, trembling with anticipation.

The midwife poked her head out the door. "Mr. Wu," she said. "You've been blessed by Heaven. The boy is strong, but Yu will need much care. She's had a hard time, and she is very weak."

How proud Bing was to announce that he had a son to carry on his line! The boy must be given a name without delay. He knew that you had to be careful here to avoid offending the gods, and then there were also family considerations. He could hardly remember what his own father's name was, and he wondered if they dare give the boy Mr. Li's personal name, Guang, which meant "light." Yu was delighted with the idea and she was sure that her father would be too. After some time, Mr. Li sent word that he would be pleased and honored for the child to have his name. He sent them a few lines of poetry, taken from the old books, to commemorate the occasion, and Yu was especially pleased. He was too old to travel nowadays, Mr. Li wrote, but his son the merchant would soon be coming their way. Yu had been recovering well, and this news made her spirits soar.

There was an air of great excitement in the city, when it was announced that, out of kind consideration for the welfare of his subjects and in celebration of the triumph of the Han army over an uncivilized barbarian, His Majesty the Emperor had given gracious permission for a grand entertainment to take place, with everyone free to come and enjoy the spectacle. The Imperial Counselor invited his assistant to join him, and highly honored dignitaries as they were, they were led to the best places to see what was going on. Occasionally, the Emperor himself would attend these performances but Bing was rather glad of his absence, as there was far less tension in the air than there would have been had His Majesty been present.

Near to where they sat were a few men who were conspicuous in their dress. Bing recognized immediately that they wore the costume of the people of the north, and he mentioned this to the Imperial Counselor.

"Oh yes," he said, "I'm very glad that they are here. Once they return to the primitive way of life of those cold parts of the world, they'll tell everyone how well and comfortably we live here. Wait till they see the refreshments! They'll be astonished that we are rich enough to mount such a spread. Instead of attacking us to steal what they can, they'll try to win our friendship. That will mean we'll have less to spend on the army."

Meanwhile, the people had been crowding in by the thousands to watch, as act followed after act. There were professional dancers named "Bayu" with their twirling skirts and graceful movements. Another team enacted a sort of play, some of them taking the part of an enormous dragonlike monster. Skilled jugglers kept one's eyes riveted on the balls that they were tossing. Then a very high pole was brought on to the platform, apparently rising from a lake. Nimble acrobats with a perfect sense of balance climbed right to the top. One of them actually had a pole resting on his head and, believe it or not, there seemed to be little children clinging on to it by a crosspiece, but when Bing looked carefully he could see that they were figurines made of wood. The climax came with what was called the "bull game." Two teams of human figures wearing bulls' horns on their heads started by dancing with one another, then they took to a much more serious and dangerous act in which they were wrestling. "An age-old game," somebody said. "You may like looking at it as a piece of playacting but what you're really seeing is something much more deadly. They're acting out a fight to the finish between two gods, each one determined to destroy the other, and so it all used to be. No, they won't go that far here, but it'll remind us all of the great battles of old."

How right the Imperial Counselor had been. When the performances were finished it was time for the refreshments to be brought in, and no one could have complained that the Han Emperor was frugal. Bing remembered reading something with Mr. Li about a very bad old king who used to feast on a mountain of meat and a lake of wine, and my goodness there was enough here to merit that description. That man of old had been wicked because he had kept all that luxury to himself, but here it was spread out for everyone to enjoy. The drinks included some of that special grape juice that was usually reserved for the palace and a choice few. How the mob scrambled to get at it now! But it was bad luck for the patrolmen who had to pick up the drunks and never tasted a mouthful themselves.

Notes to Chapter Nine

None of the eleven tombs of the Western Han emperors have been excavated fully, and the details given here may not necessarily apply to those of Gaozu and Jingdi. It is not certain that a list of military equipment kept in store in 13 BCE applies to the arsenal at Chang'an that has been excavated (see *Kaogu* 1978.4, p. 261; *Wen wu* 1982.2, pp. 78–81) or elsewhere. Fires broke out in the arsenal of the Eastern Han Dynasty, at Luoyang, in 117 and 161 CE; see Hans Bielenstein, *Lo-yang in Later Han Times* (Stockholm: Museum of Far Eastern Antiquities, 1976), p. 57. For the spectacle and games described, see A. F. P. Hulsewé, *China in Central Asia: The Early Stage, 125 B.C.– A.D. 23* (Leiden: E. J. Brill, 1979), p. 201; and Michael Loewe, *Divination, Mythology, and Monarchy in Han China* (Cambridge: Cambridge University Press, 1994), chap. 11.

Chapter Ten   *At work in the central government*

T HERE WAS A RULE THAT NOBODY COULD SERVE AS ASSISTANT TO THE
Imperial Counselor for more than two years. Over ten had
passed since Bing was first enrolled in the civil service at the lowest
level, and he now found himself moving through a series of changes.
For a time he was in the office of the Commissioner for Transport,
then in the office that received foreign dignitaries, and for a time he
had worked in that very important office responsible for collecting
various forms of tax and for supplying all the services and materials
that the Emperor needed. He learned a lot in all this, meeting
colleagues who had to find musicians and entertainers when they
were wanted, or prayer reciters, such as those he'd seen at work that
day in Yong, when he had hidden on the hillside and spied the ritual
events going on down below. He remembered how those who aspired
to that sort of work had been tested, back when he was beginning
work as a clerk.

It was that same department that looked after the Emperor's well-
being in his daily life. By all accounts, he had a poor appetite and
the cooks called up by the department were hard put to satisfy him.
Bing had once observed the doctors on their way to work, when
His Majesty had been struck down with alarming stomach pains, or
perhaps because he had found himself useless in bed. That was a serious
matter. As yet, no heir to the throne had been born, and there was
much gossip on that subject that passed from one palace to the next.

There had been much to fascinate Bing during his years of service.
The small group of men and women who worked in the Visitors'
Department, for example. They had an astonishing command of
languages. Not only could they understand what people from some
of the most remote areas said, they could even talk to these people
in their own tongue. Most of them came from the northwest, as you

could see immediately on looking at them, and they never failed to show off their skills. Some had been born to women of the Xiongnu or Xianbi people, who never settled down to live in a town. But, as Bing had been told, these groups were known to ride into the countryside and wreak havoc among the farms, taking what they could, raping the women, and setting fire to everything they could find. Some of the translators might have been the offspring of girls who had been beaten, raped, and then taken from their family farms to the cold north. Others were not of Han birth; they were Xiongnu through and through, but had pledged their loyalty to the Han Emperor.

Duty once took Bing to an office that was heavily guarded by armed servicemen. He had been given special permission to go inside, where he was to check a list of all the items that were in stock. The office had a name which in no way disclosed what its purpose was or what was likely to be found there, and it was only now, accompanied by the director, that Bing discovered the reason behind the secrecy. After passing through several gateways, where even the director had to show his pass, they came to a large hall where glowing lamps shone on shelf after shelf of treasures. Bing held his breath, staggered by what he saw: row after row of wonderfully fashioned objects of lacquered wood, bronze, and jade. His eye caught a shelf containing beautiful sets of tableware in black and scarlet. Bing could not imagine that anyone would dare to fill those cups with the hot soup for which they were intended. Some of the pieces were made in unusual shapes, and he wondered what on earth they were for, and if they had special names under which they would have to appear in a list.

The next room was just as large and was filled with shelves of bronze containers, square and round, to hold solids or liquids. Some reminded him of the vessels that he had seen on the altar that day at Yong. Others had ringed handles attached at each side. Some had a lid secured by a chain. Some really special ones were inlaid with gems or silver to form a pattern. The director explained that the large bronze vessels, unusually shaped, were used in special sacrifices that the Emperor attended, and Bing was glad to learn the names by which they would have to be registered. Other shelves supported musical instruments, mainly sets of bells neatly arranged according to their size and note, and there were sets of weights and measures made out exactly to the size specified in their inscriptions. A bronze lamp made in the shape of a serving girl, whose hands were poised to manipulate the lamp's shutters and vents, particularly fascinated him. Somehow or other, the director said—and he could not explain how—when one of the shutters was closed, light still came through glowing, but no smoke seeped out to fill the dining room and make the diners cough.

There was nothing quite so dazzling in the next room, which housed plates, cups, and dishes that the skillful potters had turned out on their wheels. Some of these were dark and unimpressive; in others the gray background had been overlaid with paint in white and red, and some of them were shaped to resemble some of the objects made in bronze. Bing had to get close to the shelves in the front of the room before he could see what was there. At first he was at a loss to understand, then suddenly the memory floated back of the funeral he had attended at the rich man's house, where he had once worked as a servant. He was looking at row after row of pottery models of the things you knew in everyday life, but all in miniature. Nobody had decorated the rough uncolored clay with which these wellheads, model granaries, and plow teams had been fashioned, but they were all true to life—the wells with their buckets and ladles, the wide wooden boards that could be raised and lowered so as to pound grain with their iron hammers, the pens with sheep herded inside. Right at the end, and rather larger than the other models, there was a farm wagon pulled by an ox, and a row of model houses several stories high, some with a miniature man or woman standing at the door.

"You know what these are for?" the director asked, and Bing nodded. "One of these days you may be involved in arranging a really high-class funeral—you know for whom I mean but I'm not going to say. You have to include all sorts of things in the tomb in case they are needed in the next world, stuff to eat and drink, clothes to wear, all the equipment needed to prepare and enjoy a meal. Or they may require tools with which to earn a living, as you see in those farms over here, all small enough but quite real. This office is responsible for keeping a supply of these items in case there's a sudden call for them. Thank goodness we don't have to stock the books that are sometimes included in case anyone in the next world wants to read."

Bing thought it all very odd. He could see no possible way in which his father, long dead, would be able to draw up water from those wells, let alone find time for reading, even if he had been able to do so.

Finally, the director brought him to a beautifully lit hall. Here there were treasures even more magnificent than those he had already seen. Every object was of jade, light green, dark green, or even black. There were circular disks, with small apertures at their centers, some almost the size of an open hand. There were long, heavy rods, beautifully carved, lying flat on the shelf. These were the scepters with which the kings showed their authority, and eventually, they were among the items buried in their tombs. This hall also contained jewelry of all sorts that high-class or rich women liked to wear, bracelets around their wrists, or pendants, and a variety of ornaments in the shapes of birds and animals.

Bing had seen craftsmen at work on jade while he was traveling with Shang, and he was aware of the power of concentration, the acutely accurate eyesight, and sense of touch that were needed to work on this extra-hard substance, so that a neat hole was drilled in the correct place, or enough, but not too much, of a surface was filed away to leave the rest thin without breaking. Polishing the finished object demanded untold skill. He could only imagine how long it must have taken to produce such gorgeous objects.

Bing thought he had seen everything, until the director paused before a curtain.

"There is one last thing I want to show you," he told Bing, "but you must swear never to tell anyone about it."

Bing agreed, and the curtain was drawn aside. The sight that met his eyes was breathtaking. It appeared to be the separate parts of a suit of clothing, made to encase a person's entire body, arms, hands, legs, and head. But none of these pieces were made of silk, let alone hemp; they were each formed of innumerable little pieces of very thin jade, and each one had a hole at each corner through which threads or sometimes gold or silver wires had been drawn. In this way the pieces could be made to hang together as one suit, with all the square, oblong, or triangular pieces in the right places.

Bing took a step closer and leaned forward to examine the section meant to encase the head. "Who on earth would wear this?" he asked.

The director looked rather grim. "No one on earth," he answered. "When the highest in the land die they are encased in one of these suits before they are buried. Jade is a wonderful thing you know. The ladies like to wear it because they think it gives them good health and energy, and a sparkle that attracts the men. Noble lords are entitled to possess and display rings of jade to show off their high position. Many people think that once you're dead it's only jade that will forever preserve your body from decay. But only very special men and women are allowed burial in a suit such as this. We are not allowed to let any of them out of this storehouse without a special decree from the Emperor, or after his death, from his Empress or his mother."

Behind this office were the workshops where all these amazing objects were made, all paid for by the Lesser Treasury from the taxes they were responsible for collecting. Some of the pieces of bronze looked very old to Bing's eye; they were decorated with extraordinary figures, repeated time after time, very different from the designs seen on modern goods. These old pieces had line after line of straight or curly decoration, always around a face that looked straight at you. For all you knew, that face was either conveying a blessing or uttering a curse on anyone who stood in the way. Bing thought some of them looked rather frightening and he wondered what they meant to the people of long, long ago when they were made. Obviously they were very important, otherwise nobody would have gone to the expense of having them repeated so often on these bronze vessels. Years ago, he had seen a small grain holder decorated in this way for sale, and nobody had bought it. Much too frightening and ugly was the general verdict, and no one worked in that style anymore. However, ugly or not, and no matter whether they brought good or bad fortune, Bing had to include them in the inventory he was assigned to draw up.

One day, none other than the Chancellor, the highest official in the empire, sent for Bing, and there was a serious expression on his face when Bing presented himself.

"This is a matter of the utmost secrecy," he began. "One of the Emperor's distant relatives who fancies himself a scholar was given a very responsible job to do. I've never met Liu Xiang, but I'm told that he is a learned man who is used to expressing his opinions openly. Some years ago, when he was young, he got himself into serious trouble by dabbling in secret arts. He was trying to make a fortune by use of magic and was lucky to escape a death penalty. Well, all that seems to have been forgotten and he was given the task of leading a team to scour the provinces in search of any traces of written matter. They were to bring all copies of books that they found here to the palace and then to go through them all comparing one copy with another and deciding which was the most accurate text to be preserved."

"That sounds fine to me," said Bing.

"Ah yes, but there's more to it than that. There were two reasons for ordering this search. First, His Majesty had every intention of setting up a library, which is to contain copies of everything that has been written and is worth preserving: those old books the masters wrote, and those in which their lessons were carefully copied; all the histories of our people, going back to the beginning; the books that tell the way to spend a better and longer life; all the poems that the men of letters have written; and the manuals that tell you how to recognize and cure diseases or how to determine what the future holds. Years ago, the Emperor of the last and cursed dynasty gave orders to destroy much of this material, and Liu Xiang was to find any copies that survived. But there was another reason. They were also looking for anything in writing that might be treasonable, for example anything that told of a plot that threatened His Majesty, or a plot to disrupt the dynasty that, by the grace of Heaven, he has inherited from his ancestors. Any documents of that nature had to be found and destroyed.

"Well, Liu Xiang and his colleagues finished their work some time ago and made an excellent job of the lists that they drew up of what has been deposited in the imperial library. But there is still much that we need to know. Did all the members of the team do their job honestly and completely? Did they ferret out everything that might stir up a movement against the throne? Is there anything in the library that should not be there? It's a difficult job I know, but I want you to see what's been going on. If you can bring back a list of what they've got, please do, and next year we'll send someone else to see if any additional and subversive materials have been added. I don't have to tell you that you'll have to tread carefully, or else we shall all be in trouble."

This was not the first time that Bing had heard talk of a danger of disloyalty or even treason, but he was surprised, even shocked, that such dangers might exist in these high and mighty circles, and he didn't relish the task in the slightest.

"But, Sir, I'm not really qualified for this task. Surely you need somebody who has had a fine scholarly training to review all the texts they have collected and judge their contents?"

"That is just the sort of person I don't want," the Chancellor replied. "They are all members of the same group of academics who praise everything old and curse anything new, and there is no doubt that they'd gang up with Liu Xiang and his colleagues. I want somebody who stands apart from that crowd and won't be tempted to cover up for them."

So Bing had no option but to undertake this highly confidential and potentially dangerous job. If only he could take Yu with him. She had learned so much from Mr. Li about the handling of books, and her help would be invaluable. He knew that he'd been told not to breathe a word to anyone but he was going to risk it.

Taking great care that he was not being overheard, Bing revealed to Yu the nature of his new assignment.

"I wish I could get you to help me," he told her. "Your experience in such things far exceeds my own. But the situation is so delicate that I can't even let on that I've discussed it with you."

Yu said nothing, and Bing could see that she was pondering the matter. "Here's some simple advice that will help you," she said at last. "Do not simply look at the surface of things. Study very closely the words in the title of each book. They will seem innocent enough on first glance, but you may find that some of them carry a wealth of inner meaning."

"I should approach the task with suspicion?" he asked.

"Approach it with an open mind," she replied with a smile. "And if they are discarding any books, do ask if you might take them home instead."

Bing was very uneasy, just as he had been the time he was sent to report on the management of the imperial tombs. He had been a much younger man then, but age and experience had not dampened the apprehension he felt in such situations. Once again, he was going somewhere as a spy rather than as an officially acknowledged inspector. His only way of carrying out his mission would be to ingratiate himself with the library's staff, including its director, while knowing that he was not going to be completely honest with them.

He was not surprised when he received a rather cold welcome upon arriving and could well understand why. Here was a fairly junior official who apparently had authority to examine their work. What did he know about literature or history or the teachings of the masters? In any case, a visit from a deputy of the Chancellor would make anyone nervous. He'd decided to do his best to play the part of a naive admirer, and sure enough once he was inside the main hall with stack after stack of shelving, it was all too easy.

Years ago, long before Bing had any knowledge of what went on in Chang'an, Mr. Li had proudly shown him his own collection of writings and told him what they were all about, how old they were, and what they had to teach. Yu had taken part in these exercises as well, carefully unrolling the scrolls and explaining some of the books to him. These were early days, and he was anxious not to let Yu see his ignorance, so there was a lot she said that he could not follow. Of course, Yu knew very well when Bing was pretending.

Mr. Li's collection was nothing compared to what was now before him, and he hoped that at least he'd be able to read the titles of all these books. Most of them were made up of rolls of wooden strips the usual length of a foot, but there were some that had been packed together in another stack that were at least twice as long, and every so often there were some carefully stored rolls of silk, and even some squares of silk, neatly folded. In a few cases there was a wooden box in which documents, whether of wood or silk, had been stored.

As the staff took Bing around the halls, they saw how impressed he was, and when his questions revealed that he knew something about literature, the assistants warmed to him and became quite friendly. He soon understood that everything had been arranged in marked categories, so that all the texts used for training cadets, and which officials had to be able to recite by heart, were together in one place. There was a special place where you could find the records of how kings and others had ruled the land in days gone by, and how the present great empire of Han had been founded.

"Look here," said one of his guides. "These are the written thoughts of the wonderful ancient masters of wisdom. We keep them separate from the writings used to impart instructions, such as how to behave properly, or how to administer a county, or how to become truly wise by escaping from all this to a mountain to live on pine cones and leaves."

Then there were the technical manuals on a whole variety of subjects, explaining how best to make a living from the land or how to treat an illness. And there were documents on silk that described how to recognize the stars and illustrated their movements. Bing showed his interest by pulling some of these rolls out for inspection. Nowhere did he see anything that might be construed as disloyal. There were no messages announcing the forthcoming end of the dynasty. He did find some books entitled *Arts of the Bedchamber,* which gave him something to think about, but he did not think that a work on that subject could pose a threat to the Emperor.

Indeed, if the assistant staff were not hiding anything, there appeared to be nothing here to worry the Chancellor. As Bing sampled the books at random, making sure to check those that the assistants had not singled out for special mention, his thoughts were flooded with memories. There was that traveler he had met on the way to Chang'an who was determined to spend the rest of his life on Huashan; all the books in this library would not have changed his mind. Then there were the officers up on the pass who had struggled to read their crudely written orders and lists; how astonished they would be to see these rooms one after another filled with books. Friend Shang would have found the library useful; if he had been able to read some of the handbooks available here, he might have made a far larger profit.

To his surprise Bing saw that it was possible for a diagram to be written on a wooden roll. It also surprised him that all the books here, whether written on wood or silk, seemed to be in perfect condition.

"Have none of these ever been dropped?" he asked. "How is it that none of the wooden pieces have come apart or been broken?"

From such simple questions Bing learned how the library had been built up and what it contained. Very few of the items that he saw were the actual copies that Liu Xiang and his colleagues had collected from all over the empire, or writings that had come in subsequently. Once any material was brought in, he was told, Lord Liu Xiang carefully compared all the copies of a particular text that they had on hand, taking notes of any differences there might be, and then he had his clerks write out what he judged to be the correct text. Some of the copies he had got hold of had been written in a script that was very difficult to read, and some of the rolls were obviously incomplete, with places where wooden strips had indeed fallen out, or where the roll had been broken. One copy of a text might be complete, with twenty chapters, but another copy had only ten. The commissioners also had to make quite sure that the strips were strung together in the right order.

"So you see, Sir, that all the items here are written in a regular hand that is easy to read, with a text that is as complete and correct as we can ever hope for. Of course, all the books are fairly new copies and still in excellent condition."

As all offices responsible for government property were required to keep records, Bing was fairly certain that the library assistants had a list of all their holdings.

"I assume you keep an inventory," he said. "Would it be possible to have a look at it?"

"Of course, Sir, we have one; in fact we keep two copies, and every so often we make sure that they are up to date. That clerk over there is making sure that the latest items are on the list, but the duplicate copy here will shortly be out-of-date and no use to us now. Please take it away if it's of any interest."

Bing could hardly believe his luck, especially when he saw how many categories of books were entered on the register. Once this copy was in the Chancellor's hands he could give orders to see the new one from time to time.

"By the way," said one of the assistants. "You see those books on the floor there?"

He was pointing to a pile on the floor. It consisted of dozens of documents, some apparently complete, others broken into fragments lying in a heap. "We've got the finished copies on the shelves, and we are throwing the old versions away. Anything there that you'd like to take?"

What a help these would be in drafting his report. "Yes, indeed," said Bing. "I'll take anything that's not wanted."

The assistant turned to a porter. "Get all those documents properly packed for the honored official to take with him," he said.

Bing felt ashamed. He was being treated with kindness, when his visit had been made on false pretenses. Well, duty was duty. When he delivered his report, the Chancellor, who was not known to lavish praise, seemed very pleased with the job he had done.

"There is just one thing, Sir," said Bing. "Please, if I dare mention it, I would be very grateful to have any of those books once they are no longer needed. My wife is a great reader."

It was an audacious request and Bing was nervous as he awaited a reply hardly daring to look at the stern face of the Chancellor.

"It is true that we will only want to keep documents that show evidence of impropriety. All right, we won't throw the rest away; tell them below where the materials should be delivered."

Bing could not contain a smile. It was not often that he could do something special for Yu. She would be so pleased!

Notes for Chapter Ten

We have no firm evidence to show how goods and treasures were stored in the *Shangfang*; nor do we know for certain that a list of items was kept. The privilege of burial within a jade suit was reserved for the emperor and some members of the imperial family, and, exceptionally, for a court favorite. The *taotie* device that is a characteristic of the décor of bronze vessels of ca. 1200 BCE appears only rarely on artifacts of Han times. The collection of books that was to form the imperial library was ordered in 26 BCE. There can be no certainty that while the search was intended to preserve literature, it was also directed to find subversive writings. A summarized version of the catalog of the library's holdings still exists.

Chapter Eleven   *Appointed magistrate*

DURING THE NEXT FEW YEARS, BING WAS CONTENT WITH HIS LIFE. His son, Guang, was healthy and bright enough, and Yu was happy, teaching the boy to read, tending their home, and studying when she could. She knew very well what sort of a life she was going to lead as the wife of an official and that there were not many excitements that she could expect. In all probability Bing would be moved from one post to another, but she didn't think that he would ever reach a very high position, such as governor of a commandery. It was anybody's guess where they might be sent, and she could only hope that she would not have to move to one of those desolate places out on the borders, where there would be hardly anyone to talk to.

In any event, Yu had other thoughts on her mind at the moment. Both she and Bing had hoped that they would have more children, preferably one boy at least so that if anything happened to Guang there would still be somebody to keep Bing's name remembered and honored. Now, after two months . . . she couldn't be sure; she would have to ask the nurse she knew, but she would not tell Bing until she was certain.

One chilly spring morning, Bing arrived at his office to find that he had been summoned to see the Imperial Counselor. He had never been called there before. He had some idea of how he would be received in that eminent place and how he should behave, as he had once been called to the office of this man's senior, the Chancellor, the only official who ranked above the Imperial Counselors, to receive his confidential orders. But that had been a long time ago, and Bing had never met the man who was Chancellor now. At one time, Bing had worked in one of the departments that the Imperial Counselor directed, but it was a very long time since he had seen him.

Bing listened, intently and with some anxiety, as an aide read out the report on his performance of duties in the previous year. These reports were nothing special; they were made out every year. But you usually heard about them when you heard that you had been named for demotion or dismissal. Bing was relieved and thankful to hear that there was nothing in the report to his discredit. With his best manners, he was just about to leave when he was called back.

A somewhat senior post had recently become vacant as the incumbent had died, he was told, and it needed filling as soon as possible. Bing had a good record, and was serving at the grade of four hundred bushels; he came from the north; there was no reason why he could not be posted as magistrate of a county, so long as it was not in the same commandery as his place of birth. The county in question, named Zuyang, lay well away to the south in Donghai commandery. It was of medium size, with some six thousand households and including twenty districts, and the post of magistrate carried a salary of six hundred bushels.

"So," said the Imperial Counselor, "we are proposing to appoint you."

Bing could hardly believe his ears. He had sometimes envied those officials who had been through the usual procedures that led to a position such as this, though, from what he had seen, many of them were not likely to be much good at such a job. If they had been selected from their home areas and sent up after competition with others from throughout the empire, they might have been better qualified, with a proper sense of duty, to govern as many people as there were in a county. But Bing was not so sure about those who had been appointed to a senior position simply because an important relative had the privilege of sponsoring them. He himself was no more than a rough country fellow who had knocked around here and there, without any of the advantages of privilege, and now he was to become a recognized figure, taking part in the structure of the empire and its government. What would his elder brother, who had predicted such a dire future for him, think now? Bing well remembered the endless taunts of his early years.

But how would it be living in such a remote place? There were not all that many people working in a magistrate's office; would he miss the company of the friends he had made here in the capital? He'd never met anyone from the south and wondered what sort of language they spoke.

"Don't you worry," said one of his friends. "It's anything but a backwater."

Yu, who knew something about the place, backed this up with her usual enthusiasm. "Why, Lanling is in that same commandery. It's one of the most famous places in the whole empire, known for the number of scholars who live there and the excellent schooling they provide. That famous old master Xun Qing came from Lanling. It's a real home where the old traditions are kept up and the things that Kongzi and others taught are respected. I only hope that Lanling will not be too far from where we're going, as there'll be plenty of people to meet and things to interest us there."

Bing was not so optimistic. To be truthful, although he had heard of Kongzi, Xun Qing was a new name to him, and he knew very well that it might not be that easy to visit Lanling from Zuyang. Poorly educated as he had been he could not possibly keep up with the conversation of those men of learning, and he'd seen before how the professionals looked down on anyone who had risen to a high office from the low ranks of the clerks. Stuffy old men they might be, but they knew well enough how to make a colleague feel miserable if they wanted to.

Of course, one of the first things that Bing did was to send a long letter to Mr. Li telling him of his luck and thanking him once again for all the training he had given him. He framed his letter very carefully as the last thing he wanted was to make the old man envious. He never learned how far Mr. Li had reached on the official scale, but he had found out that somehow or other his departure from official service had involved a scandal.

Bing learned from Yu that her father had been torn by the news of Bing's promotion. He was happy about his son-in-law's new prospects, but he was desperately unhappy at the thought that he might not see his daughter for a very long time, perhaps never again. Would he ever see his grandson? It was Yu who pointed out that a stop in Luoyang would not take them much out of their way on the journey to Zuyang. Bing agreed. Mr. Li was delighted with this news.

On their arrival, Mr. Li greeted his daughter and grandson warmly. To Bing, he said rather gruffly, "There are matters we must discuss privately."

Once more Bing found himself Mr. Li's pupil.

"You must proceed carefully," said Mr. Li. "You'll soon find yourself in the company of other magistrates and they won't like the arrival of a youngster, particularly one who hasn't gone through all the boring book learning that they were obliged to undertake—very different from what you and I did together. But I'll give you one suggestion. They'll all know those stuffy old texts, speeches of kings long dead, popular poetry, whatever that may be, and one of them will want to see how well you know these things. He'll hope to trip you up, but there's a step you can take against that. Here's a copy of the ways of behavior that the government has long approved; we actually read some of it together, if you remember. Make sure that you know exactly how to behave in every situation, whether you are with your superiors or juniors, and see to it that you never err in your behavior on special occasions such as a wedding or a funeral, particularly on official business. It's all here in this book, and if you learn it well enough you'll find ways to show the others that you know what's what better than they do, but on no account humiliate them.

"Are you sure you know what you're entitled to do as magistrate and what you have to pass on to somebody senior? I've seen officials brought down by exceeding their authority. Your real difficulty will be if there's an emergency—storm damage that breaks communications with your neighboring counties, or a sudden outbreak of crime that looks threatening. You'll have to take action on your own initiative and hope that it will be approved. When you report what you have done, make sure that you point out what disasters would have happened if you had acted otherwise; and if possible quote something from the statutes, or better still a saying from Kongzi. Or suppose that your immediate boss has been called away from his duties for a few months, perhaps to meet his mourning obligations for a parent. You need to make sure that there's a record of all that goes on in his absence."

As he listened Bing became more and more depressed. He couldn't see how he was going to avoid trouble. But there was more to come from Mr. Li, and it was even more helpful.

"Whatever you do, you must keep on good terms with the clerks who serve you, especially those who have been there for a long time. They'll know far more about local conditions than you possibly can, and they'll be anxious not to lose their jobs as might well happen, if you make a foolish or uninformed decision and are dismissed. Some of these clerks might try to hoodwink you, but you must find some whom you can trust. They're the people who will know why a particular district is always late in sending in its tax, why one district is free of crime while in another it can't be suppressed. They'll be able to tell you of the age-old quarrels between the dominant families and how to avoid stirring up their anger. You'll do well to learn the local dialect. The clerks will want their bribes, of course, and for Heaven's sake turn a blind eye to that."

Some years earlier Bing had been sent to Chang'an to do some work in one of the offices, which was only separated from the one next-door by a curtain. After a while, he realized that there were at least two men in there, and they were talking in low voices, but not always beyond Bing's hearing. Something was badly wrong, apparently, very high up. Someone had made a decision to send out an enormous force of soldiers and collect thousands of horses to strike a blow against the Xiongnu, but when you thought it over, it was a crazy thing to do. One of the men was bemoaning the fate of such expeditions. They marched miles, and were exhausted when they arrived. For a while they were able to keep the raiders off, but they never found them close enough to engage in a battle; at least they did stop the farms from being raided, and then the leader of the expedition would come back to Chang'an to be crowned in glory. But next year, sure enough the raids would start again, perhaps with greater intensity. Nothing had been gained from sending an expensive expedition out, and the treasury had to meet the cost.

"Who on earth was responsible for such a stupid decision?" Bing heard one of the men ask, and he pricked up his ears, just when the voices were hushed.

"It's the Agencies in the Counties," he thought he heard. "They're too young and inexperienced."

"Agencies in the Counties" was something new to Bing and he had no idea what it meant.

"It's just as well you asked me and not one of those highly placed senior officials," Mr. Li said. "As you know, all decisions of the empire come eventually from His Majesty, may he live forever, but, truth to say, although he authorizes them, he may not have always been properly advised and may order something that he comes to regret. Now, as you well know, none of us can ever refer to the Emperor in person, nor would we dare to speak or write his name. But there may come times when some of his most senior advisors cannot avoid referring to him, and the only safe way to do so is by using some other expression. The 'Agencies in the Counties' usually mean some of the offices that the central government has set up in the provinces to manage jobs like salt mining, and you may find that there are some of them in your county. But when it is really necessary for anyone to refer to His Majesty, and to do so without being charged with treason, he may well talk of what the 'Agencies in the Counties' said or ordered. If those two men you heard talking had said something openly about the youth and inexperience of the Emperor, they would have been clapped into jail and brutally executed in public, even though they were only doing their duty. But by talking about the 'Agencies in the Counties' they would not have been liable to a charge."

Mr. Li had, as usual, set out to give good advice for which Bing was duly grateful. At the same time, it all left Bing feeling quite worried about how much he had to learn and how on earth he was going to manage. As they settled down to their evening meal, Yu realized how depressed Bing was. Well, she knew how to cheer him up, and how to give her father something to think about; she would choose her moment carefully.

Yu chose to whisper her secret to Bing before they left Luoyang, and she was delighted to see how he seemed to forget all about his worries. Together they told Mr. Li, who wept with joy. As they were leaving, Mr. Li drew a battered scroll from his shelves. "Take this with you," he said. "It may be of use. It's ages old, written in an old-fashioned type of writing that isn't so easy to read. It lays down the ways in which you're going to have to think. I'm too old to make any use of it now. You may find it heavy going or even a bit pompous, but when you've finished with it, pass it on to somebody like yourself who needs to learn the ropes."

Bing took the book, with very grateful thanks; its title read "How to Be a Good Official."

At the age of forty-one, Bing found himself appointed magistrate of Zuyang. He and Yu left Luoyang with feelings of both excitement and apprehension. They had never traveled so far to the east and they looked forward to seeing the sea for the first time. One of Bing's friends, who had served in that part of the world, had actually been out on a ship, and he told Bing something of what it would be like. Fierce winds rose up in the autumn, and sometimes cascades of water overwhelmed whole villages and the surrounding lands. Bing resolved to be optimistic. He would see for himself in due course.

They had never before traveled in such comfort, as they had the use of one of the carriages that the great Imperial Counselor had at his disposal for just such a purpose. They were attended by a coachman and servants, with all their belongings stowed in another, less grand, wagon. There were soft cushions inside their own carriage, which was fitted with a wide umbrella, or canopy, to shield them from the scorching sun. The whole journey had been planned down to the smallest detail. The Imperial Counselor's office had mapped out the various postal stations where they were to stop along the way, and advance notice was sent so that they would be expected. They stopped at one or another of those stations every night, and were housed comfortably and given a good meal. The officials at each one well knew that if they gave poor service Bing would report it, so they did their best to please both him and his attendants, whose gossip could be just as dangerous. This suited everybody. The postmaster had written authority to provide the newly appointed magistrate with whatever he wanted. With luck, there would be ample leftovers from his high table for him and his wife to enjoy.

The routine changed one night when the carriage arrived at a postal station on the high bank of a river. This place was of greater importance than the previous stations, as the master had other responsibilities in addition to receiving and accommodating officials on their journeys. Boats were always pulling up at the jetty, and he had to ensure that the travelers could be allowed to disembark, with all their goods and chattel, to continue on their way. Some of these people had come from a long way off, and some had a long way to go. They were interrogated in much the same way as Bing had witnessed—and sometimes conducted—in his days up in that cold country of the north. As it happened, there were no such arrivals the night that Bing and Yu arrived. The postmaster told him that his main worry was that criminals, who had escaped from hard labor, or deserters from the armed forces, might pull up in a boat upstream, quietly in the dead of night, and make their way through. Certainly it would take some doing, as the banks were very high and all sorts of barriers had been built to block the more obvious ways of getting in. Even so, he kept two fearsome husky dogs, trained to give the alarm. "Come and see them," he said, and he led Bing to the cages where they were kept.

The next stage of their journey was downstream by boat, and Bing and Yu enjoyed the luxury of traveling on a comfortable craft, which was kept at the station for just this purpose. Though it was much smoother going than it had been on land, some of Bing's staff were nervous. They had seen too many accidents on the waterways, usually involving boats that were used for hauling goods. These were nothing like as sturdy as the boats made to carry important government officials. They were difficult to steer, particularly if the current was strong, and a sudden squall could drive them off course. A floating tree trunk, brought down by a storm, could cause serious damage. Very few of the people on board had any idea how to swim.

Neither had Bing, who did his best to calm his staff. Finally, he and Yu were able to relax and enjoy the smooth glide down the river.

"The trees along these banks are so beautiful," said Yu.

"You should see them in spring," one of the boatmen said. "Over there now—no, a little farther down past the bend—there's a copse where the trees are a wonderful sight, all brilliant white, and later in the year when all the blossoms have fallen, those trees will bear the most luscious peaches you ever saw. There's an old story that they were so special that they were reserved for the table of the Queen

Mother of the West, and no creature on earth was allowed to touch them. I don't really know much about it, though some say a monkey once stole the peaches, artful creatures as they are. But even those peaches are nothing compared to the ones that grow down a narrow inlet just a little farther along." Abruptly the man fell silent.

"Nothing more about it, then?" Bing asked.

"Well, yes there is, but it's not generally known. I wouldn't tell this to just anyone, but I suppose it's all right to tell Your Honor. Some of the people who live here say that they once knew a fisherman, one of their neighbors, who made his way to that narrow inlet one lovely spring day, all on his own, and he was never heard of again. I did once try finding the place myself. It was hard going, getting darker and darker, with the trees closing in over the little stream like a canopy, and then you got to a point where you couldn't go any farther. Up ahead, I could just see a glimmer of light, but I was hemmed in, with no way forward. There are those who say that the fisherman who disappeared did actually get through to where it was light, and what's more they claim he actually came back and had all sorts of stories to tell about a very strange world and the people he'd met there, as if he had been lost in a dream. Well, as I say, nobody has laid eyes on him to say for certain what really did happen. Maybe he stole some of the Queen Mother's peaches and she kept him with her as a punishment."

Eventually they reached the county town where Bing was posted. Sure enough, as he'd expected, there was a fine, well-built imposing set of quarters facing the south, and in front of them a large open space, with sophora trees and ginkos running down each side, and when he looked hard he could see in the distance what must be the wall that ran around the town. Yu was very pleased with the grounds, and once they were inside, they found that the magistrate's residence was in good shape. Part of the place had been empty for some time as the outgoing magistrate had left rather hurriedly and Bing needed to find out why.

The senior man there to welcome them was called Wang. He had been the personal aide to Bing's predecessor and could speak both the local patois of the low-grade servants and townsmen as well as the more formal idiom that Bing had learned to speak when talking with other officials. Bing's first impressions of Wang were favorable, and he thought that he might do a lot worse than keep him on as his own aide, but of course he would have to make discreet inquiries first. As late in the day as it was, and as tired as he felt, Bing gave his first orders to Wang.

"Tell them that I will always want to see all postal messengers and look at their mail before they have undone their packs; and will you give my orders at the gates to let me know immediately the names and details of any merchants who come this way by name of Li? And please bring me, here and now, the most up-to-date list of all officials and staff in the county, and the latest annual reports from all the districts. I'll see all who are coming to pay their respects, not tomorrow, but the next day, if you think that will be convenient for them. And, oh, one thing please; what's the total number of officials in the county? About sixty?"

Wang liked the crisp way in which the new magistrate spoke, but he could not suppress the thought that it would take a lot of time to inspect all incoming mail, and it could lead to trouble. "Very good, Sir," he answered. "Altogether there are fifty-seven men on your staff."

Bing spent the next day in his new office, surrounded by the documents he had sent for, and he was studying them hard. They were written out clearly enough, even though some of them were second copies of an original, which had been sent to the governor of the commandery for scrutiny. As he read on, he began to see that something was amiss. When he was commissioned with this appointment, the staff of the Imperial Counselor's office had told him that there were twenty districts in the county and that the registered population of the county was on the order of six thousand households and some twenty-five thousand individuals. It was on that basis that his salary had been fixed. All this was fine, but there were no more than seventeen districts named in the documents he had been given, and the number of registered inhabitants was far less than what he had expected. Why had the people in the governor's office given him those figures? Had they been hoodwinked? Or had they bumped them up for their own purposes? How could he submit the correct returns for taxes if the number of farmers and fields was far less than what the officials in Chang'an believed?

This was a serious worry. Was somebody in the governor's office preparing the way to blackmail him? And there was something else. No one had warned him that one of the central government's detached offices, responsible for some particular type of activity, such as salt mining, was situated in the county. Bing had no idea whether the officials in that office had senior authority that would allow them to countermand his orders. He knew that he had better act quickly if anything had to be done. When Wang came in, he found his new master sitting amid a vast pile of documents.

"Yes, what is it?" Bing asked rather curtly.

"May I be of any assistance, Sir?" asked Wang, hoping he hadn't given any offense.

Notes for Chapter Eleven
The notation of grades in the civil service corresponded to officials' salaries being calculated in measures of grain. Officials were not appointed to serve in their home areas where their interests might be divided. The dates of 551–479 BCE are usually given for Kongzi (known in the West as Confucius), and those of 310–235 CE for Xun Qing, whose writings are known as *Xunzi*. A copy of a text entitled *How to Be a Good Official,* not known previously and dated 217 BCE, was discovered recently. The theft of the queen mother's peaches by "Monkey" and its consequences form the subject of one of China's most famous novels, by Wu Cheng'en (ca. 1510–1580), translated by Arthur Waley as *Monkey* (London: George Allen and Unwin Ltd, 1942), though the Buddhist allegory therein would not have reached Han China. The tale by Tao Yuanming (365–427) of the fisherman whose journey took him back into happy worlds long since past is one of the most famous short stories in Chinese literature. See the translation by Herbert A. Giles, *Gems of Chinese Literature: Prose* (London: Bernhard Quaritch, 1926), pp. 104–5; and A. R. Davis, *T'ao Yüan-ming (AD 365–427): His Works and Their Meaning,* 2 vols. (Cambridge: Cambridge University Press, 1983), p. 195.

Chapter Twelve   *The governor and his residence*

O N THE APPOINTED DAY, BING RECEIVED THE CALLS FROM HIS subordinates that both courtesy and duty prescribed. With proper ceremony he took his seat, high up on a stage, where he could look down on his inferiors. At first glance he saw that they had all taken great care to appear at their best. There they sat, in quiet dignity, not daring to move or speak. He knew it all well enough, as it had not been so long since he'd been in their position, wondering when the great man would deign to appear and whether he would have anything to say. One by one they were called up for their turn to present themselves to His Honor, each one somewhat hampered by the stiff official robes that he was not accustomed to wear. Each of them carried a large wooden tablet that he handed over to the magistrate's clerk, who then handed it to the magistrate. These had been beautifully inscribed in clear majestic script that was very different from writing on the documents that they were used to handling in their day-to-day work. Of course, as Bing knew, they had all hired a professional letter writer to make out these very special boards with their names and postings and their respectful greetings to their new master.

Back in his office Bing settled down to take another hard look at the documents that he had called for on his arrival. Yes, as he had seen, they accounted for no more than seventeen districts. The names on the list corresponded with those that appeared on the register that he had been shown in Chang'an, all except for one, where the graph for "virtue" as seen there, appeared in the commandery's records as the one for "meaning." Well, he knew very well how mistakes could creep in and this one was fairly easy to explain. Unless . . . could this have something to do with why three districts were missing? All this was very worrisome. He must find out what was going on. But how far could he trust Wang? Well, he was going to get to the bottom of this somehow, and if Wang had taken part in any deception it would all come out.

He took care to raise the matter in a casual way that would not arouse Wang's suspicion or antagonism.

"Wang," he said offhandedly, "I've yet to see a map of the area. Tell me, are all the districts much the same size, or are any of them exceptionally large or small?"

"Oh, there's not much difference now, much the same area and the same number of inhabitants, except for two which are about double the size of the others."

"Why so? Was the land so fertile that many people came to farm it? Or, perhaps there were special features of the land worth exploiting?"

"Nothing like that," Wang answered readily. "But until about fifty years ago, the area of one of those districts was divided to form two districts, one named after the Zhang, and one after the Zhuang family. I have no idea why that was changed, but it's now administered as one district."

Well, Bing thought, that may very well be the answer, all fair enough and aboveboard, but for some reason or other the authorities in Chang'an had not recognized the change.

Bing now raised the question of why the name of one district was given with different graphs in the different sets of documents. "Just a clerical mistake, I suppose."

"Oh no," said Wang. He seemed genuinely pleased to see how acute and quick-minded the new magistrate was. "Certainly, the two characters do indeed look much the same and can easily be mistaken for each other if they are written too hastily. But there's a story, which explains this difference. This particular district is of poor-quality land, unlikely to yield a good crop. There's a wide river dividing it almost into two halves, but it is situated awkwardly so that it is very difficult for the farmers to raise the water and use it for irrigation. This gave rise to a dispute, as irrigation was easier to do in one of the two halves than in the other. From the early days of the dynasty, the whole area had been within the estate over which the Lord Fu had rights, and it had been simpler for him and his steward to treat the two halves as separate districts. But when Lord Fu's family died out and his estate came to an end, his lands came under the jurisdiction of our commandery and then of this county, and the governor of the day decided to administer the area as one district only. *De,* the graph for 'virtue,' had been part of the name of one, and *yi,* the graph for 'meaning,' had been part of the name of the other, but when the land came under our charge, some of the registers retained 'virtue' as the name for the now larger district, while others used 'meaning.' It's all very confusing, and may well make some people think that there are still two districts."

All this sounded plausible. It was just the sort of thing that happened in the course of provincial administration. Only rarely did it involve any wrongdoing. Bing was fairly certain that he could get the whole matter straightened out, at least for two of the missing districts. But what about the third? He decided to come clean with Wang.

"I'm most grateful for all this information," he said, "it has helped me understand the shape of the county and its divisions. But I have to tell you that I am worried. They told me in Chang'an that there were twenty districts in the county, and I think they must have been working from the reports that they had from the governor of the commandery. However, yesterday we had officials here from only seventeen districts. You've explained to me why there were none from two others and that brings us up to nineteen, but have we any idea what has happened to the third one? Have you any idea why the governors have persisted in reporting the existence of a total of twenty?"

Wang was puzzled. He knew nothing of the missing district. Bing had no direct access to the files that lay in the governor's office, and his sense of worry grew. He could be charged with a serious crime if he returned reports for twenty districts, when no more than seventeen existed, but he would be in equally serious trouble if he sent in registers for no more than seventeen, without accounting for the disappearance of three. In either case, he shuddered to think of the punishment. Should he write to the governor immediately to tell him of the difficulty? That could be dangerous; the governor might have his own reasons for concealing things. Of course he couldn't possibly write directly to Chang'an, as that would be seen as trying to go over the governor's head, and in any case it was strictly laid down to whom he had the authority to write or appeal. Fortunately, it was still only the second month of the year; he would not have to submit his report until the sixth month, and the governor would have until the eighth month to make his report. There was still time to ferret out the truth. He resolved to himself that he would look closely at all the reports that came through to him. As it happened, Bing saw how to solve the problem—and relieve the anxiety it produced—far sooner than he had dared to hope.

Bing's first and immediate duty was to present himself to his superior, and within days of his arrival he was on the road once again, accompanied by his close staff. Bing took care to include Wang in the party, as he already thought highly of the man's abilities, and was considering reappointing him to be personal aide to the magistrate when they returned to Zuyang.

Bing had his letter of appointment, beautifully written name cards, and his official robes, specially cleaned and pressed thanks to Yu's foresight. She had considered how best to ensure that the garment would arrive looking fresh, and had decided to fold it neatly in a wicker basket with some sweet-smelling herbs. Bing also had a smaller case that he always kept by his side. "Writing brush, knife, wooden tablets, and my official seal," he would say if he had to describe its contents. He would not have mentioned the presence of a lower layer underneath all his equipment, secured by a lock. His old friend, the merchant Shang, had had just such a contraption made to keep his gold pieces away from prying eyes, and it was when he was traveling with Shang that he had managed to acquire a few pieces of jewelry, jades and the work of a fine silversmith.

Bing would be expected to bring presents for the governor and his wife, and these he had to choose carefully. They must be fairly valuable and preferably something the governor and his wife had never seen before; however, some of the treasures he had come to possess had to be ruled out. These included a fine, beautifully decorated bronze mirror, inlaid with silver and bearing all sorts of images on it, prayers and spells. But on no account would this be suitable; no one used mirrors of that type in daily life, as they were made for burial with the dead, as Bing had once witnessed, and all those magical signs would convey exactly the wrong sort of message to the governor and his wife. For all that he knew, they might be given to dreaming and would understand what those strange images and emblems mean. He could imagine the man's wife shrieking with horror at being given such a thing. There was another worry as well. Heaven knows how Shang had acquired the pieces that he had given to Bing, and of course he never let on why he was willing to part with them, but Bing had an idea. Shang could hardly read. Each of the pieces was clearly engraved with the name of the imperial office that had made it. In some instances even the name of the inspector, who had passed the item as properly finished, was included. Some, as Bing had noticed, had been made by no less an authority than the Shangfang, the very store whose contents Bing had once been sent to check, and he knew that only members of the imperial family or a few special favorites were entitled to possess these fine things. If the governor was of the right sort and knew what went on in the wide world, he would look at the inscription, say nothing, and be glad to keep the treasure. But if he was one of those sharp, punctilious characters, whose only concern was that all the regulations are obeyed, all hell would break loose. Bing could be flogged or tortured, and if that happened, he doubted that he would be able to keep Shang's name out of it.

To avoid all such risk, Bing had brought with him some pieces of exceptionally choice red and black lacquerware. They came from the south where the lacquer trees grew plentifully, and skilled artists and craftsmen spent hours and days producing platters, cups, and ladies' toilet boxes in the finest finishes possible. North of the Yangzi River these lacquer items were scarce and therefore valuable. Bing hoped that the governor and his wife would find them distinctive, particularly as they were painted in a rare pattern. He knew that they were finished with many, many layers of lacquer of the best quality, each one laid on with unblemished brushwork. Sometimes they were inscribed with the name and title of the noble for whose house they had been ordered, and this meant that you could not be too careful. Bing had taken great pains to identify the pieces that he brought and had found out that they once belonged to a house of nobles that had died out in disgrace, ages ago. The last holder of the title, rich as he was, had been charged with immorality and treason, and executed in public in the marketplace.

At the appointed hour Bing drove out from the guesthouse where he had been lodged, two fine horses pulling his carriage, and accompanied by armed attendants, as suited his rank. They passed down a wide tree-lined avenue that led to the governor's seat. Far more imposing and grand than the residence of a mere county magistrate, it faced south, opening on to a broad open space. Bing had been summoned to the offices of his superiors before, but never to their homes, and he hoped his manners would pass muster in such august surroundings.

Doing his best to conceal his nervousness, he made his way through the long hall to where the dais lay, as yet empty and awaiting its rightful occupant. As a magistrate receiving his subordinates just recently, Bing had been seated in his place before they had arrived, following the procedure he had observed when he had been an underling in one of the departments of the central government. But this was a very different matter and he was obliged to wait some time before the governor appeared and took his seat. Finally, Bing was ushered forward. A grim-looking man, and probably rather severe, was Bing's first impression as he handed over his name card, bowing very low. No more than a nod signified His Excellency's mood, no word of greeting or acknowledgment, not even when Bing presented his gifts. When he returned to his place however, he realized that the governor continued to stare at him. If only there were some other officials here of his own rank, Bing was thinking, when he was startled by the voice of His Excellency.

"His Imperial Majesty, with his enlightened virtues and never-ending love for the people of His realm, saw fit to command me to bring his magnificent bounties to bear on the people of this commandery of Donghai. Thanks to the dutiful way in which He had himself received His charge and thanks to His constant care for His people, and thanks to His persistent efforts by day and night to attend to His duties, for some years the commandery of Donghai has been free of incident or turmoil. Thanks to the blessings imparted by Heaven and all the other spirits, the splendors of the skies have shone without disturbance, journeying in their courses as moved by yin and yang; the earth has given forth her abundant gifts of the fruits of the fields and the trees; all manner of living creatures have been at peace. The harmony with which these three realms of existence abide together without constraint or malcontent has been undisturbed. The changes of the seasons follow one another in due accord. Look around the lands of Donghai and you will see how that ever-present energy, which brings life and movement to all the many creatures of the world, has never withheld its gifts of sustaining mankind.

"As governor of Donghai it has been my constant care and duty to ensure that no action of mankind endangers or destroys the blessing of this great harmony; that all baleful influences that might do so are expelled; that all men and women live and work in calm contentment, thankful to do so in the lands beneath the skies where His Majesty's rule runs supreme.

"So also is it your duty in the county submitted to your care to see that these blessings prevail without loss or damage. His Majesty's commands are to be obeyed strictly. Any crime against the order of nature, or any infringement of the respect due to others must be eliminated without fail; all dues to be paid from the produce of the fields and the orchards, or from other occupations are to be collected and delivered to my headquarters regularly at the appropriate time. Accounts of the supplies consumed and the monies spent in each county must be submitted here by the appointed day, together with the full and accurate registers of the households and their individual members.

"All bounties which by virtue of His everlasting charity the Emperor orders to be distributed must be given to those correctly entitled to receive them. Should He command that a man in each household be honored by the gift of a high rank, such an order is to be conveyed to those who receive it without delay. The annual reports must state clearly how many men and women are aged seventy, eighty, or ninety years old; how far the numbers of the population have grown during the past year; how much land has been reclaimed and put under the plow for the first time; how many vagrant families have been brought to notice and their names included in the register.

"Probably, Magistrate, you have already learned of these regular instructions and the records made by your predecessors will help you to carry them out. But you must do more to fulfil the chosen wishes of His Majesty. See that the people of the county which is committed to your charge fully understand their great fortune; that as human beings they are set apart from all other living creatures and that they possess powers of intellect superior to those of all others; and that of all peoples who live beneath the skies they realize how blessed they are to enjoy the rule of a beneficent Emperor. See that they understand how important it is to keep their families united, free of anger and enmity, each member treating his and her kin with the respect that is their due and rendering respect where they should; and see that they do not fail to render their due services to the spirits of the soil and the crops, the hills and the rivers where they live.

"See that you and your colleagues and subordinates conduct yourselves correctly and perform your official actions with one aim; that of treating your fellow men and women as human beings such as yourself, while seeing that their actions conform with the hallowed ways of life and the regulations of His Majesty. There are times when it is difficult or even impossible to achieve all of these purposes, as you may well know, and the decisions that you take must follow the everlasting principles of the world.

"See that schools are set up to teach the youngsters these things, and make sure that any boy of promise whom you think may be fit to serve as an official is duly named and sent here for selection and training."

Well, the old boy must have made that speech dozens of times, Bing thought as he drove back to his lodgings, "and he didn't tell me much that I hadn't heard before. But perhaps he's not to be blamed for being so pompous, as he could hardly have done otherwise with all his underlings listening." Maybe Bing would find out more about the governor when he saw him at the dinner to which he had been invited that evening. With luck, Wang would have learned something from the household staff. By and large, the governor had confirmed Bing's idea of how to fulfil his duties, and after all, Bing himself had been one of those who were governed and he'd seen officials at work. He hoped that the six thousand households (if indeed there were six thousand), each with their four or five members, would remember him, when eventually he was moved elsewhere, as a magistrate who had genuinely tried to put an end to officials' cruelties and to bring relief to anyone who was suffering. Bing was also wondering what his own subordinates, who had presented their cards to him so recently, were thinking of him.

Before Bing knew it, the time had come to return to the governor's residence for dinner. He hoped that once the formalities were over it would be possible to relax and to learn something more about his superior. He guessed, correctly, that the entertainment would be at the middle range of the three types of expenditure allowed. He'd get a good plentiful meal with some choice and expensive local delicacies. As a county magistrate he would not warrant the very special treatment that a high-ranking official of the central government, or an army general, might expect, but the occasion called for a higher level of treatment than the monthly assemblies of low-grade staff who took turns coming in from the counties.

When he reached the residence, the governor's staff welcomed him and offered to show him around.

"I'd very much like to look at the gardens first," he said, and around they went to the north side of the mansion. As was to be expected in a governor's residence everything was beautifully kept. Well-clipped trees and bushes gave you shade if you wanted to walk; baskets hung down from the branches and Bing could hear the birds calling to one another from above. Soon they came across a lovely arbor, and Bing sat down on a wide bench apparently made from beautifully polished stone blocks, which had been cut to size and shaped and assembled in their right positions. As he looked more closely, Bing could actually see some simple numbers or other marks that had been scratched on the surface of the stone. He reckoned that they must have been cut there back in the quarry so that when they were unloaded the workmen who received them would know the order in which to fit them together.

"Well," he thought, quite wrongly, "that didn't involve really skilled craftsmanship." Next he was led to a more spacious enclosure surrounded by trees with a trickle of running water that dropped into a lake. Here was something that Bing had never seen before. Bronze figures of birds stood with their unfolded wings at the waterside, and there were models of musicians, men and women, in stone. But what really caught his eye and kept it riveted was a small island in the lake, pure white, rising up stage by stage, and shaped just like a vase. He asked if he could get a little closer to look and stepped into a small boat tied up to the bank and ready for just this purpose.

Close to the island he could see that there were figures on some of its stages, just a few of them, all clothed in white. They seemed to be looking after another figure, a majestic woman. Unlike the others, she was clothed in the finest drapery of many colors and patterns. Right at the top, as far as Bing could see, there were two full circles cut in the stone. If he was right, the one on the east side carried the figure of a fine bird in red, which curiously enough seemed to have three feet. On the west side the circle enclosed a newly rising moon; inside the crescent there ran a hare with his long ears and loping legs. Bing was at a loss to understand what it was all about, but he felt bound to make some remark.

"It looks rather like a bottle, at first sight," he said to his companion, "but I don't know what it's doing in the middle of this lake, or what on earth those two circles are meant to tell me."

"It's quite a secret," came the reply. "The governor's wife loves to look at it; she comes and sits here for hours, never mind how cold it gets. She's rather a sad person, as you'll see at dinner, always thinking of her mother who died last spring. I wouldn't advise you to ask her what the island means to her."

Bing's curiosity remained unsatisfied, but he was thankful for the advice. Time was getting short and his companion was urging him back to the residence where he could rest before dinner. Soon he was taken to a wide, spacious hall with a roof supported by stout wooden pillars. Lamp stands with their candles stood around the walls to provide a dim, soft lighting, and one of these in particular drew his attention. It was shaped like a tree on whose trunk and branches the artist had fashioned a number of birds and woodland creatures, and some dozen lights shone out from small cups. Must have cost a pretty penny, Bing thought, remembering his days with Shang.

Wide spaces on the walls separated these lamps from one another and here again there was something that made Bing wonder. Richly colored drapes covered nearly all the space between them, attached to the wall firmly at the top and falling gracefully to floor level. Silk like that could only have come from Wuxi, Bing thought, as he tried to pick out the designs and to understand what the artist was trying to convey. A few written characters had been worked in, but they didn't reveal anything to Bing about the meaning of the designs. Perhaps, if there was a lull in the dinner conversation, he could ask His Excellency to explain.

Meanwhile at the head of the hall the house staff were getting things ready for the evening. There were three tables set to form a square, with one side left open. Servants were scuttling to and fro, setting out plates, dishes, and cups, together with chopsticks. Bing could not be certain but he guessed that the governor would take his place at the center of the middle table, with his wife at his left side and he himself on the other. He supposed that there would be about five or six persons seated at each of the three tables; and presumably there would be a small group of musicians ready to play.

As the governor came in, Bing greeted him in the correct way and was led to take his place at the table. Fortunately, he was close enough to be able to talk to the governor with ease, though he could hardly hear the governor's wife, who sat on the other side of her husband. Not that she would have thought it her place to address Bing, though he was prepared to make complimentary remarks about the garden and lake if an opportunity presented itself. As the meal started, servants filled the cups all around with a dark red liquid which Bing realized must have been made from the grapes that he had seen in the grounds of the summer palace at Chang'an. Well, there was something he could talk about. Up until then, the atmosphere had felt rather strained. Encouraged to do so, he began to say what he knew about the drink made from grapes.

"Yes," he said, "I was told that not too long ago one of those brave adventurers, who had set out to explore the Western Regions, brought back bunches of berries that were not known in Chang'an. They were still attached to the bushes on which they had grown. He also brought back some of the liquid that these berries produced after a special treatment before they are sealed up in jars. It was known by a strange word that must have come from a long way away. His Late Majesty, Wudi the Dutiful, grandfather of our present Emperor, had enjoyed the drink to the full; so much so that he ordered the gardeners to plant the bushes in his grounds acre after acre. Yes, I actually did see some of them at the summer palace west of Chang'an."

The governor had never been to the summer palace and he was certainly not going to admit it to his junior. But he found all that Bing was saying quite fascinating and asked him if he knew anything more about it.

"A little," he answered, feeling slightly embarrassed, but daring to say more. "I was told that very little of that drink ever goes outside the walls of the palace, it is so highly prized; and there is something else too. Drinking the wine makes you forget all your worries. But if you aren't used to it, it very soon makes you noisy and even boisterous, forgetful of all the good manners you have been taught. Sometimes people are so badly affected that they have to be taken away to bed, before they make fools of themselves. There is no danger of that here, but, Your Excellency, I do congratulate you on getting hold of such a fine supply. How fortunate I am that you have invited me to come and share it with you!"

Dish after dish followed; a special minced fish, caught from the sea but two days ago and served with a rich, peppery sauce; tender pork, spiced mutton, bean curd, and leeks, and many more succulent rarities. Bing wondered whether this was a dinner for a special occasion or whether throughout the empire the governors of the commanderies were doing themselves proud like this every night, whether or not any guests were present. It could hardly be like this in some of the outlying lands, Bing thought, remembering the Spartan conditions of the northwest when he had been there as a conscript. And although, as he had heard, down in the south all sorts of delicacies were grown, they might not have reached the tables of the senior officials posted there, as they were not yet enjoying the luxurious lifestyle to which His Excellency was accustomed here in Donghai.

At first Bing had been too shy to take much initiative in the conversation, and he had been glad of the opportunity that the governor had given him to talk about grapes and wine. He spoke with the greatest deference, and was glad to notice that as the meal progressed and the wine cups were refilled, the governor was relaxing quite noticeably and getting quite talkative. He seemed nothing like the stuffed shirt who had harangued him only hours ago, and Bing realized, not for the first time, that those who took a front place in public life often combined two persons; one was the official, forbidding and severe, and determined to behave as his position demanded; the other was a human being, who cared for his fellow men and women, with his good side and bad side, his loves and hates like everyone else.

Bing came to like his superior, as they talked of the offices that they had each held and the parts of the empire they had visited. The governor seemed interested when he heard Bing's tale of how he had been a very low-ranking clerk for a short time in the Transport Office in Chang'an. It was a time when the palace was very short of horses.

"Oh yes," said His Excellency, "I know that very well. At the time in question, I was serving at the office of the Privy Purse next door. Your superior was asking for more and more money to replace the dead animals, many of whom had died in a plague. My man, as usual, was short of funds and gave away as little as he could. I even had to draft a sharp reply that he sent to one of your superior's demands."

The atmosphere became more and more relaxed, and Bing hoped that he was making a good impression. The governor's wife had long since withdrawn and eventually all the others had left, excusing themselves with pleas of urgent work, which would require them to rise early. Bing saw that it was time for him to make a move and started to do so with the most polite manners that he could muster.

"Well, if you must," said the governor. "As it happens I won't be able to see you tomorrow. I have a host of things to do. No, nothing desperately urgent, but there's been a bit of trouble over the administration of the granaries. Before you go, there's just one thing, please. When you get back to your county, would you please check the latest maps that you have and the list of districts? I'm sorry to say that my own copies here are seriously flawed. I think they must be out-of-date, and I'd be grateful if you could help me to get them straight. Once I've done so, I'll send a special report to Chang'an and let them know to put their records right. Usually it's the clerks there who make the mistakes, but this time I'm afraid it's due to lazy work down here, long before my time, of course. I wish you a good night."

Bing could not have hoped for a better end to the evening. And to think that he'd been so apprehensive! The governor had set the way in which to solve the problem that had been nagging him. Once back in his office, he would dig out all the details and send the governor a report ready to be copied to Chang'an.

Notes for Chapter Twelve

The present-day forms of the graphs for *de* ("virtue") and *yi* ("meaning") are in no way alike, but one of the forms used for *de* in Han times could easily be mistaken for the graph for *yi*. The old and obsolete graph for *de* is 悳; *yi* is written as 意. We have no record of a speech made by a governor of a commandery when receiving a county magistrate. The presence of figures or other marks to enable a workman to assemble pieces of a structure together correctly is attested by finds of stones probably used in the construction of imperial tombs of Eastern Han and more recently in a Western Han tomb in Hunan (see *Wen wu* 2010.4, pp. 7, 8). The island and its figures as described for the governor's garden are suggested as a three-dimensional representation of a theme of a painting from Mawangdui of 168 BCE. The word used in Chinese for the grape, *putao,* is explained by some as being derived from the Greek βότρυς (Botrus).

O N THE WHOLE IT HAD BEEN A PLEASANT ENOUGH EVENING. ONCE he'd begun to feel at ease, Bing felt sure that he would be able to work with the governor, though he'd have to find out where his particular aversions lay. But before doing anything he must make sure that he knew what regular tasks he had to see completed month by month, season by season, and year by year, and taking a careful look at his predecessors' documents for the last few years would help. As would all the records that he found on the shelves of his office.

There was a list of the titles of the Statutes and Ordinances of the empire, together with full copies of some of them, and other documents showing how the statutes applied. Altogether they were so voluminous that Bing wondered how on earth he was going to get through them. They covered all sorts of activities that he would have to supervise, and some of the orders that they laid down were highly detailed, such as the way in which grain should be stacked, the rations that were allowed to convict laborers, and the correct way of drafting documents. There were also accounts of actual cases where it was unclear what action had to be taken, if the correct procedures had not been followed. Worst of all, Bing had already seen two instances where different statutes gave contradictory rulings, and for all that he knew that great bundle of strips might well include others that countermanded what had been ordered earlier. Bing also found a copy of the Emperor's decrees, beautifully written and, as he noticed, with spaces left in the text to ensure that due respect was paid to any mention of an Emperor's actual words or deeds.

Cowed by all these formidable documents, Bing turned to some of the other scrolls and found that they promised to be extremely helpful, if he ever had time to read them. There was a set of criminal cases that had been taken through all the formalities but instead of

140

using real names, they designated all the people mentioned as A, B, or C. Bing couldn't be certain that these were accounts of actual cases or imaginary ones made up to show how the laws worked. Some of them sounded real enough, such as the case of the robbers who had tunneled their way into a house and stolen the occupant's best clothes, or the pregnant woman who had got into a brawl with another woman. But Bing noticed that none of the cases recorded were clear-cut. There was always some question that had to be decided—just how someone had broken a law, or which one of the statutes covered the actual circumstances. Well, these examples might prove very helpful when he had a doubtful case brought before him. So too would another of his finds—a long list of questions that might arise in implementing the laws, together with the answers.

From his predecessors' records, Bing learned that he had to send in information which he had gathered from the districts in no less than five types of report, keeping duplicate copies in his office. The governor would make a summary of all the information that the counties gave him, and he would send this to Chang'an. This was all part of the annual Submission of Accounts, and he would have his clerks check that all the figures provided really added up in the way that was claimed. Any discrepancy in the figures for Zuyang would come back to Bing for explanation.

Very shortly after his arrival at his post, Bing called for the register of incoming mail. Usually this was written in a good clear hand and neither Bing nor the clerks had much difficulty reading it. In any case, much of it was of a routine nature, and so long as you could be sure that the figures were legible, you had no difficulties as the rest of the document followed the usual form. True, sometimes, when a document had originated at a very low level it did cause trouble.

There was one document issued by the central government that every office up and down the empire needed and with which Bing had had experience very early in his career. This was the calendar for the next year, essential when you had to calculate work schedules and rates of pay, and of course, any outgoing report or letter that Bing sent must be dated correctly before he could sign it and affix his seal. Delay in receiving the calendar could make things awkward. It was no use trying to work one out for yourself; some months in the year had to be long at thirty days, some short at twenty-nine and you had to know how this had been decided. There was one other difficulty; every two or three years you had to put in an extra month, making thirteen months in that year, and here again you needed to know at what point this was to be done. Somebody had once tried to explain to Bing why the months could not all be set at either twenty-nine or thirty days, and why some years had to be longer than others, but he had quoted a lot of technical reasons, mainly to do with the movements of the sun and the moon and it had all been too much for Bing.

There was another reason why a delay in getting the new calendar could be awkward, because the way in which you named the year could be changed. This was because years were numbered in a series such as first, second, or third of a catchphrase such as "The First Light"; but every so often, usually once every five years, the government ordered the start of a new series with a new title, so that the years were known as first, second, or third of, perhaps, "The Grand Beginning." If news of such a change was late, you would probably be dating your reports incorrectly according to a system that was obsolete. Bing didn't want to be caught doing that. However, there was nothing that he could do about it. Up in the capital, he had once had to copy out calendars for distribution to the commanderies; down in a county in Donghai, he would now have to wait to get his copy from the governor's office.

Bing also learned, from Wang, that some of his colleagues had been finding difficulties with the way in which the days were identified, by means of two written graphs that together formed a series of sixty terms. Bing himself had learned how to work the system when he was up on guard duty, but it was not everyone who mastered how the terms were formed and what their correct order was. Dunderheads, Bing thought, when he learned that they were simply identifying the days by their number in the month.

From his experience as a low-level clerk, Bing well knew what was involved in getting all this work done and seeing that the results were put together in the correct forms, but he did not yet know which members of his staff were responsible for the different tasks that were involved. He must have a personal assistant who knew which clerks were doing what tasks, and which ones were simply not competent for some of the work, and he would have to be sure that he could trust the man he chose. From what he had seen of Wang, his predecessor's aide, Bing thought that he could do a great deal worse than take him on in the same capacity. Wang's knowledge of how the country was administered would clearly prove beneficial. In any case, if he appointed somebody new, there would be two of them who had everything to learn.

Wang seemed to be a man of even temper, unlikely to be flustered by difficulties. Bing had noticed that he treated the junior staff with kindness as well as with firm authority, and he guessed that the lower-grade clerks would prefer to work under Wang, a devil whom they knew, rather than under somebody else. Wang said that he was honored to be asked to continue in the position.

With Wang's help Bing went through the list of the county office's staff, reading their service reports, which in fact Wang had drawn up. Wang gave his advice about any changes that should be made, and he confided to Bing any confidential information that pertained to one or another of the clerks and how he had, on occasion, overlooked a misdemeanor and thereby earned a man's steadfast loyalty.

Before he could comply with the governor's request, and thereby, as he hoped, relieve his mind of anxiety, Bing had no choice but to get down to the immediate tasks that lay before him, and of these the most important concerned taxation. There had been a bumper harvest the year before and it had not been possible to stack all the grain in the existing stores. The temporary ones that had been erected were not weatherproof; the rats had been having a fine time, and some of the stuff lay rotting on the ground. As a result, it had not been possible to send all of what was due as tax to the granary that the commandery had named.

"Why on earth not?" Bing asked. "It's now the third month and it should have gone long before the winter set in and it started going to waste." Nothing but evasive answers were forthcoming; one party blamed the next. Nobody could be named as the culprit. If anyone should take the blame it would have been Bing's predecessor.

It would probably take at least six days to get the wagons loaded and the grain delivered, and it would be far more difficult to do this now than it would have been before the harsh winter had done its work on the lanes. There was no party of convicts on whom Bing could call, as he was allowed to do; most of the conscript laborers who were assigned to the county were at work on other jobs that could not be delayed, such as repairing the roads. In an emergency, he was entitled to use hired laborers, which is what his predecessor had failed to do. Bing knew very well that there were drawbacks in doing so; people like that were not well disciplined or honest and might give up the job halfway through if it suited them, especially if they had been able to pilfer enough of the cargo to make it worth their while. Wang solved the problem by getting a mixed crowd of conscripts and hired men, with no love lost between them, under the control of the right sort of overseer.

The next thing that arose was again due to his predecessor's failure or incompetence. As much as Bing was tempted to report these derelictions of duty to the governor, he thought better of it, knowing full well the code of procedure to which all officials subscribed. You only reported adversely on a colleague if something vital and irremediable had taken place, or if he had been guilty of a crime; otherwise you did your best to cover up for him. This time Bing had to implement an order that had come from Chang'an, through the commandery, some months previously and which had been sent to the magistrates of all the thousand and more counties of the empire. To celebrate the occasion when the Heir Apparent of the Imperial Throne came of age, the Emperor decreed that the head of each household was entitled to one extra degree of the social status that he held.

What an excellent bounty this was, to be sure, and how well it would encourage everyone to thank His Majesty! But what about the long wearisome labor that fell on the shoulders of every one of those county magistrates? They had to see that all those who were entitled to receive the new benefit were duly informed of their new status and that this was registered on any documents that they held. This was of no small importance as it meant that officials now had to treat these persons in a somewhat privileged way, particularly if they fell afoul of the laws. So far, so good. A great deal of clerical work was needed, but not much more.

Yet there was something else to these kind gifts of the Emperor that took far more time and effort and which could not always be carried out completely. This was to see that the recipients of the newly bestowed honors came to possess the land and living quarters that the grants brought with them. Thank goodness that, however frequently the Emperor bestowed these bounties, nobody was entitled to rise above the eighth grade, otherwise there would have been far more work to do. The easiest way of distributing the extra plots of land was to tell the households to go into the bush, hack down the undergrowth and start planting. Not always so easy, if there was no immediate access to water; but where it could be done, Bing would get credit both for reclamation of unused land that he had put under the plow and, in time, for the extra taxes that he would be delivering.

Then there were other ways in which the Emperor's bounteous order could be implemented. When the head of a household died, those who were left behind would probably not be able to work the whole of the land left in their charge, particularly if the head had received several orders of honor; nor was the household entitled to retain such large holdings, as there would no longer be anybody there with sufficiently high social status to merit them. In such cases, Bing's officials were entitled to mark off some of their land and make it over as the new decrees required. Not an easy or pleasant thing to do, to take away land from a family that was in mourning, and not at all easy to measure how much land was involved. That old book of sums that Mr. Li had given him helped a lot.

All these changes had to be recorded and Bing could not be confident that there would be somebody in each of his districts capable of writing it up correctly or indeed honestly. Bing was by no means the only magistrate to wish that His Majesty would not be quite so lavish so often, as sometimes hardly two or three years passed by without a bounty of this sort. All very well for him, just to sign and seal the edict, but it could mean a perpetual chore for his loyal, hardworking officials out in the country. Well, Bing could not oversee all this personally, and Wang advised him how it could best be managed. First, he must send an order to one person in each district ordering him to be responsible for the work, and Wang would choose the right people for this task. Secondly, he must make it quite clear to them that he was going to scrutinize their work personally. Finally, he must make a few sudden, unannounced visits to the districts, perhaps two or three, before they had sent in their returns and demand to see how they were getting on with the job.

Bing had in no way forgotten the last thing that the governor had said and he was only too anxious to get relief from his anxieties. Together with Wang, he took a long look at the maps of the county and the annual reports of his predecessors. For his part Wang had picked up that there had been days when the governor had left his room in a fury, after spending a long time at his own maps and documents, and leaving them all on his table for his aide to collect and put back in order. After quite a search, Bing and Wang found the reason for the third anomaly that had so far eluded them. Some long time ago, perhaps eighty years or more, seven kings of the empire had staged a dangerous rebellion against the Emperor, who had been hard put to suppress it. One, the older king of Liang, had been loyal throughout, and as he was in control of some really important territory, as well as that great granary of Ao, which Bing had seen. The Emperor rewarded him by making some of his sons nobles, and one of them had been given rights over lands that were in Zuyang county. The nobility had not lasted long, as the grandson of the first noble died without an heir. As a result the estates wherein the noble had been entitled to collect taxes had been amalgamated with the adjoining district, inside Zuyang county. All this was clear from the records, once Bing had been able to see them all, but it was quite likely that news of the change had not reached the governor's office, in which case, they would have believed that the nobility still existed. Back at Chang'an they would have known for certain that the nobility had ended and assumed that it had been formed into a district. Very sloppy, if this was the case.

Bing was only too thankful that he now knew why the officials of the central government still thought that Zuyang consisted of twenty districts, and he hoped that he could put the governor's mind at ease, if indeed this had been one of his problems. However, he had to find a way whereby he could make the necessary corrections in his annual report without incurring any blame for carelessness or hinting at inaccuracies that had been overlooked in the past. Wang agreed with him that the best way would be to draw up a formal proposal.

Naturally he took very great care in what he drafted. He started by begging leave to append maps of the county, which showed the rivers, roads, and bridges in all the seventeen districts. His Excellency would observe that in earlier documents these seventeen had sometimes been shown as twenty, and Bing further begged leave to propose why the number should be reduced to seventeen without in any way diminishing the size of the county or affecting the tax that it yielded.

In this way it would appear that it was the county magistrate who was humbly suggesting a change, and it would be for the governor to approve and forward the matter to Chang'an for confirmation. So Bing set out the reasons why he thought it suitable to make a change from the division into twenty districts. Of course he praised the manner in which the county had been set up long, long ago, with the result that it had benefited for many generations from the rule of the blessed earlier Emperors and just ways of the government. It had been only right and suitable that in those days the county should be administered in twenty districts. But Heaven had brought about a number of changes since the days of the founding Emperor, may he be praised and revered. A fast flowing river had once divided two districts, but fifty years ago this river had begun to dry up so that the people of the two districts could easily cross from one side to the other. From either side of what had been the river they were now paying their dues to the same spirits of the mountains, hearth, and soil; they were members of the same community.

Bing turned to the history of the second case, how the nobility had died out, and in order to collect the taxes that were due the magistrate of the day, his own predecessor, now no less than secretary of the Commissioner for State Visits in the central government, had ordered the adjoining district to take over the duties that the noble had discharged, so as to ensure that there would be no loss of revenue. Bing would not dare to go against a decision taken by so eminent a person, now a high-ranking official of the central government. In the same way he explained why the third district had in fact disappeared, again without affecting the administration of the county adversely.

Throughout, Bing was able to point to decisions that were taken or certainly approved, by an authority that was higher than that of a county magistrate, and he added that he had not seen any orders revoking these changes or ordering the division of the county to revert to twenty districts. He was conscious that he had been posted to Zuyang so as to ensure the peace and prosperity of all the people there and he ventured to hope that the governor would concur that the present arrangements should stand without change.

He got no word of acknowledgment from the high and mighty officials at commandery headquarters nor did he expect one, and he felt rather relieved that they had apparently accepted his proposal without demur. For his part the governor drew up his own report, worded at the somewhat higher level at which His Excellency wrote to his superiors at Chang'an. While he took over a great deal of what Bing had written, he somehow managed to give the impression that he himself had been responsible for effective and beneficial changes in governing the commandery. His introductory statement was highly deferential.

Notes for Chapter Thirteen
For a recently found set of legal cases, including one of a thief who had tunneled his way into a house, see A. F. P. Hulsewé, *Remnants of Ch'in Law: An Annotated Translation of the Ch'in Legal and Administrative Rules of the 3rd Century B.C. Discovered in Yün-meng Prefecture, Hu-pei Province, in 1975* (Leiden: E. J. Brill, 1985), pp. 183–207 (especially pp. 202–4). Informative documents found at Zhangjiashan arose from administrative work, such as the submission of accounts or the distribution of imperial benefits for early Western Han. The change from identifying days by terms of the sexagenary cycle to chronological numbering seems to have occurred early in Eastern Han. It is far from clear in what ways it was possible to distribute landholdings so as to comply with the orders of the frequent imperial bounties. A few maps on wood or silk, showing typographical, military, or administrative features date from early Western Han.

Chapter Fourteen

B Y NOW YU'S TIME HAD ARRIVED, AND TO HER GREAT JOY SHE presented Bing with another boy, whom they decided to call Fu, which meant "good luck," hoping that this would always be so with him. The months and years passed by, and as the two boys grew up Yu did her best to see that they were taught enough to fit them for a cultured and comfortable life when they went out on their own, without going through the same sorts of hardships that Bing had suffered. Guang had responded well, patiently learning how to read and write without always interrupting to ask, "Why?" So Yu hoped that in time Bing or one of his colleagues would sponsor him as a candidate to go through the regular stages and become an official. But it was a very different story with Fu, who had both of his parents worried and, in Bing's case, angry. Fu showed every sign of being bored stiff as soon as Yu took one of her scrolls down from the shelf, and so far from obeying his father when he was told to attend quietly to what his mother said, Fu showed how sulky and bad tempered he could be.

In the warm spring weather Bing loved to drive out into the countryside to see how the farmers had survived the winter. He wanted to make sure that they were getting on with the tasks set for the season in a long list of instructions that he had found in his office. These were not framed as the Emperor's commands, in the same way that certain matters were laid down in the Statutes and Ordinances. They were more in the nature of straight lists of guidance for the timing of the work that had to be done in each month of the year, to coax the best produce from the earth with the least possible labor. The lists were very detailed and they showed clearly how a farmer's work should be suited to the seasons: you planted in spring, gathered the crops in the autumn, dug the ground in winter, hoed out the weeds and poured in the water in the summer.

Much of this was familiar ground for Bing, even though his personal experience of working the land had been in a different type of country and climate than that of Donghai commandery, but there was still quite a lot in the list that he did not understand. Somehow or other each month was connected with the stars. The spirit who should be worshipped then was named. It was puzzling that for each of the twelve months the name of a person, or ancestor, or perhaps yet another god was mentioned. Bing had no idea of the stories that lay behind those names.

If the lists were to be taken as a regular practical guide for the year's work then there was another thing that puzzled him. They set down all the activities that were proper for twelve months, but as he well knew, every so often the year had thirteen months, as laid down in the calendar. However, there was no provision for a thirteenth month in these lists or "Ordinances for the Months" as they were called. Bing supposed that you continued working in the same way until the guidance for the next month, with its own schedules, applied.

One morning, Bing's work was interrupted by a special messenger. The man had come by foot from the farthest district in the county, a lovely part of the world with snowcapped mountains overlooking the settlements and the fields. He seemed ready to collapse from exhaustion, as he blurted out his grim news. The God of the Mountain was angry. Lightning and thunder had heralded the collapse of one of the hills; trees had been uprooted; the roads were blocked and half the place was flooded, with most of the harvest to come flattened in ruins. They were clearing the place as fast as they could, but the river was running at a terrifying speed, washing away their repairs as quickly as they were made. They desperately needed the help of a dozen men armed with the right implements for clearing away the broken trees and building a new bridge. The appeal was heartrending, and Bing had no option but to answer it. One of his major responsibilities was to ensure that communications were intact, and he remembered how, as a conscript laborer, he had been put to precisely that sort of work. At the cost of putting off other projects actually in progress, such as the maintenance and repair of the city wall, he was able to find enough men to send to the stricken area.

But reports that soon came in told Bing that the team he had sent was not making any real progress. The roads were still blocked and their attempts to set up a bridge that would last longer than a couple of days had failed. Every structure they put in place had begun to sag after only a night or two, and had finally fallen into the fast flowing river, just adding to the trouble.

Bing decided to go and see for himself; he was up to date with his routine work and could safely leave, trusting Wang to see that everything would be kept under control in his absence. The journey was pleasant enough, though for the last few miles he had to make his way on foot, as there was no possible way for a carriage to pass. When he finally reached the place where the village bridge once stood, he was shocked to see the results of the incompetent way in which the workmen had tried to repair it. All around him, preventing any passage along the road, lay the broken struts that they had tried to fit together, and Bing could see at a glance that the timber they were using was in no way strong enough to withstand the ordinary pressure exerted on a bridge, let alone the force of the fierce waters that never stopped bearing down.

The villagers who watched were astonished to see Bing take personal charge of the operation.

"First, we must have lengths of wood much stronger than what you've been using," he told them. "Yes, I know they are difficult to shape, but just watch me." When the right sort of wood was gathered, he began to show them with his own hands the skilled techniques he had learned as a carpenter. Next, he showed them how to place and adjust the timbers so that the force of the rushing water, instead of pulling the structure apart, would actually strengthen it. Only when he was satisfied that the bridge was securely supported did he instruct them to cover it with planks strong enough to allow carts to cross.

Finally, he turned to the repair of the roadways. "You must stop shoveling all this debris into the river," he told them. "That is only adding to the blockage."

"What can we do, then?" someone asked.

"Burn it," said Bing, biting back what he thought of their stupidity. "Collect all the rubbish and burn it."

Gradually order was restored and the farmers could set about repairing things in their own settlements. Before he left Bing had them all do two things. He wanted an account of what had been destroyed during the disaster, and he ordered them all to gather at their shrines and pay dutiful homage to the local gods, with particular attention to the gods of the mountains and the rivers.

One year, the annual reports had come in from all seventeen districts in the county and Bing's staff was drawing up the comprehensive statement of accounts for delivery to the commandery. Anxious to keep on personal terms with the county magistrates, the governor, for some time, had made a point of inviting them all to deliver their reports in person, on the same day, so that he could entertain them all with a good dinner. This would mark the end of the fiscal year and with their work done they would all, he hoped, be ready to relax and enjoy the evening. On this occasion, Bing looked over all the necessary documents that had come in, and he noticed that the yield and tax returns from one district, a large one at that, was remarkably lower than the average of the others. When he looked at the records for earlier years he found the same difference, and wondered why the district had been performing so badly. Wang couldn't explain it, and although there was nothing that he could do about it, Bing made a mental note to investigate.

At the governor's dinner Bing was seated next to a fellow magistrate, who started talking about his recent travels. These were all on official business, so he stayed at the official post stations, just as Bing had done on his way to take up his appointment.

"Comfortable?" asked Bing.

"Oh yes, except for a rowdy bunch of drinkers at a house attached to one of the stations. They were obviously celebrating something, but I did notice one odd thing. At one of the station houses—I can't remember now exactly which one it was, but it certainly was not in your county—I noticed that there were a dozen or so of your wagons, all marked with your office's mark, parked together and empty. There were plenty of stalks and leaves on the ground and clearly they had just been unloaded. They must have been carrying straw or hay, or some newly harvested millet. In fact, when I say 'marked,' somebody had tried to paint over the marks but hadn't quite succeeded. Well, this was none of my business; they gave me a good dinner and I slept well, despite the hubbub."

Bing would dearly have loved to know where his carts had gone astray, but his colleague had little more information. However, he did mention where he had been traveling, and it occurred to Bing that he had been very close to the district whose harvest had been registered as below average. As it would, the talk turned to other things, but Bing did not forget the matter.

Once back in Zuyang, Bing told the whole story to Wang, who had a shrewd idea of what had been going on, but said nothing. Shortly before the next harvest, Wang suggested that they both go on a tour of inspection of some of the districts to see how the crops were growing. He took care to include in the itinerary the district whose returns were always low. As it happened the weather had been poor that year and nobody expected a bumper crop.

"How have you been doing?" Bing asked the district official.

"Could be worse; we have a total of four hundred households," and he named the number of bushels of grain he was expecting.

"What do you get in normal years?" Wang put in.

"Oh, about twice as much," slipped by the man's tongue, and the figure that he named was just about twice what had been entered year after year in the district's returns.

After supper, once Bing and Wang were alone, Wang found an opportunity to speak his mind. "You remember that tale last year of a dozen of our carts being seen, empty, way out of our own county?"

"Indeed I do."

"Well, last year was an excellent harvest, but this district's returns, as reported and indeed as usual, were well below average. Before he could stop himself that district official let slip the amount he would expect in a better year, such as the last one. I am just wondering . . ."

"So am I," said Bing. "We'll see what the fellow has to say tomorrow morning."

It didn't take long for Bing and Wang to get the truth out of him.

"What would you do if we changed the county's mark of recognition and you had to get rid of the old one?" was Bing's first question.

It was taken as an innocent question, and the man began to explain how he would do it.

"Well, that's a quick answer," said Bing, "and it sounds easy enough to do. I suppose that's the way it's been done here, year after year. You get rid of the county mark on our carts and make it right again once they are due to return home?"

Within a few minutes the man had confessed to everything. Yes, each year they'd loaded part of the harvest on those county carts, painted over the county marks, and sent them away for sale to one of the districts outside the commandery. Some of his relatives lived there, and he had connections.

"That was smart of him," said Wang. "He'll have known that we can't do anything outside the jurisdiction of Donghai."

Of course, they could not get any account from the man of the amount sold, nor could they pinpoint the blame on anyone else.

"Take the man back to Zuyang," Bing ordered. "We'll deal with him when we get back. I'll appoint someone to take his place."

Back in Zuyang city, Bing was expecting to receive an official sent from the central government whose rank was probably higher than his own. A decision had been taken at a high level to increase the extent and production of fruit orchards. Special agencies were being appointed by the Commissioner for Agriculture to whom they would be directly responsible and then sent out with full authority to get the work done. Bing's county had been named as one where this should take place. So Bing was expecting a man called Liu and he only hoped that Liu would not be so conscious of his own authority as to make cooperation difficult. Bing at least knew that his visitor would have no right to interfere in the administration of the county, but he might be authorized to demand material help in the form of government-held farming implements or consumable stores, or even the use of conscript labor.

Liu arrived in Zuyang with a grudge, as he hated having been sent out of Chang'an and felt that he had been humiliated. So he made no effort to conceal that he was very conscious of his superiority over his country colleagues. In return, Bing found himself standing on his own dignity. But however stiff their relations were, between them they had to make some decisions, such as where the agency would be situated, what lands should be made over for fruit orchards, and who exactly would be working them. Bing set out with Liu to prospect the ground, taking good care to have Wang with him, and Bing talked it over with Wang when they returned.

"Not an easy man to work with, is he?" said Bing, and Wang had to agree that the outlook wasn't too good.

"He's one of those silent fellows who seems to be concerned with one thing only, the grade of office that he reaches. It was no use trying to share a joke with him; I was soon put in my place. He's out to get every ounce that he can from our resources, particularly transport. If we let him have some carts and he damages them, is there any way in which we can get him to be responsible for repairs?"

Notes for Chapter Fourteen
The "Ordinances for the Months" are preserved in several sets of writing. A recent discovery of the text, painted on a wall, suggests that it was displayed in public for literate members of the population to read.

Chapter Fifteen

Enforcement of the laws

GUANG WAS NOW APPROACHING THE AGE WHEN HE WOULD BE called up for his time in the service. Bing did his best to warn him of what he should try to avoid and to tell Guang what sort of things he would have to face in company that would be very different from what he was used to.

"None of it will hurt you," Bing said, "and you'll find out a lot about the way people live up and down the empire. You're a good son and I don't have to tell you to make sure that you don't give the officers any reason to scold you."

It was the younger boy, Fu, who was worrying both Bing and Yu, more and more. When Yu gave up trying to teach him, in despair, Bing had stepped in. He was all too conscious that in his own time he had had to rise from a humble background and low standard of living to a way of life that was refined, and he knew well how difficult that could be. But now he saw how his younger son was choosing to tread a path in the opposite direction.

"Have you no idea that your first duty is to obey your father and thank your mother for all the loving kindness she gives you?" his usual lecture ran. "Here we are doing our best to prepare you for a comfortable life, and all you can do is rush into the markets and mix with the rowdies and criminals there. One of these days I've no doubt that you'll be caught by one of the patrols and don't expect your father the magistrate to save you from punishment. For goodness sake, remember that you're not just a low-class boy looking for fun and games. You have been born to something better and, as the son of an official, you're supposed to set a good example of orderly conduct to everyone else."

Fu would listen to his father without a word, but the defiant look on his face never flagged, and the situation, to Bing, began to seem hopeless.

Bing was not happy altogether when he had to perform the duties of a judicial officer. He knew that only too often there was much that had been left unsaid and much to make him feel that the man or woman who stood charged before him had a human heart and a family to look after. Very often he had to suppress such feelings and carry out his duties regardless, particularly if another official was in any way involved. Although the laws left precious little scope for a magistrate to exercise his discretion, he hoped that somehow, while punishing those who were guilty of a foul crime, he could save a man or woman who was innocent from the severities of the Emperor's punishments.

Bing was also responsible for the county's prison, a small one with no more than two officials to look after it. Criminals were not sentenced to spend a term in prison by way of punishment; they were simply kept in those ghastly quarters while they were facing a charge and the case was under investigation. The wardens were obliged to supply them with food but Bing was pretty certain that they demanded their price from the poor devils inside.

A loathsome stench met Bing when he went to inspect this place. Adjoining it was a grim courtyard. All the tools and implements needed for inflicting bodily punishments were fastened around the walls, some used for the most horrible ways of torturing or cutting up a man's body. Bing could see that there might be a reason for cutting off a convict's foot to ensure that, once posted to his work, he would not be able to run away. And as he had seen up in the north, the telltale mark of a tattoo and even the removal of a man or woman's hair meant that, once punished as a criminal, no one could escape recognition as such.

But there were times when Bing felt a deep revulsion against all that this stood for. Was this really the way that one person should treat another, never mind that an Emperor ordered him to do so? He thought back to his traveling days when he had passed by that famous mountain Huashan where there were folk living by themselves, independent of others and free of any official's interference in their lives, and he remembered how for a short time that way of life had appealed to him. Thank goodness he hadn't tried it. If he found such people in the county now he would have to call them vagrants and force them into a controlled way of life. He would much rather let them be, even though some of them were scallywags. He could only respect those of them who chose that austere way of living in their belief that men and women are in no way superior to other types of living creatures; that they should live as nature saw fit, without being organized into groups or put to work. The trouble was that such people saw no reason why they should obey any rules that were imposed on them. All that was very well but you couldn't keep the country free of criminals without some measure of discipline. Bing thought that he'd feel a lot easier in his mind if the Emperor would decree an act of grace more frequently than he did, thus eliminating a lot of human suffering.

For all this, Bing was a fully paid official of the Emperor and he could not evade his duties. One man was brought in with a serious offense, theft of official property, and he had been sent down for five years of hard labor. But there was more to it. It was a case in which the magistrate was entitled, sometimes even ordered, to take the man's close relatives into custody, and there they were, the man's wife, seventeen-year-old son, and seven-year-old daughter. Bing couldn't help but think of his own family, of the way in which his grandmother had been seized by officials and how she had only just been able to survive.

"I'll keep the boy on duty here," he told Wang. "They're short of staff down below and he'll do until his time comes to be called up. Tell the steward to take the wife and daughter and keep them together; they can work in keeping the house and garden in good order. And you better tell him not to treat them roughly; if anything goes wrong, he'll be up on a charge of negligence, and I won't be merciful."

Bing was on one of his excursions into the country. It was a lovely day, and the spring sunshine felt pleasantly warm on his legs, which had grown rather stiff of late. It was with joy that he saw the trees springing into life and the millet plants sprouting. He decided to stop at one of the farms to see for himself how the household was making out. As he grew nearer, the rhythmical sound of work being done caught his attention. Yes, please, he would like to go around to the back to see how the stream was flowing. The farmer did his best to dissuade him, but Bing was adamant and once there he saw why the man had tried to stop him. A lanky youngster was chopping down a tree with the help of a fine axe, gleaming in the sun.

"What in Heaven's name is going on?" Bing demanded of the farmer. "Don't you know that you must never cut down anything that is growing at this time of year, when yang and the power of life is thriving? It's all laid down in the 'Ordinances for the Months'; even if you can't read, you must have heard of it. What's more, by law it's a punishable offense. What do you have to say for yourself?"

The man muttered to himself but said nothing.

"Arrest them both," Bing told his attendants. "And see that they hand the axe over to you for my inspection; and then straight back to the lodge."

Bing was furious at what he had seen and in no mood to think well of the farmer, or of his son, a surly, ill-mannered oaf. He did feel sorry, very sorry, for the wife that the man had left behind in tears, and once in his office, Bing summoned two of the conscript men at his disposal.

"You're to go to this man's farm—my staff will tell you where—and do the farmwork; I want no trouble. His wife's there all alone but for a five-year-old child and she's young and pretty. If I hear of anything that is wrong, you'll get a sentence of five years' hard labor with a foot chopped off, and a brand mark for life; you'll never get it off your cheek."

When the two came up for charge the next day, the boy looked just as oafish, but rather scared. They'd probably frightened him to death down in the guardroom, Bing thought. If anything, his father looked even more antagonistic than he had before, and Bing wondered whether this was the first time he had been in trouble.

"We'll start with getting their particulars down," he said to his clerk. "Name, age, height, complexion, degree of social status, and then the commandery, county, district, and village where they were each born and where they now live." He had already told the clerk to make two copies of this, and one of these was immediately passed to another clerk, for checking in the register. "Has he put in any written statement, or confessed verbally that he acted criminally in any way?"

Neither of the two had done so and Bing's first duty was to get an account of what had happened down in writing.

"I, the magistrate, saw for myself that, on the day after the spring equinox, the boy was cutting down the tree with an axe. He said that his father had told him to do so and to take good care of the axe. It had been against the father's will that I, the magistrate, went behind the house to see what was going on." Bing looked at the two culprits. "Any questions." Neither of them said a word. Bing went on to give them a chance to explain what they had been doing and state a reason why they had so blatantly broken the law; and a law it was, as Bing had carefully checked by looking at his copy of the statutes. It was quite an old law too, so it would have been known about quite generally. Well, of course they had nothing to say. "Didn't mean no harm," the farmer finally growled. "Just wanted to clear the way to build a pigsty."

Bing then raised another matter. "There's one other thing. That's a very valuable axe that the boy was manhandling, and it deserved better treatment. Can you tell me how you came by it?" Of course nothing came of the question, but Bing pressed hard. "Who sold it to you?"

"What do you think? Unlike some folk I'd never have the money to buy it."

"Did somebody give it you then?"

"Who'd you think would ever be foolish enough to do? That old Shen Nong whom you people talk about?"

"Silence in the court," Bing called out, knowing that he had been beaten at his own game, and he could get no further with this one. Eventually the prisoner said that he'd been told that the axe had belonged to his grandfather, but he had no idea where it had come from.

These procedures always followed four stages. Bing had now come to the third, which had to be put off for a day or two. This meant interrogating the group of people responsible for reporting any suspicious or criminal activity on the part of their members, of whom this man was one. Bing had ordered his staff to bring in as many members as they could find, and now four old men shuffled in, with no idea why they had been called. None of them had anything to say against the prisoner and his boy, or at least none of them was willing to say anything.

"Did anyone of you ever see him with that axe?" Bing asked. No, they had not. "Ever hear of him being out at night, after the curfew?" At this one of the four said that one night he had seen the man carrying something heavy in a hemp sack, but that had been years ago. Bing knew better than to press this question as it would have incriminated the witness, who would have had no business being outside at night.

Nothing else was forthcoming from the four old men, and Bing was about to close this part of the proceedings, when one of them blurted out, "You might ask him what's happened to his youngest boy. I once found him stealing some of my property." But neither of the two prisoners owned up to anything, even after they had been flogged to restore their memory. Bing suspected that, as a younger son like himself, the lad had made off somewhere to better himself, and he asked the clerk to check whether anything was known.

Finally Bing came to the last stage of the inquiry, to see how the provisions of the law applied to the case in question and to take appropriate action. Clearly the man had acted deliberately. The youngster had simply done what all youngsters should do, obey his father's orders. The law must take its course or else Bing would find himself in trouble.

"Well," he said, "it's all laid down quite clearly. There are many other worse crimes, with punishments far more severe than they are for this one, and we simply have to do what the book says. You will be sent as a convict to hard labor for three years, and your hair will come off so that it will never grow again. You are very lucky that I don't have to order you to be tattooed, and that's only because you've risen up to three grades in the social scale. Don't forget to thank the Emperor for that.

"Now we'll attend to you, young man, and you'll bow down to show your respect when a magistrate is addressing you. You acted illegally, though you were too ignorant and stupid to know it, not that that's any excuse. Had you refused to cut down the tree, you would have been disobeying your father and that would have been an even worse crime. You'll go back to the farm tonight. Tell your mother what has happened and see that you get it right, and you can expect to be called up for your normal duty as a conscript laborer very soon. Case dismissed."

Bing made sure that indeed the lad would be called up soon, but he still had one thing to decide—what to do about the axe. In all his earlier years as a carpenter he had never seen such a fine example, beautifully sharp and well balanced with a fine slot to fit the handle. He had looked at it with some care and eventually found the telltale stamp of the original owner, no less a person than the King of Wu. Well, that kingdom had come to an end years ago and somebody had obviously been able to get hold of all the valuables that had been in the palace. Did willful possession of such goods constitute a crime? He wondered, but he could find nothing to guide him. If only he could talk to his old friend Shang; he'd be able to advise what should be done. In the meantime, Bing had the axe put into the county's store of tools, with a written account of where it had come from and a sharp notice that it was to be used only at the express orders of the magistrate.

When the mail carrier arrived, he was shown straight to Bing, as Bing had ordered when he first took up his post. Travel-stained, weary, and dirty, he was still carrying his bag.

"Sit down," Bing called to him in a welcoming voice, "you must be very tired so we won't do any business now. Go and get a good meal down below and come back tomorrow morning. Just leave your bag here, along with any notes you've got of your time schedules. Oh, if there are any letters addressed directly to me as magistrate, could you just get them out for me now before you go?"

Off went the postman, glad to be dismissed so quickly, but with some anxieties about leaving the bag in hands other than his own. "Oh, forget it," he said to himself as he settled down to the warm soup they had provided along with a large satisfying meal to go with it. "With luck he won't notice anything."

But Bing was not unaware of what might have been going on. His own mail, he knew, would be concerned entirely with routine matters, and he knew that anything that was really interesting would come to him directly from the governor's office. This fellow had come from up country. Nonetheless, he felt entitled, or even obliged, to check what was passing through his hands for forward delivery elsewhere and he took out all the documents from the bag in order. Fair enough, there was nothing abnormal or suspicious to be seen as the rolls lay there, with their address tags all saying "Southbound" and giving their precise destination. Except that one item was evidently going to the wrong place. Donghai, of course, did lie in the south, but this roll was addressed to Donglai in the north. Some damn fool in Chang'an had been careless and put it into the wrong basket but that would not have been the carrier's fault. Judging from the times that were noted, the man had not been delayed beyond his schedule, except once. But there was something odd that struck Bing as he lifted up the bag to put everything back. At the lower end the fabric, rough hemp cloth, was firm enough as if it was supported, and it was uncreased, but at the top it had slipped into irregular folds. What was keeping the bottom part so rigid, he wondered, as he carefully stowed everything back in the bag in just the way that he had found it.

The next day the young fresh-faced serviceman who had brought the mail duly presented himself to the magistrate. Bing made a great show of opening the bag, going through the items, noting all the particulars and confirming that they were correct.

"Had a bit of trouble here did you?" he said, and he named a postal station where some of the items had originated. It was a station he did not know.

"Oh yes sir; I was held up for the best part of a day while they had to clear a landslide, and that's why I was late." Fair enough, Bing thought as he packed everything back in the bag, the young man only too eager to help him.

He hoisted the heavy bag to his shoulder. "Thank you very much sir," he said as he started to go out.

"Just one thing," said Bing, and the man stopped in his tracks. "If you don't mind, we went through all those items just now and they were fine, but . . ." and Bing pressed and prodded the lower end of the bag, "what goes on here? You better speak up."

Shamefaced, the young man complied.

"I thought so." Bing's voice was not as genial as it had been before. "A letter addressed to a woman who lives in Zuyang, is it? Sent privately, and not to an office? How much did you get for carrying this?" Out came the whole story. Yes, he'd been given a string of cash for bringing it by a very old man who was from his own village. Years ago he'd lost his wife, and the son who lived with him had been killed in the earthquake last year. There had been one other son, but he had taken off somewhere to make his living in the towns. The old man had begged him to get the letter delivered, as he was desperate to find somebody who would keep up the family sacrifices when he had gone, and this was the only chance.

Bing thought back to his early years and could only hope that he would have helped the old man in the same way. As he looked he saw before him the face of an honest young man who meant no harm and who, like himself, recognized how great the call of a family was. Nevertheless, Bing was an official of His Majesty with prescribed duties, and he had to see that all regulations were upheld.

"Do you know what the punishment is for messengers who carry private mail along with official documents?" The young man learned that he was liable to be flogged. "Come back later today," Bing ordered, "and not before you've given all this some thought."

Fortunately, Bing had dismissed the doorman and nobody had witnessed what had taken place. Should he have the postman punished and probably turn him into a dissident or even a criminal for the rest of his life? Or, should he think how right the fellow had been to try to keep family ties going, as the Emperor would surely wish? And what about the old widower whose only hope of contentment lay in getting that letter through? Bing soon knew how he was going to handle the case.

Again he saw to it that nobody would hear what he was going to do when the postman came back, frightened and looking ashamed. Had he changed his attitude with a sullen look, Bing might have thought again.

"First, hand over all of that cash that you've got left. Is there anything more that you can say to excuse your actions? You had no idea of the laws? Sorry, that won't do, as the regulations don't accept that as an excuse. I don't suppose that the old man who paid you had any idea of them either. In any case, it's up to me to decide how you are to be punished.

"As I told you, if the law takes its course you'll be brutally flogged; for the rest of your life you'll bear a grudge against everything that the Emperor and his officials order and never think of what you owe to his kindnesses. You'll probably also wonder what's the good of trying to keep a family's life together if it lands you in this sort of mess. So you'll be set against all the ways in which members of a family, old and young, male and female, act together on the occasions of birth, marriage, and death. The wise men of old always made a point of teaching how important all this is, and the Emperor has been showing how he wants everyone to realize it."

By now the young man was almost in tears. Bing went on. "Strictly speaking, I have no option but to send you down. However, I don't think that you acted deliberately in defiance of the laws, and I think you do know how much it means to keep a family closely tied together. I've a book here which tells me of a number of cases in which an official could not decide what he ought to do, particularly if there was nothing to show that although somebody had committed a crime, he had never intended to do anything wrong. Years ago there was a man called Dong, a wise man who had read an awful lot of what the old masters had written. He was asked about cases of this sort and he came down very strongly by saying that it is always the intention that really matters. I feel sure he would have seen that although you have in fact broken the law, you hadn't planned to do so for your own benefit, and he would have said that no charge should be brought against you.

"So, off you go on your way. I shall hand over this cash to the spirit who gives safety to travelers, and I shall get the old man's letter sent on as part of my own official mail. Best of luck—no, don't thank me."

Notes for Chapter Fifteen

It might seem to be unlikely that sons of a privileged person such as a magistrate would be obliged to serve as conscript laborers or in the armed forces, but I have yet to find evidence that they were exempted from those duties. Shen Nong was the culture hero of Chinese mythology who had taught human beings how to till the land. Members of the public would not have been admitted to the court where Bing tried criminal cases, but a number of junior officials and clerks would have been there. Considerable documentation attests to the importance placed on the delivery of official mail according to schedule. The intention or motive that lay behind an act against the laws could sometimes serve to dismiss a charge of criminality. The Dong who is mentioned is Dong Zhongshu (ca. 198–ca. 107 BCE) a few of whose judicial decisions have been preserved.

Chapter Sixteen   *Final years*

FOR SOME YEARS BING SERVED AS MAGISTRATE OF ZUYANG, responding to the changes of the season, regularly filling out the necessary documents, checking the accounts and their figures, which he was finding rather boring, and trying to see how any newly ordered laws would fit the existing book of rules without contradiction. But he was getting old and his limbs ached in the winter cold. What's more, Yu had never really liked it down in Donghai— so different from the lovely mountains and rich bamboos of Shu where she was born.

In any case, Bing had reached the grade of one thousand, quite a significant place in the ranking of official salaries, as it marked the highest point that most of them could ever attain. Bing thought it very unlikely that he would be chosen to rise any higher in the service, such as in a senior post of the central government, let alone as governor of a commandery. After all, he had gotten where he was by starting as a humble clerk, unlike most of his colleagues who rose far higher; and he had not been chosen by one of the provincial authorities for recommendation by reason of his personal qualities or his degree of learning. To tell the truth, he was finding some of his routine duties irksome.

As it happened, the senior people in Chang'an had concocted a scheme to settle quite a number of families just west of the capital, at a place called Maoling. Bing had never been there though he had heard of it as the place where the tomb of that long-lived emperor Wudi had been set up, but he was not clear what the point was of moving families there. At one of those meetings that the governor called every year, he had heard that the central government wanted to get control of a lot of really rich people who had acquired possession of large tracts of land. Some of them had built up strong local connections. They had been acting as local lords of creation and were quite capable of turning against the Emperor and launching a revolt against him if the opportunity arose. That was why the government had hatched this scheme to tempt them to move. They certainly needed to have a stack of money to qualify for the privilege, and for reasons that he could not quite understand many of them had jumped at the chance to do so. By all accounts living conditions in Maoling were comfortable enough and there was every chance of meeting some interesting people there. He'd even heard of at least one man who really understood how the empire should be governed and had retired there. Not that this man had had a successful career as an official, but it was evidently worthwhile for some of the most senior men of the day to go out to Maoling and see what that old man thought of their problems.

Some years earlier Bing had discussed the idea of moving to Luoyang or somewhere with Yu. "Anything to get away from this backwater," she said. "We never have made that trip to Lanling that you promised. But how on earth can we afford to move?"

Bing, in fact, had been seeing to it that they would be rich enough to do so. He knew very well that Yu had been sadly disappointed at not going to Lanling, but he had always found some excuse to refuse her pleas. Good grief, how that learned bunch would have sneered at him and his lack of education!

Bing taxed himself with looking after his own interests like this. In addition there was a further reason why both he and Yu were sick at heart, as a personal tragedy had struck them. They had been happy to see Guang grow up. Yu had taught him to read and write, and in due course he had been sent to Chang'an for further training. He'd done well and prospects were good that he would enter the civil service and enjoy a career far more successful than his father's. But Fu, the younger son, had worried them all along and things went from bad to worse. He still resented any instruction or example of behavior that he received. He was given to being quarrelsome, and he often expressed his scorn for the traditional way of life that was being planned for him. Mixing with all sorts of people in the town, he fell in with a crowd of his own age who shared his views. Frequently, they criticized the way that public life was being organized, at the whim of a few officials; they even went so far as to blame the Emperor. Fortunately they knew enough not to refer to him directly, but rather in the roundabout way that Bing had once learned as a way to avoid being accused of treason or subversive talk.

Then things got out of hand. There were a few men, who were older than these boys and should have known better, but instead they went much further, saying that the Emperor's dynasty had been going on for so long that it must surely be close to its end, unless somehow or other it was given a new lease on life with a new sense of purpose. This was just the kind of stuff that appealed to the young; they were far too inexperienced to think of the ghastly things that might follow the end of a dynasty, and they were far too ignorant and self-centered to learn anything from the past. So of course they talked, and of course their talk came to the ears of the authorities. The older men who had led them and argued that a change was bound to come were all arrested and punished, with horrible severity.

The officials who were responsible for the case had good cause for worry. They knew that if they let even one of the dissidents go, sooner or later he would talk, and sooner or later they would find themselves denounced for negligence. They were all aware of the punishment. So they rounded up all the youngsters they could find who had been involved and had them all charged on suspicion of treason. Bing and Yu's second boy was among them and was sentenced to five years hard labor, with no possibility that he would be let off, even if the large sum that would secure a ransom was paid.

Bing and Yu could hardly bear to talk about it. One day Bing took a chance with an idea that had come to him and which he hoped might give Yu something else to think about.

"You remember when we were in Chang'an," he began, and Yu tried to smile. "Well, over away to the west of the city there's a place called Maoling. That Emperor who lived and reigned so long—you know, Wudi as his title is—is buried there, along with some of his very close supporters. But what's more to the point is that a settlement of a rather special sort has grown up there. For some reason the government took a hand in establishing it, inducing a number of prominent persons to move there, and they tell me that as quite a few distinguished writers and poets have settled down there it's an interesting place to live in."

After all she had been through, this time Yu could hardly have shown less interest in the idea of moving, but slowly and persistently Bing managed to show her that life might be much more comfortable and interesting in Maoling.

"Not all that far from Chang'an itself," he noted. "We'd be able to see something of young Guang and it would be very easy for people to ride out to see us. Anyway, we'll have to move somewhere away from here; the man who takes over won't like me hanging around." So whatever she felt when Bing's appointment came to its natural end, the two of them journeyed back to Chang'an. When they passed one of the narrow tree-lined creeks, Bing remembered it. It was there that a fisherman had once ventured, never to be seen again, some said, while others claimed that he had indeed come back with extraordinary tales to tell about people he'd met there who lived in idyllic bliss. Well, well, Bing thought, perhaps this is a good omen for the new life we are about to start in Maoling.

Once settled, Bing was relieved to find that he had not been misinformed. While he had been apprehensive about the reception he might have received from the learned men of Lanling, he felt confident that he could hold his own with former officials. Certainly it was a much larger town than he had expected, with almost as many people living there as in Chang'an itself. There was a somewhat choice and secluded quarter of the town where people such as themselves had come to live after retirement from the service. Some of the people he met had grown old and were difficult to understand. But they were friendly and wanted to talk and, once Bing became used to their ways of speaking, he was glad to hear about life as a county magistrate in their day, some thirty years or more before his own service. Looking back, they all seemed to agree that the job had been much easier, and therefore better, in the good old days.

None of his neighbors would talk directly about the Emperors whom they had served or the things that went on in the different palaces of the city. Bing longed to hear the truth about how the women there had intrigued against one another so as to secure the great prize of being nominated Empress, determined as they were to produce a son who would be named Heir Apparent, but here he was frustrated. He had heard a great deal of gossip about these matters and how some of the highest officials in the land, who were related to one of the consorts, had been involved; for the better if their own sister or daughter had managed to succeed, as that would almost guarantee a promotion; for the worse if some other young girl caught the Emperor's fancy, and they would find themselves degraded, or even dismissed. One of Bing's neighbors who had enjoyed a high position at court did let down his guard once, after an especially good dinner. He more than hinted that it was usually the Emperor's women or their relatives who exerted a far greater influence on public decisions than the Emperor himself, but he did not dare to say openly that there were times when a young Emperor had had to give way to somebody else's wishes or opinions.

One day an intense argument broke out as some of them were discussing the time when fierce fighting had broken out in Chang'an city. There had been talk of witchcraft. Troops that the Heir Apparent had raised were engaged in deathly battle with those of the Emperor and had eventually been brought down, but the affair had been disastrous, ending with the suicide of the Empress and the death of the Heir Apparent. Nothing would stop one of the men in Maoling from believing that the trouble started thanks to the underhanded plotting of the Empress's family, but someone else insisted that that was pure nonsense; it was that family's rivals who had been to blame. Bing realized that family connections were playing a part here and he was sure that the two men were on the verge of coming to blows, they felt so strongly, but somehow he was able to change the subject and eventually they calmed down.

Some of these reminiscences seemed to go back a very long time, and maybe some of those old men were definitely out to impress Bing and put him in his place. Bing also wondered if they had actually witnessed the incidents they talked about, or perhaps they were repeating what others had told them. Had any of them really been there when raiders on horseback galloped into sight of Chang'an, as one of them claimed?

"If they got that close, why didn't our own forces stop them?" he asked, but the storyteller could not answer.

"That incident wasn't nearly as dangerous as things were in the next Emperor's reign," somebody chimed in. He was obviously anxious to tell Bing what he knew for certain had happened on one very dangerous occasion. So out came the story, which Bing had heard before about how, almost immediately after that Emperor's accession to the throne, seven kings teamed up to get rid of him.

"It was touch and go for a while, I can tell you, and it was only because another of the Emperor's relatives, a brother I think, or perhaps a cousin, stood by him that the forces that the seven had mustered were defeated. You can imagine what became of the seven kings."

Bing could, but he doubted that the speaker had been present to witness all that he was talking about. For one thing, he knew far less than Bing did about the changes in the ways that the seven kingdoms were then administered and which would have mattered a lot to anyone in an official position at the time.

Life in Maoling was comparatively uneventful, but news filtered through of strange and frightening happenings elsewhere. Incessant rain one year caused widespread damage in the countryside, and even in Chang'an, protected as it was by its mighty walls, people rushed around in a panic.

"Shouldn't the Emperor get away while he can?" some asked. It was only thanks to the steady voice of a senior official that they were calmed. Another time, wise, high-ranking officials had been hard put to keep order in the city when terrifying things happened. An eclipse of the sun occurred on the very same day that an earthquake shook the city and was felt right inside the palace; events of both these sorts were always seen as omens that could only spell disaster, and now they were taking place simultaneously! It took a long time to put everyone's fears to rest.

There were also happier times, such as when Yu's brother, Li the Younger, arrived unexpectedly to see them. For a number of years they had not been able to meet, and by now his business had prospered and he had become very rich. He had a lot to tell them of news from Luoyang, where Bing's old friend and onetime employer, Shang, had died. Yu had been very worried about her father, as she had not heard from him for some time, and she was happy to learn that he was in pretty good shape, considering his age, and he still spent as much time as he could with his books.

Yu's brother then told them of a terrific commotion that had recently taken place, and as this had been widespread through a number of commanderies, he thought it odd that they knew nothing about it. Crowds and crowds of people had massed together, leaving their fields to run amok, and moving from one place to another. "The Queen Mother is coming!" they cried, and whatever they did they could not be stopped. Some of them were carrying little figures of the queen made of straw and they all ran about, barefoot and with their hair disheveled. Some of them took flaming torches up to the roofs of the houses. Meanwhile, they beat their drums incessantly, and nothing would stop them as they broke down gateways and climbed over walls. They felt compelled to take images of the Queen Mother around, as widely as they could, even seizing carriages and horses to do so.

Bing wondered what it was all about, particularly when he learned that these crowds had been singing and dancing, crying out how wonderful the Queen Mother of the West was and what blessings she would bring to anyone who sang her praises.

"There was more to it than that," young Li explained. "They seemed to believe that if they all carried one of those straw images, the queen would see to it that they would never die, and that was what they all wanted so desperately. I really am surprised that you never heard of this," he said. "I understood that frenzied crowds were acting like this in Chang'an itself."

Well, maybe they had, thought Bing and Yu. Old now with gray hair, they knew well enough that their own lives would soon come to an end, and Yu had been thinking hard about what some of those old masters had had to say about the mysteries of living and dying, and how those different phases all fit together as parts of the whole way in which the world ran in its eternal, never-changing cycle. Bing's thoughts fastened on what he had often heard old people talk about; there were ways to make life beyond the grave tolerable, provided that your followers had done their duty and not left the tomb without the supplies that it needed.

No tablet marks the resting place of Bing's bones or those of Yu, his wife. Nobody saw fit to have an inscription cut in stone to praise his good qualities and record the steps that had led him forward in his official career. But then, he had not risen to be more that a county magistrate, and he would hardly have expected such honors. Just as Yu had wished, he gave orders that when her time came the books that she had so loved would be buried with her. "You never know," she had begged Bing. "Perhaps I can go on reading in the life of the world to come."

Notes for Chapter Sixteen
Senior officials would go to Maoling to consult Dong Zhongshu (ca. 198–ca. 107), who had moved there after a not too successful career. Of the two men who had voiced subversive talk toward the end of Western Han, Gan Zhongke died of illness, just in time to avoid punishment; Xia Heliang faced the death penalty. For the fighting between the emperor and the heir apparent in 91–90 BCE, see Michael Loewe, *Crisis and Conflict in Han China, 104 BC to AD 9* (London: George Allen and Unwin, 1974; reprinted London and New York), chap. 2. The floods and panic at Chang'an took place in 30 BCE, and the coincidence of the earthquake and eclipse, the following year. The movement seeking the blessing of the Queen Mother of the West took place in 3 BCE.

Appendix:
A Brief History of the Han Empire

Since perhaps 1600 BCE, kingdoms ruled over limited areas in what
we now call China for varying periods of time, but it was only in 221
BCE that an empire was formed, ruling as a single authority without
challenge from others. Short-lived as that of Qin was (221–210 BCE),
it was followed by that of Western Han from 202 to 9 CE with its
capital at Chang'an (present-day Xi'an), Xin (9–25 CE), and Eastern
Han from 25–220 CE, with its capital at Luoyang. As the first long-
lasting empire, Han drew on the institutions, experience, and practices
of the previous kingdoms, now amalgamated under single control.
Based in the northwest, Western Han ruled at first over lands that
led into the lower parts of Gansu province, the Liaodong peninsula,
and the fertile lands of Hunan and Sichuan. As yet, the emperor did
not rule in the deep south (Guangdong and Guangxi) or far west
(Yunnan), but from around 100 BCE his servicemen and officials were
penetrating more widely and setting up their offices as far afield as
Dunhuang, the Korean peninsula, and Hainan Island.

Imperial government was designed to maintain law and order,
defend the realm, suppress crime, collect revenue, and to control the
work of the population and the production of the land. The extent
to which these aims were achieved varied widely, between areas that
had previously been governed intensively and those that had been
unworked and were only recently brought under a government's
attention; between those that were populated deeply or sparsely;
those where natural conditions favored official supervision, and the
woodlands and marshes that allowed inhabitants to live in rough or
primitive conditions beyond an official's view. It was thus only in
particular areas that government could exercise a pervasive influence
or maintain a complete control. At times the authority of the emperor
lay open to attempts by rebels to displace him and establish their own
regime. Local outbreaks of dissidence were not infrequent, particularly

during the latter years of Eastern Han, when a strong-minded and popular local leader could sometimes set himself up with virtual independence, with the support of his own armed followers and control of large areas of land.

The position of emperor passed from father to son on a hereditary basis. Only a few of the eleven emperors of Western Han and the fourteen of Eastern Han can be judged to have been men of a compelling personality capable of leadership, decisiveness, and initiative. In most cases they were below the age of twenty at the time of accession or indeed no more than infants, and as such they were subject to the immediate control of their mothers, grandmothers, as agreed with the latters' own relatives. The emperors' function was rarely that of an active head of an empire who gave direct orders to his subjects or played a leading role in determining matters of policy or administration. Nevertheless, it was of paramount importance to the government of the empire that emperors existed with an acknowledged title.

The founding emperors of Qin, Western Han, Xin, and Eastern Han had won their position thanks to their military success and it was due to their personal leadership and enduring strength of character that they could command obedience. But with the passage of time, maintenance of such authority came to require religious and intellectual support; it must be demonstrated and believed that they had received a position that had been conferred upon them by a higher, superhuman authority whose will they represented on earth. In this way the emperor would constitute an unquestioned source of power that he devolved to his ministers or officials; with no emperor to command them, they would themselves have no authority to give orders; their call for obedience would ring true only if it came from their own superior, and if it was acknowledged that that superior person had himself received his charge to rule from a yet higher source. For these reasons Han emperors came at last to claim and see themselves as ruling thanks to the charge that they had received to do so, from a source that they came to identify as Heaven.

There were probably thirty thousand officials who staffed the offices of the central government in Chang'an and a hundred thousand posted in the provinces. Appointment depended on merit or sponsorship, and in time on some rudimentary forms of testing and competition. Senior officials determined major policies and attended the emperor at court.

With their juniors they staffed the government's offices and agencies at the capital city and in the provinces, promulgating imperial orders and implementing the laws. They counted, registered, and controlled the population in units of as few as four or five members, calling up males to serve in the labor gangs or in the armed services. They judged criminal cases, set up schools, and kept roads and waterways in good repair. They controlled the passage of individuals from one area to another. In outlying regions they introduced the ways of life of the civilized world, such as the use of clothing and forms of marriage. In all these duties they kept records, such as financial accounts that were carefully written on slats of wood, sometimes with duplicate copies.

In addition to the unknown number of persons who lived in the mountains or marshland and evaded the eyes of prying officials, by the beginning of the Christian era the registered population of the empire had come to number nearly sixty million individuals. Social distinctions rested on birth, merit, imperial orders, or wealth. Some dozen male members of the imperial family of Liu who had been nominated as kings transmitted their titles and the lands they governed to the keeping of their sons. Officials who showed promise could rise from the low rank of humble clerk to that of minister of state in the central government. From time to time an imperial decree bestowed orders of social precedence on certain male members of the population according to a scale of twenty orders, each with its legal privileges and allotted landholdings. The highest of these, the nobilities, provided a title and the right to raise tax and an income. A merchant's wealth could buy high social status. A comparatively small number of slaves worked either for private owners or at the behest of officials. Criminals sentenced to up to six years of hard labor, and sometimes mutilated, worked as was required in the provinces.

The great majority of the population lived off the land, sowing millet or hemp in their fields and rendering part of the produce as tax. To some extent the government controlled occupation of the land but much was available for purchase. For the rich, ingots of gold coins supplemented the bronze coins of a single denomination; private minting of coins was banned. Government monopolies of the mining, manufacture, and sale of salt and ironwares operated on and off from ca. 120 BCE, to the exclusion of private initiative. Merchants could make large fortunes by dealing in jades and pearls, lacquerwares and potteries, livestock, rare fruits, and cooked meats. Conscript servicemen worked the mines and the iron foundries; skilled artisans produced the polychrome silks, ornamental bronze vessels, and potteries, and fashioned the jades that filled the houses of the rich and might make their way outside the Han emperor's domains, sometimes reaching as far as the shores of the Mediterranean Sea.

No direct contact linked Han China with such lands. Tales of other peoples who were not subject to imperial rule, examples of rare products or commodities of exotic types reached the markets of Chang'an or Luoyang. A few travelers came back with accounts of the communities they had visited, their way of life, natural resources, living habits, and organization. From perhaps 120 BCE, Han was extending its influence and expanding its interests into these unknown regions of the northwest. The Qin empire had unified a series of defense lines in the north as a protection from violent inroads, mainly by the Xiongnu. Following a series of military campaigns against them, Han forces extended those lines of forts, staffed by conscript servicemen, to reach as far Dunhuang in the northwest. They were to serve both as a measure of defense and as an armed causeway along which the Han caravans—numbering several hundred persons—could proceed safely with their bales of silk, bronze mirrors, or potteries. Officials were posted to administer newly founded provincial units; contacts with local leaders could lead either to friendly relations or to conflict. Back in Chang'an, generals of the army welcomed the arrival of horses from the north to augment their forces; their wives enjoyed the luxury of furs and pelts; the newly arrived grape and its products enriched the emperor's banqueting table.

At the same time, provincial governors were establishing offices in Korea, and the southeast, south, and southwest of present-day China, with the intention of exploiting the land, controlling the population, and raising taxes. Some of these posts were isolated, such that appointment there could in effect be a type of banishment from the cultured and comfortable life known in the interior of the empire. Administration of these widely separated inhabitants was anything but complete or permanent and there were times when the Han government withdrew altogether from these outlying regions. Several centuries had to pass before the lands that led south to Hong Kong or present-day Yunnan formed integral parts of a united Chinese empire.

The first duty that fell to a newly acceded emperor was to pay homage at the shrines dedicated to the memory of his ancestors, thereby confirming his own inheritance of their charge. Once adult, he performed the regular cults addressed to those superior powers from whom his authority derived. He would be buried in an imposing tomb furnished with valuables, such as jade jewelry, commodities such as model farms or carriages, figures of attendants such as musicians, and consumables of food, drink, and clothing. His tomb would include symbols intended to guide his soul to one of two paradises, of the east or the west, and it would be surmounted by a lofty tumulus for all to admire and revere.

Burial of those from lower levels of society followed this pattern, depending on the rank of the deceased person. Splendid tombs of some of the kings took the shape of stone-built mansions with their chambers and protective walls. For them and certain privileged persons a suit of jade, that treasured mineral which promised enduring life, encased the body, as it did that of the emperor. High-ranking officials were buried in brick-built tombs with richly decorated walls, lintels, and vaults. At the lowest level, a body was interred with no accompanying goods, save perhaps for a rough inscription of the man or woman's name. From perhaps 150 CE, stone stelae carefully inscribed with an elaborate account of a high official's career stood beside his tomb.

Apart from the emperor's religious duties, others took care to render prayers and offerings to those mighty forces of nature, be they of hill or river, of wind or thunder, thought capable of fixing the destinies of mankind. Villagers spared products of their farms and ponds as offerings to appease those spirits and deflect their anger. Festivals to herald in the new year served as rites to bring it success, and could help to forge a sense of social identity. Faith in the ideals of the Buddha and the accompanying need for self-questioning and reverence came to China's countryside from India, perhaps about 150 CE. The last decades of Eastern Han saw the emergence of self-proclaimed teachers who promised their adherents worldly bliss and perhaps spiritual happiness in return for an obedient life within a community. Such movements gave rise to a priesthood some of whose rites came to be addressed to Laozi, seen to be the author of the *Daode jing* (*The Way and Its Power*).

Insecurity at times when the forces of nature could destroy a livelihood and a compelling need to maintain the continuity of a family were among the reasons why men and women adopted a number of means of inquiring how best to order their lives. Such guidance was to be found in messages that superhuman powers conveyed, perhaps by abnormal events such as an eclipse in the skies, or the occurrence of an earthquake at a crucial time, or the mere direction and force of the winds that blew on the first day of the new year. Specialist experts could make a living by manipulating a bundle of reeds to create a pattern of six lines, whose meaning could be found by consulting an old text called the *Book of Changes* and might serve to set the anxious mind of an inquirer at rest. Other methods were in use. Instruments displayed the cycles of the universe and the positions they had reached; books set out each day of the year with advice of what actions, such as marrying a wife or building a house, should be chosen as likely to be successful and those which should be avoided as leading to failure.

From about 100 BCE, officials were paying attention to writings that were some centuries old with a view to inculcating moral standards. From perhaps 50 BCE, there was a growing tendency to quote the sayings ascribed to Kongzi (Confucius; 551 to 479 BCE) to sustain an argument; but as yet, despite some moves toward an intellectual uniformity, there was no acknowledged system of "Confucianism," which regulated public activities and individual conduct or stamped its ideas on literature. Particular moments of intense intellectual activity are recorded for the discussions on political principles in 81 BCE and on the proper interpretation of certain old writings in 51 BCE. The collection of books to form the imperial library which was ordered in 26 BCE marked a new stage in China's literary history. The opening years of Zhangdi's reign in 76 CE witnessed an active interest in intellectual and literary matters.

A new form and style of writing history that was seen in a work completed ca. 100 BCE formed a model for compiling dynastic histories thereafter. Men of letters were writing essays on matters such as the value of the past as against a need for innovation, or dialogues between advocates and opponents of imperial policies. Criticism of public life and its direction was being voiced in another literary form; short poems drew on rigors of the time such as the hardships of the soldier; structured essays discussed the workings of nature and argued for or against well-known beliefs inherent in folklore. Elegant compositions disclosed personal points of view between friends. Occasionally we hear of the literary work of a woman.

Some writers were inquiring into the nature of the universe and its changes as manifested in the skies, on earth, or among living creatures, and as affecting the destiny of empires. Scholars were laying down the correct modes of behavior that would maintain social distinctions and religious rituals in due order. Astronomers calculated the movements of the heavenly bodies and regulated the imperial calendar. Other thinkers drew attention to the part played by superhuman forces in human affairs, whether for good or ill. Working in silk paintings or stone reliefs, artists depicted scenes of the next world, figures and incidents of history and mythology, or the luxuries of a banquet. Craftsmen produced their masterpieces in jade, bronze, or lacquer. A new method of working the fields, introduced ca. 100 BCE, increased the yield of the land; builders supervised conscript servicemen in the toil of pounding earth and clay to form the majestic walls of cities.

Such was the legacy of a mighty empire, ascribed with admiration and praise to Han for some two thousand years, and on several occasions between 338 and 1360 a short-lived regime chose to adopt Han as its title, by way of emulation. A major difference of attitude affected views of the ideals of imperial government, as between Western and Eastern Han; controversies and problems were no stranger to those who governed or lived in both the earlier and the later of these regimes. On several occasions, such as 154 and 90 BCE, survival of the dynasty was in question. Jealousies among the emperor's consorts and the claims of rivals to succeed him disrupted the peace of court and capital, at times with violence. Memorials to the throne protested against the improper selection of officials or their incompetence, corruption, and oppression, particularly in Eastern Han. Against those who advocated an intensive supervision of the working population and the products of the fields and mines, others argued for a laissez-faire policy that would reduce government's interference to a minimum.

Occasionally, an official suggested plans to restrict the size of landholdings, but such attempts to soften the hardships of the poor met with scant success. Expansionist moves to promote contacts and trade with the peoples of Central Asia proved to be expensive; as against those who proposed plans to do so, others complained that they resulted in no more than the import of luxurious baubles. Advisors at court held widely divergent views both on the purposes and conduct of the religious cults of state and on the choice of ancient, revered writings that were fit for official adoption. There survives no positive disquisition on the nature of a life after death, but the design, embellishment, and furnishing of tombs reveal differing approaches to this question. From time to time mother nature reminded men and women of their insignificance and weakness in the face of happenings that lay beyond their power, such as the floods that followed the changes of course of the Yellow River (3 and 11 CE), or the earthquake that shook Chang'an on the very same day as an eclipse (29 BCE).

Notes for Further Reading

Translations of parts of the primary sources for the history of the Han Dynasty will be found in Burton Watson, *Records of the Historian: Han Dynasty I and II,* rev. ed., 2 vols. (Hong Kong and New York: Renditions–Columbia University Press, 1993); *Records of the Grand Historian, Qin Dynasty,* vol. III, rev. ed. (Hong Kong and New York: Research Centre for Translation, Chinese University of Hong Kong and Columbia University Press, 1993); Homer H. Dubs, *The History of the Former Han Dynasty,* 3 vols. (Baltimore: Waverly Press, 1938–55); and William H. Nienhauser, Jr., ed., *The Grand Scribe's Records,* vol. 1, *The Basic Annals of Pre-Han China;* vol. II, *The Basic Annals of Pre-Han China;* vol. V.1, *The Hereditary Houses of Pre-Han China;* vol. VII, *The Memoirs of Pre-Han China, Part 1* (Bloomington and Indianapolis: Indiana University Press, 1994–2008). In a number of volumes such as *Emperor Huan and Emperor Ling* (Canberra: Australian National University, 1989), Rafe de Crespigny has translated a large body of source material for the end of Eastern Han. See also below for works by Hulsewé and Swann.

Selections of the archaeological evidence are illustrated in Michèle Pirazzoli-t'Serstevens, *The Han Dynasty,* translated by Janet Seligman (New York: Rizzoli International Publications, 1982). In *Lo-yang in Later Han Times* (Stockholm: Museum of Far Eastern Antiquities, 1976), Hans Bielenstein presents a study of Luoyang city based on the literary and archaeological evidence. See also Michael Loewe, *Everyday Life in Early Imperial China during the Han Period, 202 BC–AD 220* (London: B. T. Batsford, 1968; repr. Indianapolis: Hackett Publishing Company, 2005).

For a general account of Han times, see Denis Twitchett and Michael Loewe, eds., *The Cambridge History of China,* vol. I, *The Ch'in and Han Empires, 221 B.C.–A.D. 220* (Cambridge: Cambridge University Press, 1986). This volume has been supplemented by attention to more recently found archaeological evidence and manuscripts, and research on institutional, technical, literary subjects, and studies of rhetoric in Michael Nylan and Michael Loewe, *China's Early Empires* (Cambridge: Cambridge University Press, 2010). Recent reference books include Michael Loewe, *A Biographical Dictionary of the Qin, Former Han and Xin Periods (221 BC–AD 24)* (Leiden, Boston, Köln: Brill, 2000); and Rafe de Crespigny, *A Biographical Dictionary of Later Han to the Three Kingdoms (23–220 AD)* (Leiden, Boston: Brill, 2007).

Religious movements and intellectual developments are studied in Derk Bodde, *Festivals in Classical China: New Year and Other Annual Observances during the Han Dynasty, 206 B.C.–A.D. 220* (Princeton: Princeton University Press, and Hong Kong: Chinese University of Hong Kong, 1975); John S. Major, *Heaven and Earth in Early Han Thought: Chapters Three, Four and Five of the Huainanzi: With an Appendix by Christopher Cullen*, SUNY Series in Chinese Philosophy and Culture (Albany: State University of New York Press, 1993); Roel Sterckx, *The Animal and the Daemon in Early China*, SUNY Series in Chinese Philosophy and Culture (Albany: State University of New York Press, 2002); and Michael Loewe, *Ways to Paradise, The Chinese Quest for Immortality* (London: George Allen and Unwin, 1979), and *Chinese Ideas of Life and Death: Faith, Myth, and Reason in Han China* (London: George Allen and Unwin, 1982), reprinted as *Faith, Myth, and Reason in Han China* (Indianapolis: Hackett Publishing Company, 2005).

For the production of written texts and documents, see Tsien Tsuen-Hsuin, *Written on Bamboo and Silk: The Beginnings of Chinese Books and Inscriptions*, 2nd ed., with an afterword by Edward L. Shaughnessy (Chicago and London: University of Chicago Press, 2004). Mark Csikszentmihalyi presents a selection of prose writings in *Readings in Han Chinese Thought* (Indianapolis: Hackett Publishing Company, 2006); see also David R. Knechtges, *The Han Rhapsody: A Study of the Fu of Yang Hsiung (53 B.C.–A.D. 18)* (Cambridge: Cambridge University Press, 1976), and *Wen xuan, or Selections of Refined Literature*, vols. 1, 2, and 3 (Princeton: Princeton University Press, 1982, 1987, 1996). As a translation of some Han Dynasty poetry, David Hawkes, *The Songs of the South: An Anthology of Ancient Chinese Poems by Qu Yuan and Other Poets* (Harmondsworth: Penguin Books, 1985) remains a classic. For a study of a Han writer, see Nancy Lee Swann, *Pan Chao:*

Foremost Woman Scholar of China, First Century A.D. (New York and London: Century Company, 1932).

A detailed account of the institutions of government and establishment of officials is seen in Hans Bielenstein, *The Bureaucracy of Han Times* (Cambridge: Cambridge University Press, 1980). For a more general account, see Michael Loewe, *The Government of the Qin and Han Empires, 221 BCE–220 CE* (Indianapolis: Hackett Publishing Company, 2006).

For the forms, extent, and contents of law, see A. F. P. Hulsewé, *Remnants of Han Law* (Leiden: E. J. Brill, 1955), and *Remnants of Ch'in Law: An Annotated Translation of the Ch'in Legal and Administrative Rules of the 3rd Century B.C. Discovered in Yün-meng Prefecture, Hu-pei Province, in 1975* (Leiden: E. J. Brill, 1985).

Nancy Lee Swann translates Han texts that concern economic practice and administration in *Food and Money in Ancient China: The Earliest Economic History of China to A.D. 25; Han shu 24 with Related Texts, Han shu 91 and Shih-chi 129* (Princeton: Princeton University Press, 1950). Aspects of economic practice are described in Hsu Cho-yun, *Han Agriculture: The Formation of Early Chinese Agrarian Economy (206 B.C.–A.D. 220)* (Seattle and London: University of Washington Press, 1980); Donald B. Wagner, *The State and the Iron Industry in Han China,* NIAS Report Series no. 44 (Copenhagen: Nordic Institute of Asian Studies, 2001); and Anthony J. Barbieri-Low, *Artisans in Early Imperial China* (Seattle: University of Washington Press, 2007).

For military practice and the working life of the garrisons of the northwest, see Michael Loewe, *Records of Han Administration,* 2 vols., University of Cambridge Oriental Publications Nos. 11–12 (Cambridge: Cambridge University Press, 1967; repr. London: RoutledgeCurzon, 2002); see also Rafe de Crespigny, "The Military Culture of Later Han," in Nicola Di Cosmo (ed.), *Military Culture in Imperial China* (Cambridge, MA, and London: Harvard University Press, 2009), pp. 90–112. For contacts and relations with non-Han peoples, see Ying-shih Yü, *Trade and Expansion in Han China* (Berkeley and Los Angeles: University of California Press, 1967); and A. F. P. Hulsewé, *China in Central Asia: The Early Stage, 125 B.C.–A.D. 23* (Leiden: E. J. Brill, 1979).

Essays on select topics appear in Derk Bodde, *Essays on Chinese Civilization,* ed. Charles Le Blanc and Dorothy Borei (Princeton:

Princeton University Press, 1981); and Michael Loewe, *Crisis and Conflict in Han China 104 BC to AD 9* (London: George Allen and Unwin Ltd, 1974; repr. London and New York: Routledge, 2005); *Divination, Mythology and Monarchy in Han China* (Cambridge: Cambridge University Press, 1994); and *The Men Who Governed Han China: Companion to "A Biographical Dictionary of the Qin, Former Han and Xin Periods"* (Leiden, Boston: Brill, 2004).